"I really just want to get in bed and cry," Mrs. Dawkins said, "but I think I should wait with Mel until you take him to the funeral home." She pulled the short robe closer around her slender frame and headed out the door. I'd bet that she was commando under that cover-up. I was trailing behind her when a woman's scream cut through the night like a surgeon's scalpel through flesh.

What now? I thought. *If this were one of the mysteries I read, someone would have stolen Melvin's body.* No time to speculate. I dashed out, almost expecting the body to have disappeared, but Dr. Melvin still floated in the hot tub. The screaming came from Mrs. Dawkins, and she wasn't yelling about her husband. Near the split-rail fence at the edge of the yard stood a very good-looking dude.

Ex-cuuze me. I was on a pickup call for the funeral home to transport a man I'd known and liked my whole life. What was I doing thinking about how handsome this stranger was?

PRAISE FOR

A Tisket, a Tasket, a Fancy Stolen Casket

Berkley Prime Crime titles by Fran Rizer

A TISKET, A TASKET, A FANCY STOLEN CASKET
HEY DIDDLE DIDDLE, THE CORPSE AND THE FIDDLE
CASKET CASE

Casket Case

FRAN RIZER

BERKLEY PRIME CRIME, NEW YORK

THE BERKLEY PUBLISHING GROUP
Published by the Penguin Group
Penguin Group (USA) Inc.
375 Hudson Street, New York, New York 10014, USA
Penguin Group (Canada), 90 Eglinton Avenue East, Suite 700, Toronto, Ontario M4P 2Y3, Canada
(a division of Pearson Penguin Canada Inc.)
Penguin Books Ltd., 80 Strand, London WC2R 0RL, England
Penguin Group Ireland, 25 St. Stephen's Green, Dublin 2, Ireland (a division of Penguin Books Ltd.)
Penguin Group (Australia), 250 Camberwell Road, Camberwell, Victoria 3124, Australia
(a division of Pearson Australia Group Pty. Ltd.)
Penguin Books India Pvt. Ltd., 11 Community Centre, Panchsheel Park, New Delhi—110 017, India
Penguin Group (NZ), 67 Apollo Drive, Rosedale, North Shore 0632, New Zealand
(a division of Pearson New Zealand Ltd.)
Penguin Books (South Africa) (Pty.) Ltd., 24 Sturdee Avenue, Rosebank, Johannesburg 2196,
South Africa

Penguin Books Ltd., Registered Offices: 80 Strand, London WC2R 0RL, England

This is a work of fiction. Names, characters, places, and incidents either are the product of the author's imagination or are used fictitiously, and any resemblance to actual persons, living or dead, business establishments, events, or locales is entirely coincidental. The publisher does not have any control over and does not assume any responsibility for author or third-party websites or their content.

CASKET CASE

A Berkley Prime Crime Book / published by arrangement with the author

PRINTING HISTORY
Berkley Prime Crime mass-market edition / October 2008

Copyright © 2008 by Fran Rizer.
Interior text design by Laura K. Corless.

ISBN: 978-0-425-22428-1

BERKLEY® PRIME CRIME
Berkley Prime Crime Books are published by The Berkley Publishing Group,
a division of Penguin Group (USA) Inc.,
375 Hudson Street, New York, New York 10014.
BERKLEY PRIME CRIME and the BERKLEY PRIME CRIME design
are trademarks belonging to Penguin Group (USA) Inc.

PRINTED IN THE UNITED STATES OF AMERICA

10 9 8 7 6 5 4 3 2 1

This one is for my friend Nynaeve and for all the Callie Parrish fans I've met through e-mail and at book signings, readings, and presentations. It's also for the wonderful people who keep readers and writers happy—booksellers and librarians!

Acknowledgments

More special thanks to special people—Jeff Gerecke, agent, and all the people at Berkley Prime Crime who are involved with Callie's books, especially my marvelous new editor Michelle Vega and my super copy-editor Sheila Moody.

I also appreciate the advice, encouragement, and information from Calhoun Goodwin, Gwen and Rod Hunter, Leonard Jolley, and Ray Wade.

Chapter One

Melvin Dawkins floated facedown in the steamy, bubbling water of the hot tub. As I looked down at him, I noticed that the bodice of my black dress lay flat against my chest.

Dalmation! I'd dressed so quickly when the call came in the middle of the night that I'd forgotten my bra, and my inflatable underwear *is* my bosom. I directed my attention back to Dr. Melvin.

Nekkid as a jaybird. Not that blue jays are any more nude—or is it nuder?—than other birds, but Daddy used that expression all the time when I was growing up, and it was the first thing that popped into my mind that night out in Dr. Melvin's backyard.

Next thing I thought, I said aloud. "Where's the coroner?"

"What do you mean?" asked the slender, red-haired lady standing on the wooden deck surrounding the tub. She pulled her eyelet cover-up tighter across her middle and retied the sash. "If you can't get him out by yourself," she continued, "I'll help you. I never figured Middleton's Mortuary would send a *girl* out by herself to pick up the body."

Girl? Puh-leeze. I'm almost thirty-three years old, and thanks to my inflatable bra, I'm way more than thirty-three in the bust. At least when I don't get waked up in the middle of the night and forget to put it on. I'm not a girl; I'm a woman. A lady trained by the Middleton twins to always be polite and patient with customers, even if some woman younger than I am just called me a *girl*.

"I mean that someone has to pronounce a person dead before we can transport the deceased to the funeral home." I used my best, most comforting, Funeralese tone. "And by the way, where *is* Mrs. Dawkins? I'd like to speak to the person who called."

The woman sniffed. Not a tearful sniffle, a sniff of disdain. "I *am* Mrs. Dawkins, and I called Middleton's Mortuary," she said. "The person who answered the phone didn't say one word about contacting someone else. I called and told her to come get Mel as soon as I found him. I gave her pacific directions." She pointed toward the hot tub. "You work for the funeral home and you can't tell he's not alive? I've never seen a corpse out of a casket before and I *know* he's dead!"

I was busy trying to determine what pacific directions she could give me on the South Carolina coast of the Atlantic Ocean. She must have meant "specific."

"Was Dr. Melvin under Hospice care?" I said. "If he was, his Hospice nurse can take care of the paperwork."

She shook her head no and asked, "Why do you call him 'doctor'? Melvin was a pharmacist, not a doctor."

"You must not have grown up around here," I said. "All of us kids in St. Mary called him 'Doctor' Melvin when we were growing up. I don't really know why. That's just what my daddy told me to call him. Anyway, if Dr. Melvin wasn't under Hospice care, the coroner has to come."

"Then why did you suggest that nurse?"

"Doesn't matter." In the Low Country of South Carolina,

terminally ill patients who've been under Hospice care can be pronounced dead by the Hospice nurse. A few months back, I'd heard that Dr. Melvin had retired from the St. Mary Pharmacy. I didn't know if he left because of illness, but if the shoe doesn't fit, no need to try to wear it.

I fumbled in my purse for my cell phone before realizing I'd forgotten it again. "May I use your telephone?" I reached toward the redhead.

"Don't have one out here. I called you from the kitchen. Come on, we'll go in the house." She looked at Dr. Melvin again. His silver hair swirled around on the bubbly waves like a child's finger painting. "Do you think we should pull him out before we go in?"

"No, ma'am. We have to leave him where he is."

There I was. In trouble again for not following instructions. I knew better, I promise I knew better than to go for a body pickup alone during the middle of the night. Well, actually in the wee hours of the morning.

My bosses, Otis and Odell Middleton, had left me in charge of Middleton's Mortuary for three days while they went to Atlanta for an undertakers' seminar. They'd be back before we opened the next day. Otis had told me I could transfer the phone to my apartment each night, but I was supposed to call Jake, one of our part-time drivers, if we had a pickup call.

Instead, I'd chosen to take the funeral coach, Funeralese for hearse, myself, thinking I could prove my abilities. Never crossed my mind to question what authorities would be at the Dawkins home. Now Sheriff Harmon would know I'd goofed, and he'd tell the Middletons.

Mrs. Dawkins pushed her damp hair away from her forehead and sighed. A long, loud sigh. I couldn't tell if the sound was to bring my attention from my thoughts back to the situation or to express her feelings. She turned and walked up the inlaid stone path to the back door of the house.

The paving stones were patterned with little mosaic roosters on them. I followed her into a tidy kitchen decorated with more roosters. I mean everywhere. Wallpaper, canisters, dishcloths, even one of those half-circle rugs in front of the sink with a big rooster on it. Roosters printed on everything.

Only one thing in the kitchen was more predominant than those roosters: baked goods. Pies, cakes, platters of cookies, and loaves of home-baked breads covered the table and countertops. All wrapped in Saran Wrap. "Do you like to bake?" I asked conversationally. *Duh.*

"No, Mel bakes." Her answer was short and clipped. "There's the phone." She pointed toward an old black AT&T rotary, probably been on the wall since the fifties or sixties. I dialed 9—*click, click, click, click, click, click, click, click, click*—1—*click*—1—*click*. Lined up on the counter beneath the telephone, bottles and jars of vitamins and food supplements filled four rows. Must have been thirty or forty containers of pills and powders.

After reporting what might be an accidental drowning, although Dr. Melvin could just as well have suffered a massive stroke or heart attack, I asked Mrs. Dawkins if she'd prefer to wait inside the house or go back outside with me.

It seemed disrespectful to leave Dr. Melvin alone. He'd filled all the prescriptions for nasty pink medicine when I was a child, and he'd sold me the girly things my brothers and Daddy refused to go for when I reached adolescence. He'd handled much of what my mother would have if she hadn't died when I was born.

"I really just want to get in bed and cry," Mrs. Dawkins said, "but I think I should wait with Mel until you take him to the funeral home." She pulled the short robe closer around her slender frame and headed out the door. I'd bet that she was commando under that cover-up. I was trailing behind her when a woman's scream cut through the night like a surgeon's scalpel through flesh.

What now? I thought. *If this were one of the mysteries I read, someone would have stolen Melvin's body.* No time to speculate. I dashed out, almost expecting the body to have disappeared, but Dr. Melvin still floated. The screaming came from Mrs. Dawkins, and she wasn't yelling about her husband. Near the split-rail fence at the edge of the yard stood a very good-looking dude.

Ex-cuuze me. I was on a pickup call for the funeral home to transport a man I'd known and liked my whole life. What was I doing thinking about how handsome this stranger was? Must have been hormonal. Then I realized Mrs. Dawkins wasn't just screeching. She was yelling words: "What are *you* doing here?"

The man stepped forward, closer to us. "What's happened?" he asked in a smooth voice with a heavy Charleston drawl and motioned toward the hot tub.

For the first time since I'd arrived, Mrs. Dawkins burst into sobs with giant teardrops pouring from her dark green eyes. "Mel and I were relaxing in the Jacuzzi. I went in the house to get some wine, and when I came back out, he looked like he does now. I knew he was dead, and I didn't know what to do. There's only one funeral home listed in the phone book for St. Mary. I called them. Now this woman says the sheriff and coroner have to come before she can take Mel out of the tub."

"That makes sense," the stranger said, "but did you check his pulse when you found him like this?"

"I held his wrist, but I didn't feel anything. That's why I didn't call 911. Just look at my poor Mel. He was exactly like that when I came out. I could tell he was dead or I wouldn't have called a funeral home."

The man walked to the hot tub, bent over, and lifted

Dr. Melvin's arm. He held the wrist more than a minute, then felt Dr. Melvin's carotid artery. He shook his head no at Mrs. Dawkins before turning his attention toward me. "Who are you?" he asked.

"Callie Parrish. I work for Middleton's Mortuary, and I thought that Mr. Dawkins had already been pronounced and was ready to be picked up. I've called for the sheriff and the coroner."

"I'm Levi Pinckney, a friend of Roselle's from Charleston. I stopped when I drove by and saw the hearse."

"What are you doing in St. Mary and why were you driving by my house?" Mrs. Dawkins interrupted. She wiped away her tears with the back of her hand.

"I came down here a few weeks ago, and I drive by sometimes because it makes me feel better about you. I guess I'm behaving like a jerk, worrying about you all the time."

Before Levi continued, Sheriff Harmon stepped through the gate. Jed Amick, the coroner of St. Mary, who has an amazing resemblance to Ichabod Crane, shuffled in right behind him.

"Callie," the sheriff said, "where's Otis or Odell?"

"They've gone to Georgia and left me in charge. They'll be back tomorrow. Well, since it's past midnight, they'll be back later this morning. Dr. Melvin's over there in the hot tub." I pointed. Jed sauntered over and peered at Dr. Melvin in the bubbly water. "I didn't know Mr. Amick hadn't been called when I came," I added.

"And she didn't say a word about you or the coroner when I called her," Mrs. Dawkins protested.

"You called Callie? What's your relationship to Mr. Dawkins?" Harmon asked without pausing for a response to his first question.

"He's my husband. I'm Roselle Dawkins. We've only been back from our honeymoon a few weeks. Mel took me to Greece. The hot tub in our hotel suite was so much fun that Mel had this Jacuzzi put in for us at home. Tonight was our first time in it." She burst into tears again. "We're still newlyweds."

Levi stepped beside her and even if she didn't want him there, she had no qualms about letting him hold her close against his chest while she cried. I wondered what their relationship was—ex-husband and wife?

The men who attract me are usually tall. This Levi Pinckney wasn't a lot taller than I am, and a few inches over five foot four isn't even average for a man. His disheveled dark, curly hair fell forward over part of his forehead, and his deep brown eyes reflected concern for Mrs. Dawkins, but he still projected pheromoans in all directions. I know that's not how to spell that word, but it's what my friend Jane and I call that sensuality that just seems to emanate from some men.

The man hadn't even looked at me, but I sure wished I had on my bra. Buh-leeve me. I would have been happier if I'd had it on and had inflated it a little more than I usually did. I grew up with five brothers, so I know that most males react to healthy female chests.

"Callie?" Sheriff Harmon called me. "Did you phone one of the part-timers to meet you here?"

"No, sir," I answered.

"Jed's going to need an autopsy on Melvin to determine cause of death. We'll have to send him to Charleston."

"Are you going to call in forensics?" I asked.

"No, I don't see any signs of foul play," Sheriff Harmon responded. "Jed thinks this appears to be natural, but we have to know cause of death. You'll need one of Middleton's part-time drivers to take Melvin to the medical university."

In South Carolina, we don't have medical examiners. Our coroner here in Jade County is an elected official who sends bodies to MUSC—the Medical University of South Carolina in Charleston—when a postmortem exam is needed.

"Otis and Odell are due back this morning. I can drive Dr. Melvin myself and be home before I'm scheduled for work this afternoon." I glanced at the Jacuzzi. Mrs. Dawkins had turned off the jets and was showing the coroner how to drain the tub. Levi Pinckney was helping them. The part of me who thinks I'm Kinsey Millhone instead of Callie Parrish wondered if they should save a sample of the water in case Melvin didn't die of natural causes, but I had enough sense not to mention one of my wild ideas.

"May I use your telephone again?" I asked Mrs. Dawkins.

"Sure," she answered. "I'm going in myself to get dressed. I know I won't be able to sleep any more tonight, and it's cooler out of the water than it was in the tub. I don't want to catch ammonia."

I did a quick double take at the woman's fear of catching "ammonia" in the June heat of the southern coast, then returned to the rooster kitchen of baked goods and vitamins to dial my friend Jane's number.

"What do you mean calling me before sunrise?" she demanded. "Roxanne's on the other line."

"Dr. Melvin died. I'm taking him to Charleston. By the time I get there, deliver him, and have breakfast, I won't have to wait too long for Victoria's Secret to open. I'm going shopping."

"What about the funeral home?"

"Otis and Odell are already scheduled to open this morning. We don't have any clients right now, and the mortuary phone is forwarded to my cell. I'm not due in until four this afternoon." *Mental note: Go by my apartment and pick up the cell phone before leaving town.*

"Roxanne will speed up. Can I go?"

"If you'll behave."

"I'll try."

Chapter Two

***D**almation!* I'd gone by my apartment, taken my Great Dane dog, Big Boy, out for his morning business, and showered. I changed from the black dress I'd worn to the Dawkins house into fresh jeans and a tank top with an inflated bra, then climbed in the hearse and headed toward my friend Jane's. Why can't I remember to call the hearse by its proper name—the funeral coach?

Almost to Jane's, I thought about the cell phone. After checking for any calls I'd missed while gone, I'd used my landline phone to call the mortuary number and leave a message for the Middletons. I'd explained about Dr. Melvin's death and that I was taking him to Charleston for a postmortem exam. That had been efficient. Leaving the cell phone on the coffee table again hadn't been. I needed the telephone with me until Otis and Odell opened the mortuary and transferred calls back to the business line. I was fortunate that another call hadn't come in while I was at the Dawkins house, not even realizing the business calls were going to the cell phone in my apartment with nobody there to answer. The mortuary telephone was supposed to be answered immediately twenty-four/seven. That was one of Middleton's rules.

I finally reached Jane's apartment after detouring back by my place for the cell phone and rubbing behind the ears of my joyful dog, who was happy to see me, but mad when I left again. No telling what Big Boy would do while I was gone. That dog throws temper tantrums like a five-year-old child.

Jane was standing at the top of the steep stairway up to her garage apartment. Usually, she would have started down when I turned into the drive. Born blind, Jane recognizes the sounds of her friends' cars, but since I was driving the funeral coach, she wasn't sure it was me until I called out to her.

"Hey, Jane, come on down," I yelled.

"Oh, that *is* you, Callie. I wasn't sure since you're not driving the Mustang," Jane said as she walked toward me. I got out, stepped around, and opened the door for her. As usual, Jane wore vintage sixties clothing—a crinkly lavender dress with a low neckline. She'd inherited her mother's hippie wardrobe after her mom's death following our senior year of high school. Somehow, the clothes appeared current on her with her long, straight red hair hanging down to her waist. She wore a wide-brimmed hat with a clutch of purple violets at the band and new sunglasses with deep lavender lenses.

When I was back in the driver's seat and we were both buckled in, Jane asked, "Are we in the hearse?"

I didn't even bother to correct her that we call it a funeral coach. Just mumbled an affirmative, "Uh-huh."

"Is Dr. Melvin in the back?" she asked as I pulled onto the highway.

"Yes," I said.

"I don't smell anything."

"You shouldn't. He's fresh, clean, and enclosed."

"What kind of casket is he in?" Jane shows interest in my work, but the truth is that my job is as repugnant to Jane as hers is to me. She calls herself a "conversationalist," but to call a spade a flipping shovel, Jane is a telephone sex operator. She works nights on a 900 line as Roxanne. I don't criticize this because it pays well and keeps her self-sufficient without relying on anyone for transportation.

Buh-leeve me, I *know* who would be driving her to and from work if she had to go out to a job. Being Roxanne at night works because Jane was always a late-night person anyway and frequently talks until dawn.

"He's not in a casket," I said.

Jane's nose crumpled into a disgusted wrinkle. "He's just lying back there?"

"No, he's in a zippered body bag. You can't see him."

Jane howled with laughter. "I couldn't see him anyway."

When Jane and I first became friends, I was very self-conscious about using words related to sight. After a while, I realized that it didn't matter to her. Her standard good-bye is, "See ya later."

"Did you say Dr. Melvin drowned?" Jane asked.

"We don't know for sure. His wife found him dead in their new hot tub. The coroner wants an autopsy to see if he drowned or died from a heart attack or stroke." I paused. "Betcha didn't know he has a young new wife. She's got red hair like you."

"I didn't know she has red hair, but I knew he married a young woman he met over the Internet after he retired." Jane just amazes me. She would let me think she stays in her apartment and sleeps except when she talks to me or is on the phone as Roxanne, but she's always a day ahead of me on gossip.

"The Internet?" I asked.

"Yep, he met her in a chat room and decided she's the perfect woman for him regardless of the almost fifty years between them. According to what I heard, she grew up in a poor rural part of Georgia and has never had much. When she came to visit, she thought the Dawkins house was like a mansion."

"Did you know Dr. Melvin liked to bake?" I said.

"He doesn't, guess I should say *didn't*, really like to bake. He wanted to win the Southern Belle Flour Baking Contest. The grand prize is half a million dollars. I've thought about sending in one of my recipes."

"You should. You're a great cook!" My mind shifted back to Dr. Melvin. "So he needed money?" I asked.

"I think he was comfortable, but he wanted to be able to do more for his bride."

"Do you think she might have drowned him?"

"Oh, Callie, why do you always think that way? Stick to reading your mysteries. His new wife probably killed him, but I doubt she drowned him." Jane giggled. She didn't have to say what she was thinking. We've been friends so long that a lot of the time we know each other's thoughts. To be polite about it, she was insinuating that Roselle "loved" him to death.

After riding silently for about fifteen minutes, Jane asked, "Can we have breakfast on the way? I didn't have supper, and I'm starving."

"I don't think it's a good idea to eat before we deliver Dr. Melvin to MUSC."

"To what?"

"The Medical University of South Carolina, where the autopsies for Jade County are performed."

"Oh, I should have remembered that, but why can't we eat first?"

"We need to get Dr. Melvin into refrigeration as soon as possible because he hasn't been embalmed." *Besides,* I thought, *it seems disrespectful to leave Dr. Melvin in the parking lot while we eat. What if someone stole him out of the funeral coach?*

Jane didn't answer. She was pouting. I could tell because she sat up straight and pressed her lips together. Her silence was probably because she hates to think about body preparation and the other aspects of the mortuary business just as much as I hate to think of her sitting up all night talking dirty to old men, though she swears not all her talk is obscene and not all of her clients are old. Jane considers her job a public service.

When we pulled up at the MUSC morgue receiving area, Jane sat quietly while I got out and signed papers for the attendant, who transferred Dr. Melvin's bag to a gurney and rolled him inside after signing my receipt for body delivery.

"Where do you want to eat?" I asked as I wheeled out of the parking lot.

"Are we anywhere near a Cracker Barrel? I'm starving. I want Uncle Herschel's breakfast with grits and biscuits and gravy as well as country fried steak and eggs."

I'd planned to go through a take-out window at Bojangles', but I'd asked Jane's preference, and we weren't that far away from where she wanted to go, so that's where we went. When we got out, I was immediately reminded of work. We have rocking chairs on the wraparound veranda at the mortuary. Ever since a mourner said that the rocking chairs at Middleton's made her think of the rockers on the porch at the Cracker Barrel, the restaurant brings the funeral home to my mind.

All the tables were full, so I put my name on the waiting list.

"Jane, do you want to sit in the chairs out front?" I asked.

"No, let's check out the gift shop." Looking through any

store with Jane means telling her what I see and letting her examine through touch whatever interests her.

June. Not even summertime yet. Though the South Carolina coast feels like summer as early as April, sometimes even the end of March, I always remember that summertime sometimes starts officially on June twenty-first because my birthday is the next day.

The Mother's Day items were reduced forty percent. Not that Jane and I were interested. My mother died the day I was born. Jane's passed away when she was eighteen. The Father's Day special gifts were reduced twenty-five percent. I didn't mention those to Jane either. I'd already given Daddy a nice gift on Father's Day, and Jane's dad abandoned his family right after he learned his baby girl was completely blind.

"What's new to look at?" Jane said.

"There's a lot of red, white, and blue for the Fourth of July," I said, "but there's also a lot of Halloween stuff."

"Oh, phooey," Jane joked, "I was hoping to see Christmas trees." I didn't tell her that a young lady was setting up a display of ornaments right beside a turkey-shaped cookie jar.

Jane can't see a thing, not even a shadow. She was born with no optic nerves. Since, according to shows on television, the medical profession now transplants corneas, hearts, kidneys, livers, and lungs as well as grafting toes onto hands to replace fingers, I sometimes wonder if Jane could have optic nerve transplants and be able to see. Until then, I'll just have to keep describing what she's touching for her to "see" it.

Chapter Three

"**Is** that Jane Baker? Jane?" called a tiny older lady looking our way.

The woman was hunched over one of those walkers with tennis balls on the back legs. She zeroed in on us, pushed through the crowd, and reached out to put her hand on Jane's arm. The woman's bright floral, matching skirt, blouse, and hat contrasted with her short, curly white hair. Her flip-flop shoes with bright cloth flowers attached didn't quite seem appropriate with the walker she used.

Jane doesn't like to be touched by strangers, but she knew the speaker because she wrapped her arms around the lady in an embrace.

"Mrs. White, you're back! How was your trip?"

"Wonderful, just wonderful!" the woman replied.

"Callie," Jane said, "you remember my landlady, Pearl White, don't you?"

How could I forget her? Names fascinate me because mine is so strange. I was named Calamine Lotion Parrish by my daddy, who happened to be drunk, *very* drunk, when my mother died giving birth to me. Daddy couldn't think of anything feminine except the color pink. Thank goodness he thought of lotion instead of Pepto-Bismol. Most folks call me Callie now, but my dad still calls me Calamine, and I get a kick out of other strange names.

What struck me as funny when I first met Pearl White was that her maiden name was Pearl Gray. I thought she could be a walking commercial for teeth-whitening ads. Especially since when Pearl gave up her own dental battle and got false teeth, she talked her dentist into giving her an unnaturally bright white.

"Of course," I replied and noticed the man standing right behind her. His hair was gray only at his temples, but his mustache was salt and pepper. He had cool blue eyes and a smile that said, "Hello, where have you been all my life?" I couldn't call him a *young* man, because he looked about fifty, but if he was Mrs. White's escort, he qualified as a boy toy in comparison to Jane's landlady, who was at least seventy.

"I'm really glad to run into you, Jane. I was planning to go by the apartment today to talk to you," Pearl said.

"Go by? Are you taking another trip?"

"Not exactly," Pearl said and then spoke over her shoulder to the man. "Georgie, would you change our request to a table for four? Jane and Callie can join us, and I'll tell them my exciting news."

The man squeezed through the crowd and headed away from us toward the hostess area. I noticed that he moved with that confident, long stride that smooth, self-assured men use. His khakis looked like they'd been tailored to fit, and the polo shirt he wore was one of the top name brands.

"I can't wait until we're seated to tell you." Pearl laughed and gave a silly little shimmy. "George and I are going to be married. I'll be moving to Orlando with him."

Jane opened her mouth, but before a word escaped, "Carter. Table for four for Carter" sounded over the speaker.

"Come on, that's us." Pearl led Jane through the crowd, spreading the sea of people with her walker. I followed. We caught up with George and were seated together at a big round table. The restaurant was crowded and the table would have sat eight. I wondered if George had rubbed a little green across a palm at the hostess desk, but I must confess, I've never seen or heard of that happening at a Cracker Barrel.

The landlady's expression beamed with unabated joy. "Georgie, this is Jane Baker, my tenant in the garage apartment, and her friend, Callie Parrish. Ladies, this is George Carter, my fiancé."

"You're getting married? How wonderful! Are you going to Orlando for your honeymoon? When will you be moving back to St. Mary?" I promise, I promise I didn't mean to, but I babbled.

"We won't be," George said as he patted the older woman's veined and wrinkled hand. We'll be living in Florida at my place. Pearl is selling her South Carolina property."

"And that's what I needed to tell you, Jane. I'm afraid I have to give you thirty days' notice to move unless you want to buy the house and apartment."

Jane's eyes don't demonstrate emotion, but her face does. Fear and dismay replaced her happy expression. "Thirty days? But what will I do? You worked for the Commission for the Blind, Pearl, and you know how hard it will be for me to find another place. I've been in the apartment for years. It'll take more than thirty days to pack everything."

"Ridiculous! You're one of the most independent visually handicapped people I know." Pearl paused. "And I'll help you pack."

We ordered and consumed breakfast foods, but Jane ate very little. Pearl described her love for *Georgie* and how the engagement might seem quick, but they'd been communicating hours at a time on the Internet since meeting in a chat room for older singles.

Having been interested in a younger man earlier in the spring, one I hadn't heard from since he left St. Mary promising to be in touch, I felt a pang of identification with Pearl. I'd never thought of her as lonely, but she must have been. The change from drab brown and gray clothing to the brightly garbed peacock sitting with us was obviously a result of finding love.

Picking at my breakfast cheese potato casserole and scrambled eggs, my mind wandered to this Internet phenomenon as Pearl and Jane talked. I caught occasional bits of their conversation. Pearl continued her joyful account of love at first sight, or was it first chat? Jane bemoaned the thought of moving.

Both Dr. Melvin and Pearl had found their soul mates online. I wondered if I could find time to enter a dating profile in one of the chat rooms while at work. I'd been planning to buy a computer for my home, but other bills kept pushing that goal away. No one stared over my shoulder when I entered obituaries on the mortuary computer. I could check out a singles website there.

Suddenly, my mind jumped back to Jane and her problem.

"Next door!" I blurted.

"What?" asked Jane and Pearl in unison.

"You know I'm living in a duplex," I said, "but no one lives next door. Jane, why don't you rent the other side of my building?"

"Is it just like yours?" Jane asked. She dipped her biscuit into white gravy.

"It's exactly like mine. It would be like living together, but still having our own privacy." The server topped off everyone's coffee. I added cream and two sugars to mine. I used to take three or four, but I'm trying to cut back on processed sugar.

"And you wouldn't be moving my things around like you did when you lived with me after your divorce."

"That's right. No more garlic on your cinnamon toast, but we'd be close enough to visit anytime."

"And you wouldn't have to listen to Roxanne, but you could if you ever wanted to," Jane promised.

"Who's Roxanne?" Pearl asked and frowned. "Do you have a roommate I don't know about?"

"Oh, no," I answered quickly. "That's a radio show. I don't like it, but Jane listens to it." *May that lie not blister my tongue,* I thought.

"That apartment next door to your friend sounds like a problem solved," George Carter said to Jane as he continued stroking Pearl's hand. "But I've already told Pearl she doesn't have to be in a hurry to sell, so you can take your time."

"Now Georgie," Pearl said, "I want to settle everything as quickly as possible so we don't have to keep coming back and forth from Florida, and besides, I already have someone interested in buying all my property. Her name is Dorcas Lucas, so if she comes and wants to look around, it will be okay, Jane."

"Are you staying in Charleston now?" I asked.

"No, we're actually staying at a bed and breakfast in Beaufort. We came up this morning to go shopping." Pearl smiled a big shiny white smile and gave George Carter a look of adoration. "Georgie is the only man I've ever known who never hurries me."

We all walked out together after George paid the bill. He and Pearl both laughed when they saw that Jane and I were traveling in the mortuary's funeral coach. I didn't laugh when I saw George open his car door for Pearl. He was driving a silvery blue Lincoln Continental. A new one with dealer tags.

Chapter Four

"**Where** are we?" Jane asked when I wheeled the funeral coach into the space in front of Victoria's Secret. About a year ago, I discovered these wonderful blow-up bras there. I threw out all my old ones and replaced them with inflatables. Recently, when I'd tried to even out a few that seemed to have leaked down a little, I broke the cute little pump.

"We're at Victoria's Secret's parking lot," I told Jane. "I won't be but a minute. Do you want to wait out here?"

She grabbed her mobility cane. "No, I'm going in. Why do you think I agreed to ride in a hearse with a body in the back? It was for Victoria's Secret, not for breakfast."

I'd expected that response but had hoped she would stay outside. The last time I took Jane into Victoria's Secret, she faked a fall and blamed the clerk for discrimination against the handicapped. The manager had comped Jane with bags full of merchandise to keep her from suing and probably figured the store had gotten off lightly. I'd seen Jane pull similar scams when we were teens. "Don't try anything," I mumbled as I guided her into the store with her cane *tap, tap, tapping* beside me.

Both salesclerks who approached us were extremely polite. I couldn't tell if they remembered Jane or not, but she's kind of hard to forget. How many young blind women with waist-length red hair and hippie clothing could there be in Charleston? I explained that I needed to buy a replacement pump for my bras. Jane told the other clerk that she'd like to "see" some panties.

Jane and I checked out at the same time. I paid for my pump and Jane paid for a pair of hot pink satin thongs. I was so proud that she hadn't pulled any stunts this time. As we left the store, I realized the clerks had recognized Jane because I heard sighs of relief as we passed through the door.

"Do you want to have lunch with me in St. Mary before I take you home?" I asked as we rode.

"No, you can just drop me off. Roxanne was up all night, and I need to sleep." She reached into the plunging neckline of her dress and began pulling out what appeared to be tiny scraps of lacy cloth.

"What's that?" I asked.

"Eight pairs of thongs. Nine if you count the ones I purchased. I'm going to give you four pairs for bringing me to Charleston."

"Are you telling me you stole panties from Victoria's Secret?"

"I didn't steal them. I just borrowed them against the rebate they should give us for making us want such expensive underwear."

"I don't need any of your stolen goods!" I spit the words. "One of these days, you'll go to jail if you don't stop!" I've tried for years to make Jane stop shoplifting.

"Is it because you only wear the ones with the built-in foam fannies?" she asked.

"*Dalmation!* You know how I feel about your stealing!" I said it with force, but even if she'd bought me a thong, I wouldn't have wanted it. When I tried wearing thongs, they were uncomfortable, and Jane spoke the truth. I only wear panties that boost my booty power.

Jane and I spoke not another word until I pulled into her drive. "Okay," I said when I turned off the car. "You can get out now."

"I know you're angry, but will you ask your landlady if I can take a look at the apartment?" Jane said.

So mad that I wasn't sure I wanted Jane living next door, I almost told her, "Not no, but four-letter-word no." Knowing I'd get over it and miss Jane horribly if our friendship ended, I said, "Okay, but we need to have another talk about your morals."

"Later," Jane said. Then added, "See ya!"

Chapter Five

Panting like a running dog with its tongue hanging out. That's how I felt, full of fear that I was late, when I pulled the funeral coach into the garage at Middleton's Mortuary. I'd left my Mustang in its assigned space at the back of the funeral home when I picked up the hearse to go to Dr. Melvin's. I checked my face in the rearview mirror and found that while my tongue wasn't protruding, wisps of hair straggled around my face, and I'd forgotten to put on any makeup.

My bosses require that I wear black dresses, stockings, and low heels to work. I've never asked, but I think they like the way I do my hair in a reserved style and don't paint up my face on the job. Regardless of what color my tresses are at the time, I smooth my hair back into a discreet bun at the nape of my neck when on duty. My style couldn't be called sleek now, so I patted my hair down, brushed on a touch of brown mascara, and slid on lip gloss before unfastening my seat belt and heading to the rear door.

By the time I'd dropped Jane off at her place and gone by my apartment to change clothes and take Big Boy out, I was running behind schedule. I didn't want Odell to catch me slipping in late. I work for the Middleton twin brothers. Originally identical, Odell now outweighs Otis by about forty pounds because of his addiction to barbecue. Odell also shaves his head though Otis chose tinted hair implants when the brothers began balding. Otis is a vegetarian who tans himself two shades darker than Odell. Otis has offered use of the tanning bed he had installed at the mortuary to both Odell and me. I've never used it, and I don't think Odell has either. Other differences between the two brothers include that Otis is always immaculate and usually soft-spoken. Odell shares neither of those characteristics.

"Hey, Callie," Odell called as I entered. I was glad I'd made it on time and saved him from having to look at his watch and give me a lecture on punctuality. "You won't believe what's going on," he continued. "While you were gone to take Mr. Dawkins for his postmortem, we've had three calls. I can't remember the last time business has been this good!" He grinned.

I started to bypass my office and head straight to my workroom, but the telephone rang.

"Middleton's Mortuary," I answered, "this is Callie Parrish. How may I help you?"

"This is Dennis Sharpe. Can I speak to the embalmer?"

"I'll be happy to arrange to pick up the deceased for you," I said, thinking what a smooth, melodic voice this man had. I have this thing about voices. A really smooth voice is more interesting to me than good looks, but this guy sounded like he had both.

"No, I want to talk to an embalmer. By telephone or you can make me an appointment." He cleared his throat. "Come to think of it, I'd rather come by. Can you schedule an appointment for me?"

"Would you like to come in today?"

"No, tomorrow's better. Can I talk to an embalmer tomorrow morning?"

"Yes, I'll be glad to schedule that. How about ten o'clock?"

"That's fine:"

"May I tell Mr. Middleton what the meeting will be about?"

"No, just tell him Dennis Sharpe with Carefree Pets will be in to see him in the morning at ten."

He hung up, and I wrote the appointment on the message pad before hurrying into my workroom. With three clients, Otis or Odell probably had already embalmed, or in mortuary vernacular, "prepared" at least one of them.

Sure enough, an elderly man lay on my work gurney with a sheet tucked in over his shoulders, up under his chin. I didn't recognize him, but a note on the counter had a line drawing of a circle head with hair parted on the left and combed over the top. I read the note in Odell's handwriting: "Callie, this is how Mr. Johnson's family wants his hair combed. Clothes on the rack. Do *not* put polish on his nails, not even clear."

Like I've *ever* polished a man's nails unless the family asked for it. I manicure male clients, but I only buff the nails. Never polish unless requested.

A gray suit, white shirt, and red tie with blue stripes hung on the rack behind my worktable. Socks and shoes were lined up neatly beside the note. I removed the sheet and saw that whichever Middleton had prepped him had, as always, put underwear on the gentleman before bringing him to my area. White boxer shorts and T-shirt, compliments of Middleton's Mortuary.

Mr. Johnson's skin had that pale, papery look that sometimes comes with age. I opened my kit and selected an appropriate shade of base makeup. Just as I finished applying the first coat to his face, neck, arms, and hands, Otis came in.

"Hey, glad you've started. I just completed the next one and she's gonna be hard. Nine-year-old girl with cancer.

She's still on my table. Mr. Johnson was preplanned, and the family came with the garments less than an hour after we picked him up. I'll help you dress him, and we can casket him right away. I'll be right back."

While I worked, Odell stuck his head in the door. "Going over to Shoney's," he said. "Be back soon."

By the time I'd made Mr. Johnson look as good as possible, Otis rolled in a mahogany bier with a gunmetal blue casket with blue-gray satin lining on it. With the help of the body lift, we dressed and casketed Mr. Johnson. As we rolled the bier down the hall, Otis told me, "Slumber Room B." He glanced toward the door to Slumber Room A and said, "We're putting the little girl in A."

"Odell said we have three today," I said. "Is he counting Dr. Melvin?"

"No, I guess it's four if we count Melvin Dawkins." Otis smiled. "Seems terribly disrespectful to be glad people are dying, but we need the business." He made the turn into Slumber Room B, pulling the bier, while I pushed from behind.

"Is the third one here yet?"

"Nope," Otis said. "We'll be going out to Taylors Cemetery tomorrow for her."

"Did someone die at the cemetery? Why would we wait a day to go get the body?"

"Remember asking me if Middleton's has ever handled an exhumation?"

"Yes," I said and thought *Ugggghhhh.* I like my job and enjoy making the deceased look good for their loved ones. So far as I'm concerned, the bodies we work on are shells left after the soul or whatever someone else wants to call it is gone.

For me, personally, though, there's no interest in learning to embalm, and if Middleton's is opening an existing grave, I'm glad I won't have anything to do with it. I don't want to be involved in those sides of the business.

"Well," Otis continued, "some woman in Beaufort won pretty big in the state lottery, and she's having her grandmother moved to a perpetual care cemetery. We'll be handling it for her."

"How long has the grandmother been buried?" I asked as we positioned Mr. Johnson's casket with his left side against the wall in Slumber Room B. I don't know why, but we always place the body tilted just a tiny bit toward the right in the coffin, and normally the bereaved pass by on the deceased person's right.

"I'm not quite sure how long the grandmother's been dead, but this woman wants the best of everything. We'll be recasketing and installing our best vault. Middleton's is ordering the marker, too. The lady's supposed to bring the paperwork and permits by this evening."

"Will I have to do anything?" I asked.

"Don't know yet." Otis headed toward the hall. "If we're recasketing, we'll probably be redressing also." I grimaced. "Come back to the prep room and let me go over what we're going to do for the little girl," Otis said.

I hate, positively *hate* working on children. There's no way that any makeup can duplicate the beauty and freshness of a child's complexion, but I don't think that's my problem. It's the sadness of life being cut so short and the extreme grief of the parents and family. Otis and Odell have been in the funeral home business all their lives, spent their own childhood living upstairs over the mortuary, but burying children still gets to them, too.

Saved by the bell. Just as Otis and I stepped into the prep room and I saw the tiny sheet-covered mound on the gurney, my cell phone rang. Miraculously, it was charged and in a dress pocket, so I answered it.

"Callie!" Jane screamed. "Something's wrong. Something's wrong."

Buh-leeve me, I was surprised. Jane is usually a cool, calm customer, while I panic frequently.

"What's wrong?" I demanded.

"There's someone going up and down the steps and when I ask who it is, no one answers. They've rattled against the door and seem to be trying to get in. What should I do?"

"Call 911. I'm on my way." I pressed the key to end her call and told Otis, "Something's happening at Jane's. I'm going over there. Be back as soon as possible."

Otis followed me out of the building, asking, "Do you want me to go with you?"

"No, I told her to call the sheriff. It's probably a raccoon or something like that, but she's all upset that whatever's on her steps doesn't answer her." I paused. "Besides, somebody has to stay here. Odell just left."

I jumped in the Mustang and tore out of the parking lot. Good grief. I don't always think before I act. I slowed down and headed toward Jane's at a reasonable speed. No point in breaking the law and no point in risking a wreck.

Almost to Jane's, I realized that I was trying to minimize the situation, whatever it was. Jane's hearing is acute and she's excellent at interpretation. She'd know the difference between the sound of a human on her steps and a small animal like a raccoon.

Any doubt that something was happening ended when I turned into Jane's driveway.

I heard her screaming.

Chapter Six

"**T**his is *my* home, so it's *my* porch. You get off. Just get off!" Jane stood at the top of the steep stairs to her front door, screaming and shaking her finger.

A tall, slender lady, wearing a pale gray skirt suit and alligator-skin heels, stood on the tiny porch. Apparently, Jane was trying to shake her finger in this woman's face. The problem was that Jane's adversary had turned her back, so the finger was shaking behind a gray high-dollar wedge haircut.

"What's going on?" I called as I jumped from the Mustang.

I couldn't understand a word because both of them began shouting.

"Calm down, calm down," I cautioned as I bounded up the stairs and stopped on the next-to-the-highest step behind the gray-haired woman. There wasn't room for both of us to stand on the covered stoop at the top of the stairs.

"Callie!" Jane yelled. "Make her leave. Tell her to get out of here."

"Shhhhh," I said to Jane. "Who are you?" I asked the woman who faced me.

"My name is Dorcas Lucas, and I'm trying to talk to Miss Baker here, but she won't stop screaming. I'm not having some blind psycho living on my property."

"What do you mean *your* property?" Jane demanded.

"My family owns Lucas Investment Enterprises, and we're purchasing this house and garage apartment along with other properties belonging to Mrs. Pearl White. I came to inspect everything and speak with Ms. Baker, but if this is the tenant"—she turned back to Jane, motioned toward her, and frowned—"I'm having her evicted immediately." The woman's tone sounded haughty and hateful.

"Jane has lived here for years." I put on my most professional funeral home voice. "As you know, she's visually impaired. You frightened her when you wouldn't answer while she asked who was out here. I'm sure you two can come to terms." Buh-leeve me, I thought I was being diplomatic.

"I *demand* to see the inside of her apartment. It's probably filthy since she can't see to clean it up," the Lucas woman snorted.

"That's a good idea," I answered. "You'll be surprised. Jane can't see, but she's an immaculate housekeeper."

"What's that I smell?" Ms. Lucas demanded.

I'd been so upset with the screaming and arguing that I'd ignored the rich, buttery aroma coming from Jane's open door.

"Cookies!" I said.

"I'm developing my own adaptation of benne wafers for the baking contest," Jane said.

"Benny wafers? What's that?" Ms. Lucas asked.

"They're very thin cookies with toasted sesame seeds in a batter of butter and brown sugar," Jane answered.

Ms. Lucas turned toward me and shouted, "She *cooks*?" The woman actually stomped her foot. "That blind girl better not be doing anything more than using the microwave in my building. That's why I need to see in there. I don't want a blind person burning down the place before I even take possession. If there's a cooking range in there, it has to come out. *Immediately!*"

"Prejudiced effing bigot!" Jane shot her arm out and pushed the woman.

I reached out and steadied Ms. Lucas. She wobbled and I realized that the slender heel of her shoe had caught in the space between two of the boards on the porch. She wiggled her foot loose.

"See!" Ms. Lucas spat out the words. "She's psycho. She could have knocked me down the steps. I'll file an eviction notice and she'll be out tomorrow."

"I beg your pardon." I revved up a nasty tone. "But we saw Mrs. White earlier today, and she just said you were interested in the property. You can't evict someone from a building you don't even own yet, and when you do possess it, the legal proceedings take a lot more than a few days."

"You must have seen Mrs. White this morning. Just an hour ago, we set the closing with her for tomorrow at four thirty." Ms. Lucas turned to face Jane. "I want you out of here tomorrow night. I'll come back after the closing to see that you're gone." She brushed against me as she stomped down the steps, then climbed into her Lincoln Town Car and drove away. The car was the same color as her hair and suit. I wondered if her monochromatic color scheme was intentional.

Jane seldom cries, but when she does, it just destroys me. Her eyes are useless, but her tear ducts work fine. Tears flowing from those sightless orbs have always upset me. "Did you call 911?" I asked.

"No," Jane sniffled. "She called out my name right after I called you. When she did that, I thought maybe she hadn't heard me before. I opened the door. After that, we just screamed at each other until you came."

I put my arm around her shoulder and led her into the apartment.

This had been the perfect home for Jane, one giant square room with a kitchen area in one corner, a bed in another, television and love seat in the third, and door to the bathroom in the fourth. It's important for all of Jane's belongings to have designated places. The apartment was large enough for that, but not too big for Jane to keep tidy. Pearl had worked for the Commission for the Blind, and, knowing Jane through the commission, she'd let Jane have the place for a ridiculously low rental.

Once we were inside, Jane regained her self-control. She went to the kitchen area and washed her hands, then filled the coffeemaker and clicked it on. She tugged on a padded glove and pulled a baking sheet from the oven.

"Have a seat," she said and motioned toward the love seat as she set the pan on a metal trivet to cool. Then she sat in the fake La-Z-Boy.

"I guess I'll be moving soon." Jane sighed.

"No problem," I replied. "Don't you remember? I promised to check with my landlady. I'd really love to have you living next door to me in the duplex."

"Yes, that could be a cool setup." She sat silently for a few minutes before pushing the remote control. The television clicked on and we watched Paula Deen for several minutes. Well, I watched; she listened.

When the commercial came on, Jane went back to the counter, poured two mugs of coffee, and added cream plus three sugars in one. To avoid overfilling cups and glasses, Jane folds her index finger over the rim. When the liquid reaches her fingertip, she knows the container is full. That's understandable, but I don't know how she senses when my cup is empty and reaches for it to give me a refill. As I accepted my coffee, she said, "You're gonna get diabetes if you keep using all that sugar."

I didn't bother to answer her because it's probably true. I didn't tell her that I'd been cutting back to two sugars either. Instead, I inhaled the fragrance from my mug and said, "Cinnamon almond."

Jane grinned. "You're getting really good at that. The *café du jour* is Almond Cinnamon. You reversed the name, but you got the flavors right." She sipped, then continued, "I'm sorry I called you, but that woman kept walking on the steps and when I called out, she didn't answer until after I called you. I'll bet she heard me talking to you through the door."

"She does seem strange," I said before changing the subject. "Do you mind if I call Otis? He was upset for you, wanted to come with me."

"Sure," she said and handed me her telephone. *Her* phone, not the one Roxanne uses.

"Middleton's Mortuary," Otis answered. "How may I help you?"

"Callie here. Jane's okay. The woman who's buying Pearl White's property was here and wouldn't answer, stayed quiet when Jane asked who was there."

"That's *weird*. Do you need to spend more time with Jane? The little girl's family won't be bringing her clothing in until tomorrow, so you can stay with Jane if you want. Just be on time in the morning."

I thanked Otis and disconnected the phone. Turning to Jane, I said, "Otis has given me the afternoon off to spend with you. What do you want to do?"

Jane squealed with joy. She worked her phone line at night, and I was busy at the mortuary most days, so we didn't have as much time together as we'd like. "Let's pick up some po'boy sandwiches and picnic on the beach," she suggested.

I'd never shared the secret with anyone. Jane and I used to skip school and go picnic on the beach. It was still one of our favorite things to do. Sitting on the sand, watching waves, was peaceful and brought memories of when we were young and our only problems related to which boys we each liked that week.

Jane locked her apartment door, mumbling that she hoped Pearl hadn't given "that blankety-blank" keys to everything yet. I've tried to convert Jane's profanity to my kind of kindergarten cursing, but she's not always a believer. We put the ragtop down on the Mustang and headed to Rizzie's Gastric Gullah near Hunting Island.

The restaurant had been open only a little over a month, but from the cars in the parking lot, it looked like Rizzie was doing well. Rizzie is a Gullah girl, well, woman, from Surcie Island. She's beautiful—tall and dark as Godiva chocolate. She wore a red and turquoise–patterned piece of cloth that covered her breasts, wrapped around one shoulder, then circled her hips, forming a dress that exposed her toned arms. When she moved, one leg showed, but only up to her knee. She'd shown me how to wrap the long cloth to make a dress, but I never got the hang of it. Rizzie also wore a head cloth in turquoise with gold threads through it. Traditional to her West African roots.

"Huddy, ev'rybuddy," she called loudly. "Come jine we on we bittle."

"What did she say?" Jane questioned. She hadn't come to St. Mary until we were in ninth grade, and she doesn't understand the Gullah language as well as I do.

"She said," I answered, "hurry, everybody, come join us and our food."

"You got it!" Rizzie said as she motioned Jane and me to one of the small tables. Rizzie speaks Gullah for tourists, and though I understand the language better than I speak it, sometimes she enjoys laying it on for me, too.

"No table," I said. "We want you to pack us a picnic. We're on our way to Hunting Island Beach."

"Where's your picnic basket?" Rizzie asked and pushed a stray curl of jet black hair back up under her head cloth.

"We didn't bring a basket," Jane answered. "Just put it in a bag."

"What do you want in your picnic?" Rizzie said.

I laughed. "From the smells in here, I want one of everything you're cooking today, but we'll settle for some sandwiches and drinks."

"What kind of sandwiches?"

"How about shrimp po'boys?" I suggested. "That's not very Gullah, but it's what I want."

"All seafood is Gullah," Rizzie said. "My people lived on the islands for a long time and we cooked mostly what came from the ocean. I can make you the best shrimp you ever tasted. I'll put some hush puppies in for you, too."

Having eaten here several times in the few weeks Rizzie's restaurant had been open, I knew she made *the* best hush puppies, even better than my brother's. While Rizzie cooked, I described the restaurant to Jane.

"She has shelves all around with sweetgrass baskets on them. Since Rizzie makes baskets, I suppose they're her own work, but she's got framed Gullah art and other crafts on the walls with price tags on them. Probably made by her friends."

"What kind of framed pictures?"

By the time I'd described the Low Country scenes in some of the paintings, Rizzie was back with a large plastic Piggly Wiggly grocery bag. "Sorry," she said, handing me the sack. "I don't have 'to go' bags yet. I'm just using what I get free."

"That's fine," Jane said as if she could see. "Pay her fast, Callie. I can't wait to eat these po'boys. They smell delicious."

As I handed Rizzie the money, I asked, "How's your grandmother?"

"Oh, Maum's about the same. Sometimes I worry that brother Tyrone and I spend so much time working here that Maum's left alone in the house too much."

"I'll stop by and see her sometime. Take some red polish and give her a manicure."

Rizzie laughed. "That would be great, but now she's been watching television, and she wants to try some other color, maybe metallic blue."

"We haven't used that at the mortuary yet, so I don't have any in my manicure kit, but I'll pick some up and try it on your grandmother's nails."

I guided Jane back to the car. Rizzie followed us out. "Here," she said and put another small bag on the floor behind the driver's seat. "Can't have a picnic without watermelon." She laughed and said, "Ef oonah yent hab hawss fuh ride—ride pawnee." I laughed, too. Rizzie had been around enough to know my brothers call my Mustang a pony. She'd said, "If you don't have a horse to ride, ride a pony."

Chapter Seven

It's impossible to carry on a conversation riding down the highway in a convertible with the top down. We headed down Highway 21 and cut over to the entrance to Hunting Island after a few minutes.

From the parking lot, we headed to the beach area, though from the smell of our food, I don't think it would have taken much to talk both of us into eating in the car.

I carried the bag full of hot hush puppies, packets of Tabasco sauce, and succulent-smelling shrimp po'boys as well as the smaller bag with the melon. Jane brought our beach towel, and we each held a giant soda, Coke for me and Dr Pepper for Jane. The damp sand oozed through our toes as we walked barefoot to the edge of the waves.

Even sitting on the towel, water from the sand quickly wet our derrieres. Jane's through the shorts she wore with a halter top. Mine all the way through my black work dress skirt tucked around my knees as well as my padded panties. The sky and water merged a rich medium blue, blurring the horizon. An occasional wispy white cloud floated above us, and the waves broke out in the ocean like white foam. I've seen pictures of beaches with beige, even dark brown sand. The sand here was the palest possible cream—almost pure white.

Both Jane and I have decent manners, but when it's just the two of us, we don't always use them. "Callie," Jane said as she chewed a mouthful of shrimp, "you understand everything Rizzie says in Gullah. Why don't you ever answer her in Gullah?"

I took a big swallow of Coke, then said, "I understand it better than I can speak it. Rizzie wouldn't care if I mispronounced something, and the tourists wouldn't know the difference, but some of the Gullah customers might think I was making fun of them."

I chewed a delicious, oniony hush puppy—crispy on the outside, fluffy and tender on the inside.

"What about Dr. Melvin? Has the funeral been set yet? If you have to work at the service, do you think one of your brothers might take me?" Jane piled her questions one on top of the other, not giving me time to respond to one before she asked the next.

"I'll be sure you get to his memorial, but I don't know when it will be. Depends on when the autopsy is completed."

"What do you think killed him?"

"Probably had a stroke or heart attack in the Jacuzzi."

"The way you attract murder, I'm surprised you still don't think that young wife of his killed him for his insurance money." Jane grinned.

I confess that I probably blushed. Jane couldn't see it, but she sensed my embarrassment. "Oh, I'm sorry, Callie," she said. "I don't mean you *attract* murder. I just meant you've gotten involved in several of them lately."

"Let me tell you this," I said. "If I ever have anything to do with another homicide, I'll be a basket case, for sure."

Jane laughed. "A basket case or a casket case?"

"Probably a casket case. Otis and Odell will be laying

me out in one of our finest models." Even in the June heat, I shivered when I said that. I had once been locked in a casket, and it wasn't a pretty memory.

Apparently, Jane had the same thought and the same reaction. "Don't even joke about that, Callie. You're giving me the heebie jeebies."

"Tell me about it. I don't want to work on any more murder victims, nor get involved with their killers."

Several minutes passed. We didn't talk, just enjoyed the food. I hoped Rizzie's restaurant became a smashing success because I could eat her cooking forever. Seagulls flew above us. I love to watch them. They seem to flap their wings more slowly than most birds when they fly.

"Want some watermelon?" I asked as I pulled the green sphere from the plastic bag.

"Not yet."

"Jane," I said. I folded my trash and stuffed it back into the plastic Piggly Wiggly bag. "Let's talk about *you*. I know we usually spend time together at your place, but you've been to my apartment. The one next door is the exact floor plan in reverse, a mirror image. It hasn't been rented in a good while because it needs repairs, but I don't think there are any major problems. Could you look at it tomorrow if I can set it up with my landlady?"

"Sure." Jane giggled. "I'll be happy to go tomorrow, and you can tell the landlady that renovations for appearance aren't important to me. I just want a safe place with all the appliances working." She broke into a belly laugh, and added, "Especially the stove. I'm going to learn to cook as well as Rizzie."

Now, Jane is no slack in the kitchen. She's a far better cook than I will ever be and gives Rizzie a run for her money. They just cook different styles. Jane leans toward Italian and occasionally Mexican.

"I assure you, Jane, if you move in next door to me,

you'll have two ranges to cook on, because I don't ever use mine!"

I stuffed our trash bag under the towel, then put the watermelon and shoes on the corners to keep the towel from blowing away. We took a walk along the edge of the water, letting the waves wash up over our toes. I felt like I could stay forever.

"I need to get home and see how my benne wafers turned out since they cooled," Jane said. "Besides, I have to take a short nap before I start work."

On the way back to our belongings, loud seagull squawking drew my attention again. Just as I looked up at the sky, I heard a sound I knew too well. The *crack* of a rifle shot. Both Jane and I jerked toward our left as a bleeding seagull landed about twenty feet away from us. I'd followed the falling bird visually. Jane must have been able to hear the thud when the bird hit the sand.

"Isn't it against the law to hunt here?" she said.

"Not only is it against the law to hunt at this park, it's illegal to shoot seagulls even during bird season." I know these things because Daddy and my brothers all hunt, and I used to go with them.

Jane and I hurried toward the towel. We had both sat down to put on our shoes when the sound cut through the air again, with a simultaneous *splash!* Our watermelon exploded into pieces, splattering both of us with wet, red mush and scratching us with broken pieces of hard rind. I grabbed my shoes and snatched Jane's wrist with my other hand. She already had her sandals on.

"Is someone shooting at *us*?" she squealed as we ran to the parking lot and jumped into the car.

"I don't know. We're just getting out of here!" I yelled as I cranked the car, threw it in gear, and took off.

We weren't even out of the state park before it happened.

Chapter Eight

It stopped. Dead still. The Mustang died smack in the middle of the road. The car had never given me a minute's trouble except for regular maintenance like oil changes and occasional new tires. Now it just sat there.

The pony wouldn't budge at all. Jane and I still had the jitters from the watermelon exploding all over us. The dead seagull upset me, but when the sniper hit the melon, the thought slid across my mind that the shot might have been directed at us, not necessarily to kill us, but to scare us. I wanted out of there right then.

I slammed my fists against the steering wheel and said, "Shhhh . . . oooot!" *Shame on me for what I almost said.*

"Call a tow truck," Jane suggested.

Buh-leeve me, I couldn't afford a wrecker. I rang Daddy's house on my cell phone. Since three of my five older brothers move in and out of the home place frequently, I guessed right—one of them answered.

"Hello."

"Hey, this is Callie."

"I know who you are. After all, you *are* my sister.

What'sa matter? You sound upset. Did you find another homicide victim?"

Among my problems was the fact that he'd recognized me, since I'm the only sister, but I wasn't sure if the voice belonged to Bill or Frank. I took a guess.

"Bill, my car won't start! It stopped right in the middle of the road!"

"Do you want me to tell Bill when I hear from him?"

"Okay, Frank. I'm sorry. You two sound alike. Where's Bill?"

"Said he was meeting Molly. I think they've gone to register for wedding gifts."

"Where'd they go?"

"Probably Wally World." He laughed, then roared like his smarty-pants answer was hysterical because he was more sophisticated, less redneck than Bill. If Frank ever re-marries, he'll register someplace classy—like Target. At his first wedding reception, he insisted on potato chips with French onion dip.

"Can you come get us?" I asked.

"Where are you and who's with you?"

"Jane's with me, and we're at Hunting Island State Park."

"That's where you two used to go when you cut classes in high school."

So much for my big secret.

"Well," I began, expecting him to say, "A well is a hole in the ground." He said nothing. "Can you come pick us up?"

"What are you going to do about the car?" Frank asked.

"I was hoping you could get it to run," I said.

"I'll drive Pa's truck, so I can tow the pony if we have to," he suggested.

"Where's Daddy?"

"He went fishing down at the pond. It'll take me about

half an hour to get to Hunting Island. No need for you and Jane to sit out there in a hot car. Go back to the beach. I'll find you."

"Oh, no," I said, "we're not going back to the beach. Someone's shooting a gun down there."

"Did you see the shooter?"

"No, but he was shooting seagulls and then he shot my melon."

"He did *what*?"

"He shot our watermelon."

"That's what I thought you said." He chuckled. "Well, just sit in the car or by the road until I get there." He laughed even louder. "Did you call the law on the shooter?"

"No, but I will in a few minutes. I don't know what to do about the car."

"Just sit in the car. I'll take care of it when I get there."

"But Frank, the car is stopped in the center of the road."

"You were driving down the middle?"

"No, you know what I mean. It's in the driving lane."

"Put it in neutral, then you and Jane push it over to the shoulder. Lean in and steer with your right hand. You've seen me do it." I must have been more upset than I realized. I should've thought of doing that. Frank should not have had to give directions. At various times in my life, I'd seen Daddy and each of my brothers have to push cars and trucks because of dead batteries or other problems.

"Okay," I agreed, then thought about the possibility that the shooter might have disabled my car. I'd read about men who would do that so a woman would be at their mercy when they stopped to "help." "Frank, we're going to the pier. Come get us from there. We'll see you in half an hour or so." When I explained to Jane, she agreed that leaving the car and waiting for Frank somewhere crowded with other people sounded like a good idea.

Jane and I managed to push the car over to the edge

of the road and walked back to the pier. I called the Jade County Sheriff's Department and reported the dead seagull and exploded watermelon. The dispatcher informed me that Hunting Island wasn't in Jade County, but he'd relay the report to the proper authorities. Jane and I strolled out over the water and talked with some folks who were fishing. Nothing was biting.

"Hey, Jane," I heard my brother shout. We met him at the steps to the pier. Frank is the youngest boy, only two years older than I am. He'd not only made it to the beach from Daddy's house in record time, he must have showered and changed before he came. He wore a spiffy black T-shirt with "Mama Said" printed on the chest in large white letters and "Americana Music" under it in smaller print. His jeans were cleaner than usual.

"Hi, Jane," he said as though I were invisible. "I saw the Mustang on the way in. I think the best thing is for me to hook it up to Pa's truck and tow it to the house. For the car to stop like Callie said, it's probably got a broken belt, and I don't have a replacement with me."

Daddy's truck is a Ford F-350 diesel with a rear seat that he uses for storage. In other words, it stays full of "stuff." Frank held the door for me to climb in the back, then assisted Jane to the front seat like a gentleman.

Of my five brothers, the only one who is consistently mannerly is my oldest. John is thirteen years older than I am, and he was as socially unacceptable as the others until he married Miriam. She trained him well, and now he's a sweetheart, living in Atlanta, working for her rich father.

"How have you been, Jane?" Frank asked as we rode.

"Not as well as I'd like," she said.

"What's wrong?"

"Pearl White is selling her property. I have to move, and I don't have the money to hire a moving company, plus it will be difficult to pack my things so that I can put everything where it belongs in the new place. Besides, the woman buying the property is already a real pain and I want out of there as soon as possible."

"Got any idea where you'll be moving?" Frank asked. Then, without giving her a chance to respond, he offered, "I'm sure Pa would let you stay with us if you need some place."

Puh-leeze. Jane's been my friend for years. She's been in and out of Daddy's house thousands of times and knows all my brothers. As a child, she loved coming home with me, but there's no way she'd ever stay with the Parrish men now that we're all grown.

"If Jane needs somewhere, she can stay with me," I said.

"But it was sweet of you to offer, Frank," Jane cooed, just like a Magnolia Mouth. She leaned over toward him and breathed, "*Ooooh*, you smell *so* good." At times in the past, I'd wondered if Frank might have a crush on Jane. It sounded like she knew he did. Then again, she may have been practicing her Roxanne on that last sentence.

Anxiety. It struck me like that bullet hit the watermelon. What if some thief had disabled the Mustang to make Jane and me get out of the way, leaving my car to be stolen? That fear didn't last long.

There was the blue pony, right on the side of the road where Jane and I left it. We stopped in front of it, and Frank had it chained to Pa's truck in no time. He drove out of the park and back up Highway 21. When he turned, I realized that he was headed to Daddy's, not to Jane's or my place.

"Jane needs to go home and get some sleep," I said.

"I won't be long, just want to unhook the Mustang and leave it in the yard. Then I'll drive you girls home."

The driveway up to Daddy's house is classic Low Country. Old live oak trees line both sides of the dirt road, and their curved branches create an arch over it. Spanish moss drapes from the branches, veiling the house, which is fortunate because no one wants to see the Parrish house until it's unavoidable.

At the end of the road is the ugliest house in St. Mary. It's my home place. The building has dark gray shingles that were on sale, and the trim, including the front porch, is painted black. I grew up thinking I lived in the Addams Family or Munster house.

Through the years, I've described the house to Jane, but since she lived most of her childhood at a home for the blind, then spent her teenaged years as an only child with a single mom in an apartment, Jane used to love hanging out at Daddy's house with all the hustle and bustle of six kids. I think she also loves my daddy, who looks like a sixty-something-year-old Larry the Cable Guy and acts like him, too.

While Frank unhooked the car, Jane and I went inside to use the restroom. Bill was there, sitting at the computer, and he jumped up in surprise when we opened the front door. I wondered if he'd been visiting some sites he didn't want me to see.

"Thought you'd gone to register wedding gifts," I said as Jane headed into the bathroom.

"I did. Now I'm back," he answered.

"Where's Molly?"

"Took her home. She's got to take care of her new litter of pups." Bill's fiancée bred and sold poodles. My own dog, Big Boy, came from Molly. Someone traded her a Great Dane puppy for a miniature poodle. When Molly couldn't sell him, she gave him to Bill to give to me. There'd been a time that she threatened to take Big Boy back, but everything was cool now.

Jane came into the living room, and I took her place in the restroom. That Coke had been *enormous*.

"Callie almost caught me printing out the banner," I heard Bill whisper to Jane. "Do you think she knows anything about it?"

"No," Jane replied softly, "we've been together all afternoon. If she had any idea, she'd have said something."

I was ready to flush, but I wanted to keep listening. When anyone whispers, it always piques my curiosity. What kind of secret did my friend have with my brothers? Could it have anything to do with my birthday Saturday? Daddy never celebrated the day of my birth because it's also the day my mother died, but my brothers have been known to buy gifts and even a cake. I waited, snooping, until I heard Frank's voice and the sound of the front door closing.

"Did you pick out any good tools or fishing equipment?" Frank asked.

"Nah, just dishes and trash cans and shower curtains and towels and bed linens. Not one thing for me." Bill wasn't too enthusiastic.

"Why didn't you insist?"

"Molly's not totally over being mad about me spending time with Lucy. I'm not doing anything to rock the boat."

"When's the wedding?" Jane asked.

"October," Bill said.

"Where's Callie?" Frank questioned.

"John," said Bill.

"Is John here?" Jane questioned.

"No, I mean Callie's in the john. You know, the bathroom."

"Oh, the loo."

I headed out before they started naming all the slang words they could think of for the necessary room.

Bill decided to come along with Frank to take Jane and me home. Frank made him sit in back with me, mumbling something about it being hard for Jane to get in the backseat.

Ex-cuuze me. Jane can climb in and out of any place I can. Frank definitely had a crush on Jane. She couldn't see the expression on his face when he looked at her, but I did.

When we pulled around Pearl's house to Jane's garage apartment in the rear, I looked for the gray Lincoln Town Car. No sign of it. No Ms. Lucas on the premises. No other vehicles. Pearl and her boyfriend weren't there either.

Frank and Bill walked Jane up the steps to her apartment.

"Come in and taste my benne wafers," Jane said. We followed her in and each had a cookie.

"You could win with these," I said and licked the crumbs from my fingers.

"Sure could," Bill assured Jane.

As we were leaving, just before Jane closed the door behind us, I heard Frank tell her, "When you get ready, I'll rent a big truck and move you."

On the way to my place, Bill asked a question I found awkward. "Jane said she has to sleep so she can work all night. She's a telemarketer, right? What does she sell at night?"

I'd never told Daddy and The Boys exactly what Jane did on the telephone, and I couldn't think of a thing that made sense.

"Uh, she sells products to people who work at night."

"If they work at night, how do they answer their home phone, and how does she know who works at night?" Bill said.

I hate to lie, positively hate it, but I mumbled, "The supplier gives her numbers of people to call and she calls them at work."

It was a flimsy answer, but I didn't want The Boys to think less of Jane, and I didn't want them excited about her job either. "The Boys" is a collective name I use for my brothers, with a capital T and capital B. I call them that because I doubt they'll ever grow up and act like adults, although John has improved considerably since his marriage.

"I think," Bill said, "that you're trying to say she doesn't make cold calls."

I pretend-coughed to cover up my laugh. "No," I said, "Jane doesn't make cold calls."

My duplex has a common porch across the front with a door into each apartment. I live on the right side. There are two driveways, one on each side of the building. Bill and Frank both came in with me. Big Boy was excited to have three people to pet him, but he was in a hurry to get outside. He brought his leash from the doorknob to me, but Bill clipped it on and took him out.

Frank made himself at home in the kitchen. He opened the refrigerator and brought back two Coronas and a canned Coke. He popped the top off the Coke and handed it to me, set one beer on the coffee table, and opened the other. He took a long pull from it.

"I didn't see any lemons or limes in the fridge," he said.

"That's because I don't have any." I drank some Coke from the can. "What if I wanted beer instead of cola?" I asked.

"You don't need to drink beer," Frank said, sounding exactly like our father.

There had been five Coronas in the fridge. It was easier to drink the soda and wait to have a beer after they left than to argue with him. I'm over thirty, been married and divorced, but Daddy and The Boys don't think I'm old enough to drink. If Jane had been with us, he would have brought her a beer, but not me. Good grief! I'm three months older than Jane. Thank heaven I don't have to live with my daddy and brothers.

Bill brought Big Boy back in, and we sat on the couch,

each of us taking turns rubbing his belly and scratching behind his ears. Big Boy's ears and belly, not Bill's. I'd known that Great Danes grow big when I got Big Boy as a pup, but my vet says that my dog is one of the largest Great Danes she's ever seen.

When Bill and Frank finished their Coronas, Frank headed toward the kitchen. I heard the fridge open and called, "Don't drink any more of my beers unless you plan to go to the store and replace them before you go home."

"What do you buy them for if not for us?" Bill asked.

"For me and my friends."

"You don't need to be drinking beer," he said.

"Come on, Bill," Frank said as he headed to the front door. "Let's go home and fix Callie's car." He turned to me. "I'll call you when I know what's wrong." He grinned sheepishly. "I offered to help Jane move. Don't let her forget, okay?"

I assured him all help would be appreciated and mentally thanked him for reminding me to call my landlady. She readily agreed to show Jane the apartment. I explained that I'd have to see about getting my car back or renting one before I could set a time.

"No problem," she said. "Why don't I just drop the keys off to you this evening? You can show it to your friend at your convenience. Call and let me know what she thinks. If she's willing to take it as is, the rent will be a hundred less a month than yours. If she wants carpet and the walls painted, it will be a hundred dollars a month more than yours."

The day had been long. I filled my tub with rose-scented bath oil and rummaged through my books until I found a Sherlock Holmes collection. I have many favorite modern mystery writers, but sometimes, I'm just in the mood for classics. Sir Arthur Conan Doyle fills that need. I dropped my clothes on the floor and stepped into the tub. The water was perfect. I slid into the bath until only my face and hands were out of the water. I was barely into the story when the doorbell rang.

Dalmation! I considered ignoring whoever was there until I realized it was probably my landlady and if she thought I wasn't home, she might use her key to come in. She might even need to use the bathroom and walk in on me lying naked in the tub reading a book instead of answering the bell. I climbed from the tub and slipped on my terry cloth robe. I had some satin and silk robes when I was married to Donnie, but for comfort, terry cloth is tops.

I tied the sash and opened the front door without peeking through the peephole. Levi Pinckney stood on my porch. Exuding testosterone in all directions, he leaned against the corner column with a box in his hand. "Nate's Sports and Subs" was printed on the carton.

"Pardon me," he said in that smooth Charleston accent of his. "I'm looking for 1450 Oak Street, but most of these houses don't have numbers on them, and I can't find it."

"This is 1440 Oak." I closed the robe more tightly. "Fourteen fifty is on the next block."

"Oh." Those dark eyes lit up and sparkled. "I'm sorry I interrupted you." He backed down the step. "I know it sounds trite, but don't I know you from somewhere?"

"I saw you early this morning at the Dawkins home. I'm surprised you're not with Mrs. Dawkins this evening."

"You're the girl who brought the hearse, aren't you?"

"No, I'm the *woman* who drove the *funeral coach* when Mrs. Dawkins called me."

"Roselle didn't want me around tonight. I'm working part-time for Nate's Sports and Subs. The delivery guy didn't show up, so I'm filling in for him."

I'm nosy. I promise I try not to be, but bottom line is that I am a nosy and catty female. "Are you Roselle's ex-husband or boyfriend?" I asked.

He laughed—a full, rich roar. "Not at all. Roselle is my half sister. She found me on the Internet several months ago when our father died, and we were getting to know each other when she got foolish and married an old geezer three times her age after she'd only known him a few weeks."

"But she virtually accused you of stalking her."

"I was raised in Charleston by our father and my mother. Roselle grew up in Georgia with her mother. When she located me about six months ago, I liked her, but she worried me with all that online dating. I thought it might be dangerous."

Levi grinned, and I felt my toes curl. "I've tried to keep an eye on Roselle since she came to South Carolina to meet this Dawkins," he said. "They married right away and went on a cruise to Greece. When they came back, I came here from Charleston. It seemed as good a place as any to explore what kind of business I want. Besides, I felt a need to keep an eye on the baby sister I hadn't known existed until a few months ago."

"I've known Melvin Dawkins my whole life, and he's a gentleman. I guess I should say he *was* a fine man. If there was anything wrong going on, it seems it would be Roselle's doing. After all, he's dead, and she's alive to collect his insurance."

His eyes narrowed. "I haven't known my sister very long, but I don't think she had anything to do with her husband's death. Every time I've been around them, she's acted like Dawkins was the love of her life."

"Maybe 'acted' is the key word."

Before he could answer, my landlady drove up in the driveway on the side of the vacant apartment. Now I was even more embarrassed to be standing on the front porch wearing nothing but a short robe.

"Hi, Callie," she called. "I've brought the keys. Is this the friend who's looking for an apartment? I thought you said a female friend."

"No, Jane Baker will be seeing it tomorrow. I'll call you after she comes over."

My landlady is sixty-five if she's a day, but she put her hand out toward Levi and purred, "Then who is this young man?"

"Levi Pinckney," he said. "I'm delivering for Nate's and stopped here to ask about 1450 Oak Street. I can't find it."

"That's because the numbers aren't logical on this street. For some reason, 1450 is next door to 1432 up the block there. Follow me, and I'll show you." She looked back at me, and her voice stopped purring. "Callie, you should dress before you come outdoors, even when the weather is hot."

"Yes, ma'am," I said and slipped back inside, closed the door, and keyed the dead bolt.

By the time I got back to the tub, the water was cold. Big Boy had climbed up on my bed and was snoring. I gently pushed him off onto the rug. I should have been full from the late afternoon picnic, but my stomach told me it still wanted something to eat. Raiding the kitchen pantry only resulted in one Moon Pie. I slid between the sheets with my book and read as I nibbled the Moon Pie. I thought about Levi Pinckney and told myself, *Callie, you need to get a life. Thirty-three this weekend and all you have in your bed is dog hairs and Moon Pie crumbs. Maybe you should go online and see if Levi has a profile.*

I put Sherlock Holmes aside and thought about Ann Rule's true crime book, *Too Late to Say Goodbye.* I'd read it since I like Rule's writing and because that case took place pretty near where I live. The victim's husband was convicted of killing her after she fell in love with a guy named Christopher that she met on the Internet. Christopher turned out to be a fictitious male created by a woman. That would be just my luck. I'd wind up involved with someone who wasn't even real.

After a while, Big Boy climbed back onto the bed and began licking up the crumbs.

I let him stay.

Chapter Nine

Life isn't fair. I've known that since I realized that other kids had mothers and I didn't. I've known that since Jane and I became close friends. I've known that since I realized that my mother had no choice about leaving me, but Jane's dad left her because he wanted to, because he was disappointed that his child wasn't perfect.

Whenever we have a very young person to prep at the mortuary, I feel like my nose is being rubbed in the unfairness of life. I pulled on jeans and a tee over my underwear and called Big Boy.

"I don't want to go to work," I said to my dog as I clipped the leash to his collar and took him outside for his morning walk. As always, he stepped behind the young tree at the edge of the yard to do his business. He's shy and doesn't realize that his head shows on one side of the tree and his haunches on the other side. I pretended to ignore him. When he'd finished, I scooped his production into a bag and took him for a walk.

"Jane might move next door to us," I told him. "You'll like that. She'll want to pet you all the time. I hate to tell you this, but we're going to have to shorten our walk this morning. I've got to find a way to work, maybe call Otis and see if someone can come pick me up." We turned and headed back to my apartment.

On the way, we passed a young man and woman stopped by the side of the road, talking. Each of them had a dog on a leash. His, a chocolate lab; hers, a fluffy white poodle. Might have even been bred at Bill's fiancée Molly's kennels. Why didn't any nice young men ever stop and talk to me when I took Big Boy out?

Looking at my big, gawky gray dog with his black spots and long legs, I wondered if it had anything to do with Big Boy not really looking like the choice of a frilly, feminine lady. The woman with the poodle had on pink shorts and a snug white shirt with pink trim on the sleeves. She tossed her hair back with a shake of her head and smiled at the young man, ignoring her prissy poodle with its yellow hair ribbons, though the dog kept trying to get her attention.

My blue eyes were taking on that greenish tint again. Jealousy is an ugly trait, but sometimes it creeps all over me. I try not to be jealous, but I don't always succeed.

I try, I promise I try, to be a frilly, feminine girl sometimes, but I just can't make it with the Magnolia Mouth speech and the ruffles that go with being a Southern Belle.

"Southern Belle" made me think of the baking contest. I wondered if I could create a recipe that would win half a million dollars. Puh-leeze. I don't cook very well *with* a recipe. Nobody would want to eat something I made up.

The young couple continued talking while their dogs explored each other more boldly, sniffing. The poodle had it all over Big Boy as a man magnet. The next thing that happened revealed that the little dog had it over Big Boy in other ways, too. The poodle didn't tee-tee like a girl dog the way Big Boy did. That tiny, adorable creature lifted his leg and piddled on his mistress's beautiful tanned calf.

She spewed and let loose with an unladylike four-letter word.

I pulled on Big Boy's leash to nudge him into walking home with me. He might be shy and he might still squat like a girl dog to tinkle, but he'd never wet on me. I patted his head and told him what a good boy he was.

Just as we reached our yard, Frank pulled into my drive in his Jeep. Mike, the middle brother, was behind him driving the rattletrap pickup Daddy keeps at the house for really dirty jobs.

"Good morning," I called. "What got you two up so early?"

"Pa made us bring you the extra truck to drive," Frank answered. "He's going to check out your Mustang this morning. I looked under the hood yesterday, but I didn't see any broken belts or anything."

"Do you have coffee made yet?" Mike asked.

"Not yet, Mikey, but I'll put some on."

"Don't call me 'Mikey.' I'm grown," Mike said as he and Frank followed Big Boy and me inside. I set up the coffeepot and showered while the coffee dripped, leaving my brothers in the living room watching the *Today* show. I put on panty hose and heels with a black dress and joined them.

Both men had brought Dunkin' Donuts travel mugs in from the truck and wanted their coffee to go. Mike handed me keys to the pickup, and they left with their steaming hot coffee. If I'd been a Mickey Dee's, I would've needed to warn them that fresh coffee is very hot.

I pulled my hair back into a chignon on the nape of my neck and examined the color. I'd been platinum blonde for a while. Dr. Melvin had picked out the color before he retired from the drugstore. He called it "Jean Harlow, Marilyn Monroe, and Jayne Mansfield blonde." I'd heard of those women, but almost all I knew about them was that they were all dead and that Jayne Mansfield had been the mother of Mariska Hargitay.

Almost thirty-three years old, I was ready for a change. I wondered how I'd look with honey brown hair.

When I called Daddy on my cell phone and thanked him for sending me what he still calls wheels, he said, "I'll try to get your car running today and get it back to you tonight."

Some women wouldn't want to be seen driving a beat-up old pickup to work, but I had a private parking space in the back so I wouldn't be embarrassed, and I'm not scared to drive anything. I drove the combine growing up, so I had no problem with driving a truck.

Mike had installed a CD player after he let his car get repo'ed and had to drive "the spare" for a few months. He had some great music in the truck. I listened to Bon Jovi all the way to the funeral home, then found an old Eagles album that I listened to sitting out back before I went in to work. My musical taste had been influenced by what my brothers played, and we'd all listened to Daddy's music coming up. He liked a little rock and roll, a little rhythm and blues, and a whole lotta bluegrass.

Otis met me in the hall. "I've just put the little girl in your workroom," he said. "There's a picture on the counter and her clothes are on the rack."

"How'd she die?" I asked. This is a no-no question from mourners who come to pay their respects, but Otis and I were the only ones there.

"Acute leukemia. Didn't respond to treatment." He paused. "Poor little girl."

I've noticed that although Otis and Odell both insist that the deceased be called by their names, never "the body" or "the corpse," they usually refer to children as "the little boy" or "the little girl." I think it's to keep from getting too personally involved.

"Mrs. Dawkins is scheduled in at eleven to make arrangements, too," he added.

"Is Dr. Melvin coming back from Charleston today?"

"Don't know, haven't heard."

"What about the exhumation?"

"Mrs. Whitaker brought her paperwork in yesterday, but it's not complete. She has to have another permit before we even begin planning the transfer."

"Where's Odell?" I questioned as we went into my workroom and I pulled a plastic smock over my dress and disposable gloves over my hands.

"Now, where do you think he is?"

"Shoney's?"

"Yep."

I began my work on the little girl.

She was dressed and I was ready to find Otis to ask for the casket when he came in pushing a white, child-sized model with soft pink lining.

"She looks nice," he said.

"Have her services been planned?"

"Visitation is tonight. The family moved here from Connecticut. Father is a Marine at Parris Island. Tomorrow morning, we'll be shipping the little girl up north for the funeral."

I breathed a sigh of relief that I'd be spared another child's funeral. We casketed her and rolled the bier to Slumber Room A. The name on the sign by the door read "Miss Angela Lee 'Angie' Greene." The casket spray was pink rosebuds and baby's breath. I removed it from the stand and set it on the bottom half of Angie's casket.

An instrumental version of "Blessed Assurance" sounded through the funeral home, signaling that the front door had been opened.

Dreading facing the parents during a time of such great loss, I went to the entry hall. The man stood at the door alone. I wondered why Angie's mom wasn't with him. Then I realized that this man did not look like a Marine, even an off-duty one.

There aren't any mountains along the South Carolina coast, but this was a mountain man, for sure. He wasn't much over six feet tall, but he gave the impression of being a giant. He was huge in a way that wasn't flabby fat, just a solid-looking big man. He wore a farm equipment cap with camouflage pants and T-shirt. The pants were held up with leather suspenders, hand-tooled with vertical letters spelling out "Carefree" on his right side and "Pets" on the left.

When he turned to pull the door closed, I saw that his gray-streaked brown hair hung through the hole in the back of the cap in a ponytail down to his waist. His beard was a lot like one of the men in ZZ Top, and he had an unlit cigar in his mouth. It looked slobbery, like he'd chewed on it.

"I'm Dennis Sharpe," he said in that same wonderful warm voice I'd heard on the phone. A voice that didn't go at all with his appearance. "I've come to talk to an embalmer."

"Certainly, Mr. Sharpe. I spoke with you yesterday. Have a seat in the conference room and I'll call Mr. Middleton for you." I motioned toward an open door and watched as he went in and sat at the round conference table. He sure didn't look like he sounded.

I was glad this man wasn't the little girl's daddy. He didn't look like I'd pictured her father in my mind. Actually, I don't think I'd ever pictured anybody quite like him. I pressed a button on the wall beside the light switch and notified Otis to come up front. When he arrived, we entered the room where Mr. Sharpe waited.

"Mr. Sharpe," I said as Otis and I sat down, "this is Otis Middleton, one of the owners of Middleton's Mortuary. He's also a licensed undertaker and embalmer, so he can answer any questions you have."

Otis pulled out a clipboard with a planning sheet on top.

"Oh, no," Mr. Sharpe said. "You won't need any of that. I just want some information about embalming."

"What would you like to know?" Otis asked and set the papers and pen on the table.

"Well, first off, so you won't think I'm some kind of kook with a kinky morbid interest, I want you to know that I'm a taxidermist. I've made a good living preserving hunting and fishing trophies around here but it's slowed down. Last year, I started another business. I got to thinking about years and years ago, somebody made a bunch of money selling 'pet rocks.' Remember that?"

"Yes," Otis said, "I believe I do."

Dennis Sharpe pulled the cigar out of his mouth and looked at the wet end, then put it back between his lips. "Well, you know Roy Rogers had his horse Trigger preserved and mounted by a taxidermist, and I've done some pet dogs and cats. Got to thinking that while some people can't let their pets go when they die, there's probably folks around who'd like a pet but either can't afford or don't have time to feed and care for one. That's when I started Carefree Pets."

"What kind of pets do you sell?" I interrupted.

"Started out mostly dogs and cats, but I found out a lot of people who don't hunt wanted stuffed wild animals. I don't mean big ones. Little fellows like squirrels and raccoons, sometimes even possums."

Otis cut me a look and said, "Mr. Sharpe, I follow what you're saying, but what does it have to do with embalming?"

"Competition has gotten pretty fierce in the taxidermy business. Lots of folks are having their kills freeze-dried, and I've been wondering if embalming might be an alternative. In taxidermy, we stretch the fur over forms, sometimes plastic, sometimes carved from wood. Would it work to just embalm the animals?"

"No." Otis smiled. "Embalming wouldn't be suitable. It's not as permanent as your taxidermy methods."

"I saw on television that some woman named Eva Perón was perfectly preserved for over twenty years," Dennis Sharpe said. "Her husband kept her in his dining room even after he remarried."

"That's not usual embalming, though. Her body was treated with a much costlier and lengthier method than is used today," Otis said in the instructor tone he sometimes uses with me. "Mrs. Perón's body was almost plasticized."

I couldn't believe that Otis was actually using the word "body."

Mr. Sharpe looked disappointed. "Then you don't think embalming might be able to replace taxidermy?"

"Never."

"What about freeze-drying?"

"Instead of taxidermy?" Otis asked.

"It's already doing that. Do you think freeze-drying might replace embalming?"

"I never really thought about it, but from what I've read, freeze-drying anything the size of a human would be a very lengthy process."

"The equipment's expensive and it does take months, but I was wondering if you might be able to convince people their loved ones would last longer if they were freeze-dried instead of embalmed."

Otis gave Dennis Sharpe a *What kind of fool are you?* look before he responded. "Why?" Otis asked. "Why would you want to do that? The bereaved don't want to wait for months to bury their loved ones."

"If you convinced them to freeze-dry their loved ones, they could take them home with them."

I'm sure Dennis Sharpe could see my look of disbelief that he'd even suggest such a thing.

"Why would you want us to do that?" Otis asked.

"I was hoping we could go in together to buy the freeze-drying equipment. It's very expensive, so we could share it."

Otis sat silently, probably wondering how to get rid of this goofball. "I don't think so," he finally said. "Our clients want to see their loved ones embalmed and looking peaceful within a day of death. Besides, no one would want to think of a family member lying up in a freeze-dryer beside a possum or some other roadkill."

"Oh, I don't use much roadkill," Dennis Sharpe quickly said. "The only roadkill I ever use is if it's absolutely, positively fresh."

Otis stood, which is his way of dismissing people from the conference table. "Sorry, Mr. Sharpe," he said. "I'm afraid I can't help you."

Dennis Sharpe pulled two business cards from his pocket and handed one to each of us. "If you think of a way we could do business, please call me," he said.

I walked him to the door.

"You sure are pretty," he said before he left. I heard "How Great Thou Art" as the front door closed.

I almost bumped into Otis as I turned away from the door. He'd followed me. "That guy's a kook," he said. "Does he actually go out there and kill innocent cats and dogs to stuff them?"

Goose bumps rose on my arms, and I said, "I don't even want to think about it."

Chapter Ten

"**Y**oo-hoo, is anyone here?" a young female voice called before I'd even reached my workroom. I turned around and faced the front door. Roselle Dawkins and Levi Pinckney stood together by the hall tree. They must have come in right after Dennis Sharpe left. Roselle looked like death warmed over. Ex-cuuze me. I can't believe I used that expression. Let me edit myself. Roselle looked dreadful. Her hair was tangled and uncombed. She wore a wrinkled blue jumper with a beige cotton shirt and leather sandals.

"Hello, Mrs. Dawkins and Mr. Pinckney," I said. "Mr. Middleton said you were scheduled for eleven, but I'm sure he'll see you now. Just follow me to a consultation parlor."

As we passed the open door to Slumber Room A, Roselle glanced in. She sucked her breath in hard, exhaled loudly, and whispered, "Look, Levi. It's a child."

"Yes, ma'am," I replied. "A little girl."

"How sad," Roselle said. "I asked Mel if we could have children, and he said we'd try. I can't imagine losing a kid." I couldn't imagine Dr. Melvin as the father of a newborn.

They followed me into our nicest conference room and

sat side by side in two of the overstuffed green velvet chairs surrounding the antique table.

"Please pardon me," I said, "I'll call Mr. Middleton."

"Can't you help us with the plans?" Levi asked. "You work here, don't you?"

The smart-aleck side of me wanted to say, "No, I just drive the funeral coach around and always dress in black because I think it's a good color for me." Instead, I said, "I work here, but making arrangements isn't part of my job. That's usually handled by one of the Middletons."

I stepped out of the room and saw Otis headed down the hall. "Dr. Melvin's widow and her brother are here," I said. He joined them as I stood at the door and asked, "Could I bring anyone coffee or bottled water?"

Odell got this idea that if we offered bottles of water instead of soft drinks, we wouldn't need to stock a variety. Personally, I thought if we served water, it could be tap on ice in a glass. Even less expensive than bottles. Irrelevant at the moment. Roselle and Levi both agreed coffee would be fine.

When I returned with the silver coffee service, planning sheets and contracts were spread across the table. As I served the coffee, I took a good look at Levi Pinckney. The South isn't nearly so inbred as Jerry Springer would have folks believe, so tell me why I was jealous of Roselle Dawkins.

Levi said they were siblings, but he'd also said they hadn't known each other very long. I thought about one of my brothers being concerned enough to move to a strange town to watch out for me if we'd only known each other a few months. My brothers are protective, but they've known me my whole life.

My blue eyes turned green again, and I wondered if Levi's interest in Roselle was anything other than brotherly. That brought a quick consideration of brother-sister romance, and I gagged while fighting down the urge to upchuck all over the papers Otis had on the table for Roselle.

"Mel gave me this not long after we married," she said and handed a large manila envelope to Otis. She turned toward me. "Callie, this coffee is good," she said, "but could I have some water, too? I need to take some pills."

Otis looked through the papers in the envelope, smiled, and said, "There won't be any problem. Your husband has left you well provided for with insurance naming you the beneficiary and his will making you his sole heir. All I'll need is for you to sign papers giving Middleton's an assignment against the policy."

I went for the water while Otis continued examining the papers. When I returned and handed the bottle to Roselle, Otis was saying, "Here are suggestions for Melvin's funeral. It's not written in such a way that it legally binds you, but as a letter telling what he'd like."

Roselle unscrewed the cap from the bottle of water and set it on the table. She removed a small bottle from her purse and poured almost a handful of capsules and pills into the palm of her hand. She tipped the whole lot of meds into her mouth and chased them down with about half of the water. Then she looked at the paper Otis offered.

"May I see that?" Roselle reached out and accidentally spilled her coffee. I dabbed it up with some of the napkins on the silver tray. Though we use mugs and paper towels in our offices, Otis insists on cloth napkins and Wedgwood china for the bereaved. Silver coffee service and real china, but he gives people water in plastic bottles. Go figure.

"What are all those pills you're taking?" Levi asked.

"Just Mel's vitamins and nutritional supplements. He had them all counted out by days, and I figure I need extra strength going through all this." Roselle's face crumpled, and tears flowed from her eyes, but after a minute or so, her mouth curved into a smile. "Mel's done it all for me. Just follow his directions there, a wooden coffin, the church and cemetery he names. All we have to do is set the date and time."

"We can't do that until Mr. Dawkins comes back from Charleston," Otis said, "but we'll call you as soon as we hear something."

Roselle turned to Levi and said, "See? I told you I could handle this without your help. Mel took care of everything. *He's* taking care of me. Why, I'll even have enough money left from the insurance to buy a condom to lease out."

Otis raised his eyebrows at me. Levi squirmed and said, "Yes, you may be able to buy a condominium for rental property." He shot me a look that was half embarrassed and half amused.

"I told you Mel would take care of me. He really loved me."

Levi squirmed in his chair again and mumbled, "Well, you never know. I'm just trying to act like I think a big brother should." He patted her hand. "I'm really glad you found me."

Otis and I walked Roselle and Levi toward the front door after she'd signed everywhere Otis pointed to on the papers. When we reached the door to Slumber Room A, Roselle turned to Otis. "Would it be all right for me to see the little girl?" she asked.

"I don't see any harm in that," Otis said and led her to the casket.

Levi and I stayed in the entry hall. "Did you find the right house last night?" I asked.

"Exactly where the lady said it was."

"How long have you been delivering for this sub place?"

"I'm not the delivery boy. I'm learning the business and since there was no one to deliver that sub, I did it myself." I really liked his Charleston accent.

"What will you be doing after you learn the business?"

"I worked as a butcher in Charleston in my dad's meat-packing business, but I'd rather do something that's more people-oriented. When Dad died, I sold his company and I'm exploring what I want to do. I may open my own sub shop, so I'm getting the feel of it at Nate's."

"Where is Nate's?"

"Here in town. It's over on Pine Street. Why don't you come by this evening?"

"You won't be there, will you? I'd imagine you'll be with Roselle."

He looked down. "Can't you tell she doesn't want me around? I'm taking her shopping and to the bank, but I'll be going in to work at six. Her mom and family will be up from Georgia before then. Come on by Nate's. I'll treat you to dinner."

Thank heaven Roselle and Otis joined us and saved me from having to answer. A dinner invitation at a sub shop while my "date" worked the counter wasn't the best offer I've ever had—but I've had worse.

"What a Friend We Have in Jesus" sounded as Roselle and her brother left. I went to my office and called Jane to see when she wanted to see the apartment next to mine. She suggested I pick her up about dinnertime and get something to eat after looking at the apartment.

"Sure," I answered. "There's a new sub shop in town. We'll go there."

Chapter Eleven

"**S**orry," Odell said to me when he came back near midday. "I should have told you to take lunch early." He thrust a paper bag at me. "Otis and I are taking Mr. Johnson to the church for the funeral, and I need you to hold down the fort. I brought you a sandwich. We'll be back before the little girl's visitation."

"Sure." I opened the bag. I should have known even before I smelled the aroma. Barbecue. Sometimes I think that's the only kind of sandwich Odell knows.

"By the way, if you get a pickup," Odell continued, "call Jake and send him. We're taking the new funeral coach, but the keys to the other one are on the rack where they belong." This was a direct attack on me since I've been known not to return things to their proper place. Not to put lots of things back correctly, including mixing up the garlic powder and the cinnamon during the short time that I lived with Jane when I returned from Columbia after my divorce. Does anyone eat garlic toast for breakfast? Jane didn't much care for it.

There were no calls during the afternoon, and Angie's family didn't come by. I spent my time on the computer, updating our web page and Internet memorials. When I finished, I read Gwen Hunter's *Sleep Softly* until the Middletons returned.

"It stinks" was the first thing Jane said when we opened the door to the apartment next to mine. She wrinkled her nose like Samantha on the television reruns, but the smell didn't magically disappear.

"Of course," I said. "It's been empty a couple of years. We can take care of that." Thank heaven she couldn't see it. My apartment is very seventies, with avocado green shag carpet and matching appliances. That's bad enough, but it looked twenty years newer than this. Mine had been remodeled, and this one was still decorated like it was when the building was constructed in the forties or fifties.

"Okay," I said as I guided Jane through the rooms. "The front door opens into the living room. You know how my kitchen is on the right. Yours is on the left. You can see it from the door."

Outdated wallpaper everywhere. Worn, scratched hardwood floors except in the kitchen, which someone had tried to modernize with peel-and-press tiles that curled at the edges. I have butcher-block Formica on my counters and lust for the beautiful granite countertops I see at Lowe's and Home Depot. The counters here were topped with black linoleum marked by numerous cuts and gouges.

"Two bedrooms at the back with a bathroom in between, just like mine." I guided Jane to the bathroom. Whoever had stuck tiles in the kitchen had apparently used the leftovers around the commode until they ran out, leaving the rest of the broken, cracked ceramic tile showing everywhere else. I didn't bother describing that to Jane.

"What do you think?" she asked.

"I think you should take it, and if I were you, I'd rent it as is and get the cheaper rent."

"Sounds good to me *if* we can get rid of the musty smell."

"Tell you what," I said, "I'll talk to Frank about the odor, and I'll bet he'll take care of it for you."

"I hope so. That woman's been back sneaking around my place, and she still won't answer when I talk to her. Mrs. White came by with George Carter, who she calls her *fiancé,* and giggled like an eleven-year-old. She said the closing has been delayed, but she still wants me to move as soon as possible." Jane paused. "She even offered to refund my last month's rent and my deposit to help me relocate faster."

"I've never heard of anybody doing that."

"She's good people. Can you tell the landlady here that I'll take it as is and ask how much deposit she needs?"

"Let's go next door, and I'll call her from my place."

"Hi, Callie and Jane" was the first thing I heard when Jane and I walked from the piece-of-caca truck into Nate's Sports and Subs. The place reminded me of some of the sports bars my ex had taken me to in Columbia. Various sports games played on several large-screen televisions on each wall. Football helmets, baseball gloves, and other athletic equipment were displayed every place that room permitted.

The voice was masculine, but it wasn't that Charleston drawl Levi Pinckney spoke. I glanced over and saw Sheriff Wayne Harmon sitting at the counter, or in the case of Nate's, I thought it might properly be called a bar.

The sheriff was eating a foot-long sub that looked as though some of everything available was on it. Guess law enforcement officials have to eat something besides doughnuts sometime.

"May I talk with you two ladies?" Harmon didn't wait for an answer. He moved his plate and cup to a booth and motioned for us to sit across from him. I noticed that he chose a booth that was relatively secluded, not near anyone else.

I nudged Jane into the seat and looked around for a server. Oh, okay, I admit it. I was searching for Levi.

A girl, looked late teens but probably somewhere in her twenties, approached us. She had lots of tattoos that I could see, and I'd bet a month's wages that she had many more beneath her jeans and tank top. "What would you like to drink?" she asked.

"I want a draft beer," Jane answered.

Any other time, I would have wanted a beer with her, but since we were sitting with the sheriff, I asked for a Coke. He'd know I was driving, and though one beer certainly wouldn't put me over the alcohol limit, I make it a policy not to drink and drive. Wayne Harmon had been friends with my daddy and brothers so long, he'd probably give me a lecture if I drank in front of him anyway.

Sometimes Jane asks me to read the menu to her when we go somewhere new. This time, she didn't. When the server returned with our drinks, Jane said, "Do you have meatball subs?"

"Sure do," Miss Tattoo replied.

"That's what I want," Jane said.

"What's the sheriff eating?" I asked and motioned toward Harmon's sandwich.

"It's a deluxe," he answered for her. "Some of everything, including all kinds of peppers."

"I'll take one just like his, with extra jalapeños, please."

Miss Tattoo went behind the counter.

"Callie," Sheriff Harmon said, "I wanted to ask you about Melvin Dawkins."

I took a swallow of Coke and asked, "What do you want to know?"

"Exactly what was the situation when you arrived?"

"Same as when you got there."

"Where was the body?"

"He was floating in the hot tub."

"Did you touch him?"

"No, I could tell he was dead."

"Did you see his wife move him in any way?"

"No, but she did ask me if I thought we should take him out before I called you. I told her we couldn't touch anything. When her brother got there, he felt for a pulse, but the body wasn't actually moved. Left Dr. Melvin floating facedown in the tub with the pumps on."

"Callie, are you lying to me?" The sheriff used his authoritative tone.

"No, why do you ask that?"

"You're looking all over this place except at me. Why can't you look me in the eye? Are you fudging on the truth?"

Jane laughed. "She's looking for a man. She told me we were meeting some hot guy here, and from the sound of her voice, it wasn't you."

Harmon smiled. "Is it someone who might not want to join you if he sees me sitting here? Someone who might not want to sit at a table with the county sheriff?"

"No, actually Dr. Melvin's brother-in-law asked me to meet him here."

"Levi Pinckney?" Sheriff Harmon asked just as our tattooed lady returned with subs for Jane and me.

"Levi's not working tonight," she said as she placed the wrapped sandwiches in front of us. "He called in, said his sister needed him. Her husband died, you know?"

"Yes," I said, "we know."

The girl picked up Jane's empty mug and headed toward the counter. "Don't refill that," I called. "Bring her a Dr Pepper."

"Why?" Jane asked.

"Because if I can't have a beer, you can't either."

Sheriff Harmon continued chewing. Jane took a big bite. I didn't really feel like eating. I had this great big sub in front of me, large enough to feed two of my brothers, and I wasn't even hungry. I sipped my cola, then rewrapped the sandwich.

"Not hungry?" Harmon asked.

"No, not really. Why are you asking about Dr. Melvin? Is he back yet? Have you heard from the postmortem?"

Harmon motioned toward his mouth and kept chewing. I knew he meant for me to wait. He swallowed, then said, "The autopsy's complete, but we're waiting for the toxicology results. It will take another couple of weeks or so for those. There was no water in his lungs, so he didn't drown. No signs that he'd been hit or anything either, and his heart looked pretty good, too. No scar tissue. In other words, the autopsy didn't show cause of death, so we're hoping the chemical tests on fluids from the body will answer our questions."

"Are you testing for poisons?"

"Doing a basic metallic scan, but there's no reason to test for things like arsenic. Those poisons display symptoms that Melvin Dawkins didn't have."

Jane wiped her lips and fingers with her napkin. "That's about the best sub I ever ate," she said.

"I'll have to try the meatballs sometime," Harmon said. "Everything I've had here has been good." He looked around. There were a few customers, but the place was far from crowded. "So you came to see Levi Pinckney," he continued. "Why?"

"He said he's working here and suggested I try it sometime. I just thought he might be here."

"That's not what you told *me*!" Jane protested. "You told me we were meeting him here."

Good grief. Embarrass me anytime, Jane. Tell the sheriff I got stood up tonight. I thought those words. Thank heaven I didn't say them aloud.

"Well, if you think of anything else about the night Dawkins died, let me know." Sheriff Harmon stood, slapped a couple of dollars on the table for a tip, and started toward the door. Then he turned back. "Callie," he said, "I heard that Mullet Man came to Middleton's today."

"Mullet Man? I don't know anyone called Mullet Man," I said.

"Dennis Sharpe. Try to avoid him, Callie. He's extremely weird."

"I kinda thought so," I said, thinking about his interest in freeze-drying dead people.

After he'd left, Miss Tattoo reappeared at our table. "Want that beer now?" she asked me.

"No, not even a refill on the Coke. I'd like the check now."

"Sure." She handed me the ticket.

"Do I pay you or at the register?" I said.

"I'll take it."

"No change," I said when I handed her the money.

She started toward the register at the counter, then turned back to me. "That Levi is a real hottie, isn't he?"

I nodded, so Jane wouldn't know my answer, picked up my sub, and led Jane out of the sub shop.

"Are you angry with me for some reason?" she asked when I closed the car door behind her.

"Nope, just weary, that's all."

I was tired, but I had a swarm of other feelings, too. Disappointment that I hadn't seen Levi was one of them. Curiosity was another. Was Dr. Melvin's death due to natural causes or not? Why hadn't the autopsy shown a physical cause, the expected heart attack or stroke? I promise I don't seek out murders. Why did they seem to follow me?

"Well, if you're tired, let's get outta here. I want a shower before Roxanne starts working tonight."

At home, when I pulled into her yard, Jane said, "Call me tomorrow," and climbed out of the truck.

"Stairs are straight ahead, about seven steps in front of you," I told her.

Jane was inside her apartment when I realized I had that humongous sub in the backseat. I picked it up and carried it to the top of the stairway. Jane let me in when I called out to her, and I cut the sandwich in half, wrapped it in two packages, and left one part in Jane's fridge.

"Thanks, Roxanne will enjoy that in the wee hours of the morning." Jane giggled. We both referred to her "conversationalist" personality as though Roxanne were a real person, not just a name Jane used on her job. Tired and ready to have some time to myself, I breathed a sigh of relief as Jane locked her apartment door and I headed down the steps.

My relief was premature. Ms. Lucas pulled in behind me in her gray Lincoln Town Car, opened the door, and stepped out. She wore a powder blue suit, probably some expensive brand from New York that I'd never even heard of.

"Glad to see you," she said as she walked quickly toward me. "Is Miss Baker home?"

"Yes, she is. What do you want?"

"Mrs. White gave me keys to the property, but when I was here earlier, I found out she didn't give me one for the apartment. I need to get in there to inspect it."

"If you want to go in before Jane moves out, Mrs. White will have to come with you." I stepped around her and opened the truck door.

"Well, if that blind girl is in there, she's going to show me around." Ms. Lucas started up the stairs. I sat in my car, hoping Jane wouldn't answer the woman's knock. I was just too exhausted to deal with this tonight.

"Open up!" Ms. Lucas shouted when she reached the top of the stairs and banged on the door.

Jane opened the door barely wide enough to stick her head out. "Go away," I heard her say.

"I'm buying this property, and I'm coming in to look at it *now*."

Stepping out onto the stoop, Jane pulled the door closed behind her. I could hardly believe what Ms. Lucas did next. She leaned far to her left and said something I couldn't hear. Jane turned toward the sound. Ms. Lucas leaned to the right. Again, I saw her mouth open and close, but I couldn't hear her. She continued moving, side to side, dipping down low, then standing on tiptoe, speaking to Jane from different angles and different heights.

Jane twisted her head, trying to determine the woman's location. Jane was one of the most controlled people I've ever known, and her lack of sight had never seemed much of a handicap. All of that was irrelevant. Jane lost it. Totally and completely lost it. She began flailing her arms around, trying to locate her tormenter. Ms. Lucas ducked and moved from side to side, laughing at Jane's distress.

Enough was enough, and this was too much. I jumped out of my car and yelled, "Just be still, Jane. She's trying to fool you."

When I reached the top of the stairs, I screamed, "Get out of here *now*. I told you to leave Jane alone. You're not getting in here until we see a deed showing you own the place. Until then, the only person with a legal right to be in here is Pearl White or Jane's invited guests."

I couldn't believe what happened next.

Ms. Lucas shoved me. I wobbled a moment, caught my balance, and yelled, "Jane, call 911. Get Sheriff Harmon over here."

The woman pushed her way around me and ran down

the stairway. "This isn't over," she yelled as she jumped into her car, gunned the motor, and sped out of the yard.

A few minutes later, Deputy Smoak pulled up in his cruiser. I went down to meet him. "The emergency's over," I said, "but I want to file a report."

Chapter Twelve

Dalmation! *A hundred and one dalmations! Shih tzu!!!* Telling Deputy Smoak about Ms. Lucas and how she'd acted made me madder than I'd been while she was there. When he finished taking our statements, I told Jane I'd see her later, climbed in the rattletrap truck, and left.

Sometimes driving with the wind in my hair improves my spirits and removes my need for profanity, even if it is kindergarten cussing. Since I still didn't have my convertible Mustang back, I rolled all the windows down and turned the air conditioner on high.

I had plenty to do at home. Housecleaning, laundry, watering my plants, and taking Big Boy for a walk. Problem was that I was too angry to be productive. I thought about driving by Middleton's, but that didn't really have any appeal either. Stopped at a traffic sign, I peered at myself in the rearview mirror. Maybe I needed a change. I headed for the pharmacy.

Once in the store, I realized that I'd come for cosmetics. A new lipstick or shade of mascara, something different in my life. I had many, many shades of lipstick in my kit at work, but I never used mortuary makeup on myself. It wasn't because I'd used those products on dead people. I always used brushes and frequently cotton-tipped swabs at work to apply the makeup.

The problem was that, to me, teachers who took school supplies home for personal use were as guilty as Jane was for shoplifting. Those acts were stealing, and using cosmetics from work would be the same thing. I did sometimes use nail polish from work when I manicured Rizzie's grandmother's hands. I felt that was evened out by my personally buying polish for her, and using it at work whenever the colors were better matched to a client's clothing.

Browsing through the nail polish display, I thought about Dr. Melvin. He'd worked here for so many years that it seemed strange not to see him, to know that he'd never be back. He'd selected the platinum blonde that was my current color. It had been his suggestion to lighten it up from the strawberry blonde I'd been wearing. Of course, I'd bought hair color several times and colored the roots numerous times since then. I wondered what color he'd pick for me if he were here. Probably red, like his new wife's.

I didn't want to be a redhead. There was no dye or tint product that could come anywhere near being as pretty and bright a red as Jane's hair. Besides, I'd once dated a guy who'd been called "Red." I definitely didn't want to invite a nickname that would remind me of him.

"May I help you?"

I looked up and saw a middle-aged lady.

"Not really," I said. "I'm just looking." I smiled. "I'm thinking maybe I want a big change."

"I noticed you looking at hair color. We have some new shades in." She picked up a box and held it out to me. "This Honey Brown is new and Sherry Sparkle is nice, too. It's a dark auburn." She looked up at the clock and added, "We close in five minutes."

Perhaps it was the anger still in me. Could have even been PMS, though I don't acknowledge that I'm particularly foul at that time. I'm perfectly capable of being foul anytime or all the time. I couldn't make up my mind. I wound up buying a box of each with the woman's assurance that I could return the one I didn't use so long as it wasn't opened.

For a wonder, I had my cell phone with me, and it was even charged. I called Daddy.

"Hi, this is Callie. Is Daddy home?"

"Yeah," said Mike. "Pa wants to talk to you. I'll get him."

"Calamine, I got your Mustang fixed," Daddy said. "Your fuel pump was bad. I replaced it. Where are you?"

"I'm near McDonald's. I'm going to get a Coke."

"Wait there and I'll bring your car to you and drive the truck home."

I agreed and flipped the phone closed. That was nice of Daddy to offer to bring the car instead of making me drive to his place to get it. When I reached McDonald's, I dropped my half sub into my bag, went inside, and ordered a large Coke. I sat at a table and waited.

Daddy showed up with Mike driving.

They came in, and Daddy offered to buy me a Big Mac or Quarter Pounder. "I been craving a Big Mac all day," he said.

"Yeah, I thought Pa would have a Mac Attack before we got here," Mike added.

So much for the kindness of my family bringing my car to me. I declined the offer and left before they received their orders. It felt good to be back in my Mustang. I thought about putting the top down, but didn't take the time to stop and do it. A crumpled pile of satin and lace lay on the backseat. The thongs. I wondered if anyone had noticed them.

Unwrapping my half of the deluxe submarine sandwich, I drove through town. The Mustang had belonged to my ex, Donnie. It was his pride and joy. When Donnie did what he did that made me divorce him, I was madder'n a wet Rhode Island Red hen. I asked for the car, and I got it.

At first, I just took Donnie's Mustang for spite, even planned to sell it, but when I started driving that baby, I fell in love. I hope it lasts forever. That reminded me that I hadn't even asked Daddy how much I owed him for the fuel pump. He wouldn't charge me labor, but I should at least offer to pay for the parts. Finally, I drove back to my apartment munching on the last bite of my sub.

When I pulled into my driveway, I saw something different on the front porch. I have a terra-cotta pot by the door that I plant with seasonal flowers throughout the year. Marigolds blossomed like a big frilly yellow hat over the planter. Across from them, on the other side of the door, stood a container filled with mixed spring and summer flowers. Who'd brought them? They weren't here when I left the house. Levi Pinckney knew where I lived. Had he been by with a peace offering for standing me up at Nate's?

Big Boy met me as soon as I opened the door. I clipped on his leash and took him for a long walk. My mood was lifted by something as simple as a bouquet. Back inside, I placed the flowers on the counter by the sink so I could see them from both the living room and the kitchen. I filled the dog bowls with fresh water and Kibbles 'n Bits, then set the food dish on the coffee table and hand-fed the red pieces to Big Boy. Those are his favorites, and he loves being spoiled.

RRRRing. "Hello," I answered.

"Just me," Jane said. "I left those thongs from Victoria's Secret on the seat of your car, and I just remembered how fussy you are sometimes. Thought I'd call and tell you to go by and get them out before your brothers or your daddy see them."

"I told you I'm not going to wear anything you steal," I told her.

"I know that. I didn't leave them for you. I want them back. Just forgot about 'em when the car broke down."

"Well, don't worry. I've got the Mustang now, and the thongs are still on the backseat. I'll bring them in."

"Okay," she said. "That sub you gave me was almost as good as the meatballs." She paused for a moment. "Gotta go. Someone's calling Roxanne."

"Thanks for letting me know," I mumbled. I didn't want the thongs, but Jane was right. I was all grown up now, but a part of me was still the little girl who started drying her unmentionables on a clothesline in her room at puberty so her brothers wouldn't see them hanging on the line outside.

Big Boy and I went out to the car and searched everywhere, including under the seats. No sign of any underwear. That was strange. I'd seen them. They'd been on the seat when I drove the car home. Was all this trouble Jane was having with Dorcas Lucas making me crazy? Those underwear, if thongs can even be considered that, *had* been on the backseat of the Mustang. I'd seen them with my own eyes.

Thinking about panties led me to think about bras. I put all of my inflatables on the table and lined them up side by side. Using a ruler and my new little pump, I adjusted them so they were all blown up exactly the same size. Now if I could just remember to put one on before dashing out in the middle of the night. I couldn't believe I'd actually pinned up my hair, put on a dress, panty hose, and heels, but forgotten to wear a bra the other night. I wondered if Levi Pinckney noticed how flat-chested I'd looked.

After my divorce from Donnie, I went through a period of not dating at all. When I moved back to St. Mary, I went out almost every Friday night. Sometimes on dates with men, occasionally just Jane and me to a movie. About the time Jane took the job as a 900 operator, I stopped dating anyone who didn't really interest me. As Jane used to say, "I stopped dating the creeps to check out the crop." Jane couldn't go out on weekends now because of her work, and I spent a lot of time reading.

I cuddled my dog up to me and rubbed his nose. "Big Boy," I said, "do you realize how many times I've gotten really excited about someone, only to have my enthusiasm shattered? Nick Rivers made my heart go pitty-pat all the way back to high school. He turned out to be a murderer. Dr. Don Walters impressed me until I learned what a womanizer he was, and I really liked that bluegrass musician Andy Campbell, but I haven't seen nor heard from him since he hit the spring/summer bluegrass circuit."

I stopped petting Big Boy, and he licked my hand. "Don't get me wrong," I said to him. "A woman doesn't *have* to have a boyfriend. I love my family and I enjoy my job, and I love you, too, you big old dog."

I showered, put on a comfortable old nightdress, and crawled in bed with *Deadly Advice* by Roberta Isleib. It's an advice column mystery, and I thought maybe I'd get some ideas to spark up my life, especially my love life. Did I say *my love life*? I didn't have one!

Big Boy curled up against me. I went to the kitchen and brought the vase of flowers to the bedroom. Maybe my love life would improve after all.

Chapter Thirteen

Friday the thirteenth has a terrible reputation. Supposed to be bad luck. The thirteenth of any month is a miserable day, regardless of the day of the week it falls on. The only good thirteen I know of is my friend's adorable little boy Aeden's birthday, November thirteenth. That's the only good thirteen I ever knew.

Thirteen is the first of the teenaged years. So far as I'm concerned, the only females with great memories of their teenaged years were cheerleaders.

I've tried and tried to think of something good about thirteen. There were thirteen original colonies in the United States, but now there are fifty. Surely fifty is better than thirteen. I'd rather have fifty dollars than thirteen any day.

The movie *Ocean's Thirteen* was released in 2007, and I went to see it with my brother Mike, but the only thing I really liked was looking at Brad Pitt and George Clooney.

Personally, I ignore the number thirteen. It doesn't bother me at all that some elevators go directly from the twelfth floor to the fourteenth. I admit that when I was a little girl, I wondered what was on the thirteenth floor. It never occurred to me that there was no thirteenth floor. I thought it was just a secret place.

I read Janet Evanovich's book *Lean Mean Thirteen*, and was surprised that someone as smart as she is would not only write chapter 13s, but a whole book with that number in the title. Then I figured out maybe that's why Stephanie Plum is plagued by bad luck, especially with her cars.

As for me, Calamine Lotion Parrish, I have no intention of ever writing a chapter 13, and there is no way in a four-letter word that I will ever even read another book with "thirteen" in the title. (That is, unless Janet Evanovich gets up to 113. I'm kinda addicted to reading what happens to Stephanie Plum.)

Chapter Fourteen

Friday. But not Friday the thirteenth. Friday, the twenty-first of June. Thirty-two years and 364 days since my birth.

Four fifty-three a.m. I sat on the front step of my apartment wearing my heart-printed nightie. Insomnia had plagued me all night, but my distressed rolling around hadn't bothered Big Boy. He was inside, asleep and snoring.

Thank heaven he'd moved to the rug because he'd recently grown so large that when he plopped on his stomach on the bed and spread-eagled all four legs, there was hardly any room for me. But this night, thoughts, not Big Boy's legs or snoring, had crowded me out of the bed.

The moon was full—a big round yellow balloon in the sky. A childhood song played in my head. *I see the moon; the moon sees me. God bless the moon, and God bless me.* Just as the rhyme ended in my mind, a dark shadow crossed, blocking out the golden orb. An eclipse? Were we having a lunar eclipse? The blackness moved too fast for an eclipse. I wasn't watching any great astronomical event, just clouds. Sometimes my thought processes amaze me, not always in good ways.

St. Mary needed rain, especially local farmers, but I hoped any rain would be during the morning hours. Frank, Bill, and Mike planned to move Jane from her garage apartment that afternoon. The thought of Jane living next door should have brightened my spirits, but I was smothered in a dark haze.

I didn't know what had me in such a mood unless it was Dr. Melvin's death. I'd cosmetized people I knew in the past, but not anyone I'd felt as close to as Dr. Melvin. I expected him back from Charleston and ready for me by the afternoon.

Otis and Odell would be pleased for the pharmacist to be returned to Middleton's. They both panic anytime there's no one in a prep room or a slumber room, and right then, we had no clients at the mortuary. The little girl, Angie, had been sent to Connecticut. The reinterment of the grandmother awaited even more permits and paperwork.

Unless a call came in, the only work for me today was making Dr. Melvin look good if he came back from Charleston. I needed to think in terms of doing my best for him, regardless of what I thought of his young wife and how many questions kept creeping into my mind about his death.

Jane had said that I "attracted" murder, and I didn't want to think anyone had killed Dr. Melvin, but it didn't sound right that the autopsy hadn't shown the cause of death. Sheriff Harmon had mentioned waiting on toxicology reports. I hoped Dr. Melvin hadn't been poisoned or drugged to death.

I glanced at my watch again and wondered if it were too early to make coffee. Pondered going back to bed and trying to catch an hour of sleep. I looked back at the sky. Clouds now blacked out the stars as well as the moon. I decided not to make coffee yet, but to get a Moon Pie and a glass of milk. Just as I stood, the skies opened. I was totally drenched before I even got back under the porch ceiling.

Big Boy galloped up to me as I stepped into the living room. He seemed to be growing bigger and more dependent on me every day. From his avoidance of being seen doing his business to his fear of chickens and other small animals to his wanting me to be with him anytime the weather was bad, especially when thunder rumbled and lightning cut through the sky.

I wondered if I would need to take Big Boy to a doggie shrink. I hoped not. I'd already spent my savings having his ears cropped so they would stand up and he'd look like the purebred Great Dane he was instead of just a giant, spotted dog.

Big Boy wasn't cooperating with my idea that he could go potty even if it were raining. It didn't matter that I stood at the door; he wasn't having any of it. He bounded back into the bedroom and leaped up on the bed.

Giving up, I carried the Moon Pie and milk to the bed, where *Deadly Advice* awaited me on the bedside table. I shoved the dog's legs and paws out of the way, and by the time I'd finished the next chapter, Big Boy's snores were rumbling along with the thunder.

When I climbed out of bed a little after eight, I turned on the radio to catch the news and weather. Disc jockey Cousin Roger on WXZW announced the storms would probably last all day. That made me so mad that I turned off the radio and considered calling in sick and staying home to read. But that wouldn't be fair to Otis and Odell, and I would have felt really guilty if I didn't go in to take care of Dr. Melvin.

I showered, dressed, and headed to work. The rain sluiced over the windshield reminding me I needed new wipers. Gusts of wind rocked the Mustang slightly, and I was glad when I reached Middleton's.

Otis was sitting at his desk, reading the newspaper. "Where's Odell?" I asked. "Has he gone for Dr. Melvin?"

"No. I'll give you one guess where he is."

"Picking up a client?"

"No, guess again."

"Shoney's?"

"You got it. Gone to the breakfast buffet. You can work on the web page if you want. Bring everything up to date."

"We don't have anyone at all?"

"Not a single client."

"What do you want me to do on the web page? There's no info to add."

"Pretty it up some." He paused, then changed his mind. "Aw, you don't have to do anything. Just read a book and answer the phone if anyone calls." Otis stood. "I'm going over to Shoney's and see what a vegan can eat off that buffet."

The storm raged louder with sharp bolts of lightning. I read until both of my bosses returned. "What did you find to eat?" I asked Otis, knowing that he wouldn't eat eggs or any kind of breakfast meat.

"Salad bar was already set up. I had a great breakfast. Grits and veggies. Brought you a blueberry muffin." He set a small bag on my desk.

All three of us jumped when the phone rang, each hoping the call was work-related, though for it to be business, someone had to have died. I always felt guilty when I wished someone would die so the twins wouldn't have to close the mortuary.

"Middleton's Mortuary," I said into the phone receiver. "How may I help you?"

"Calamine." Daddy was the caller. "Is the electricity off downtown?"

"No, sir. We've got power."

"It's off here. Lightning musta struck something. Frank

wants to know if you think Jane's awake yet. He needs to call and let her know that even if he rents a covered truck, everything will get wet bringing it down the stairs to load the truck unless this rain lets up."

"Tell him not to call her until noon. The storm might have awakened her, but it's best to wait. She's not stupid. She'll know that The Boys can't move her until the rain stops, or at least slows down."

"Okay." Daddy paused several seconds. "Whatcha doing tomorrow, Calamine?"

"Daddy, you and I both know what tomorrow is, and I won't be coming over there, so don't worry about it." My daddy loves me, and I think he's been a great father/mother to me and The Boys since I was born, but he's never celebrated my birthday.

John was just shy of thirteen when I was born, and I remember his making cupcakes for me when I was in kindergarten. When I was in elementary school, my brothers took me out to McDonald's for my birthday, but Daddy was never a part of it. To him, the twenty-second of June was the day his wife died. Nothing more.

"Have you made plans?" he asked.

"Not really. If Jane gets moved today, I'll probably spend tomorrow helping her set up the new apartment. Frank and Mike did a good job cleaning it."

"Yeah, I heard that." Daddy cleared his throat. "Your brother John came in last night. Wants to know if he can take you to dinner."

"What time will I be finished?" I half-mouthed to my bosses. Odell waved his hand toward the door.

Otis said, "Anytime. Unless we get a call, there's nothing to be done here anyway."

"Sure," I said to Daddy, "tell John to pick me up around six. I'd like to eat dinner early. I didn't get much sleep last night."

The telephone was silent the rest of the day. I had lots of time to sit around and think. I thought about being almost thirty-three and having no regular gentleman caller. I thought about both Pearl and Dr. Melvin finding love on the Internet. I even wondered what had happened to those thongs Jane left in the backseat. Had a raccoon or some other animal like a cat stolen them? Or a squirrel? I shuddered at the thought. I don't like squirrels at all.

Just fooling around, I went to one of the singles' websites and filled in a profile. The first thing I did was change my name. No way am I going to be known online as Calamine Lotion Parrish. What was the prettiest name I ever heard for a girl? Vanessa. No doubt about it. Vanessa! I typed my name as Vanessa and felt prettier immediately.

According to the computer, Vanessa was five feet, six inches tall. *That's only two inches taller than I am, maybe no one will notice.* She weighed 120 pounds. *Well, I did weigh 120 before I gained almost ten pounds.* She had red hair and brown eyes. *Just the color of Jane's. If I try enough hair products, I could probably get my hair that color, and they sell colored contact lenses that will change eye color.*

I typed that Vanessa was twenty-eight years old. I almost put twenty-nine, but *nobody would believe anyone in a singles' chat room is really twenty-nine.*

The next part of the profile asked about likes and dislikes. Now, I *know* what I like—lasagna and coconut cake, not necessarily at the same meal. Somehow, I didn't think that's what they were asking. I put that I enjoyed walks along the beach. *Who doesn't?*

Occupation? Technically, a person who does what I do at a funeral home is called a cosmetitian. Don't ask me why. There should be a whole dictionary of Funeralese. I typed that in, then deleted it. Most folks wouldn't know what it meant. I just filled in cosmetologist so the guys wouldn't think Vanessa couldn't spell.

I guess I fooled around creating the new me on the computer for an hour or so. What if I actually pushed "submit" and someone responded? What if he was really sweet and really hot? What if Vanessa liked him? What if he turned out to be a fake like Christopher in that Ann Rule book?

"Amazing Grace" announced John's arrival a little before six. My hand acted on its own and, with no direction from me, the mouse went to "submit." Vanessa entered the chat room as I met John in the entry. He shook off his umbrella and raincoat, then slid both of them out onto the covered porch that surrounds three sides of Middleton's. Wind blew the rain so hard that it looked and felt like it was raining on the veranda.

"Wow!" John said. "This is getting worse by the minute. Have you had the radio on?"

"No," I said.

"Tropical storm Elise is skipping up the coast. It may still turn into a hurricane. That's what brought all of this, and the storm's stopped off the coast of South Carolina. We may have several days of wind and rain."

"I know hurricane season starts near the first of June, but it seems early for Elise. I'd think something this early would be called Adam or Amanda," I said.

"Storm season got a fast start this year."

John and I dashed to his Mercedes with the wind trying to wrench our umbrellas from our hands and the rain blowing directly into our faces.

Chapter Fifteen

"**Little** Sister, how about Blue Crab?" John asked as we both tried to brush water from our faces and clothing.

"Sure. You know me and seafood, and I haven't been to Blue Crab in ages."

There are times when something in my Mustang gets waterlogged, and the car doesn't want to turn on during heavy rain. John's Mercedes doesn't have that problem. In seconds, we were taking a smooth ride to the restaurant.

John and I have become closer since I grew up, and normally I babble constantly to him when he's around, but the wind and rain beating against the car made me silent. I wanted John to keep his mind on his driving.

Blue Crab's parking lot wasn't crowded, and John pulled into a space near the door. He reached across to the back-seat and brought the umbrellas out. He got out of the car, put both umbrellas up, and walked around to my side. Even with his thoughtfulness, I was soaked again by the time we stepped into the restaurant. The wind was blowing the rain at us sideways.

The restaurant interior might seem tacky to some folks, but I've always loved it. Gray board walls are hung with fishing nets, and there are crabs of all sizes displayed in the nets. Some of them are genuine shells, but others are plastic. Not kiddy plastic, but expensive crabs created to decorate places like Blue Crab.

Not nearly so classy as Andre's, Blue Crab is still several notches above where I usually eat. When the server brought the menus, John ordered a decanter of wine. John did the sniff, taste, and smile routine. The server poured mine and walked away. John lifted his glass in a toast. "To us," he proposed. "To happy futures and many long years of health for Little Sister and me."

It wasn't what I'd expected since all of my brothers know many, many risqué toasts. They learned them from Daddy. After John married Miriam and moved to Atlanta, he had changed from the rude, crude, socially unacceptable red-neck typical of our household. I've been to visit them in their McMansion with their adorable son and daughter. They even have a maid and a gardener.

"Callie!" I heard the squeal before I saw her. Pearl White and her fiancé were rising from a table on the other side of the room. Pearl came clumping over to John and me with her walker. She had on a red dress and she'd put red tennis balls on her walker.

"Is Jane with you?" Pearl asked. As if she were blind or Jane was invisible.

"No, ma'am."

"I was hoping to speak with her. Ms. Lucas says that Jane is being very difficult."

My hackles rose on that. "Mrs. White, Jane was supposed to move today, but as you know, the weather hasn't cooperated. Can't you make that woman wait until after Jane's moved out to show her the garage apartment? If not, maybe you should come with her."

"I just don't understand. I know Jane went through a rowdy spell as a young lady, but she's always been the epitome of courtesy to me." Pearl's voice was almost a whimper.

"That's because you aren't rude to her and you don't scream at her." *And you're the only person in the world who'd call Jane a "lady" during her wild time.* I didn't say the second part of that thought aloud.

"I'm selling everything off, all of my property, so no one can say that Georgie is after my money." She laughed. "You know, they say that a lot of the time when people find their soul mates on the Internet and one of them happens to be a few years younger than the other. I'm not going to have anyone saying that about my Georgie."

"I've told you not to worry about it," George said.

Pearl continued as though he hadn't spoken. "I was just lucky that Lucas Investment Enterprises came along so quickly to buy my two houses, the apartment, and the oceanfront lot."

"An oceanfront lot!" I splattered a bit of spittle as I spat out the words. "Mrs. White, there isn't any oceanfront property available around here. Hasn't been for years!"

"Well, I've owned this piece for years and not had it on the market. It's leased out to a waterfront restaurant, but I'm going to sell it. Get rid of all the responsibilities of these rentals."

"Are you sure you want to do that?" John asked.

"What's wrong with that?" Pearl demanded with just a touch of anger in her voice.

George Carter pulled out a chair for Pearl as though they were joining us. He said, "Maybe you should listen to these young people, Pearl. Wait a while to liquidate all your holdings."

"No, I want to be free and clear of everything here. When we marry and move to Orlando, I don't want any business to distract me from living happily ever after."

"But you'll still have to manage your assets," John

commented. "Just because it's money instead of property doesn't mean you won't have business responsibilities."

"You don't understand," Pearl said and sat in the chair George had pulled out for her. He sat down beside her. "Georgie here"—she motioned toward Mr. Carter—"has made it clear to me that he doesn't want anything from me but love." She smiled up at the man with a simpering look and, buh-leeve me, it was all I could do not to barf. "I'm going to donate the money to homes for the blind and deaf."

"Do you mind if we join you?" George asked the question, but it was a case of putting the horse after the cart. They'd already sat with us.

"Oh, no, not at all." Ex-cuuze me. That was John talking, because I *did* mind. I don't have many opportunities to talk alone with my oldest brother, and, besides, I'd been thinking this dinner might be a private birthday celebration.

The server reappeared beside us, and John ordered Lobster Imperial for himself and my favorite, Crab Benedict, for me. George suggested dessert to Pearl, but she said, "No, just coffee, please." He requested two coffees and one slice of Chocolate Volcano cake.

The young man brought John's and my dinners at the same time as their coffees and cake.

Pearl took a sip of coffee and screwed her face into a very unpleasant and unhappy expression. "What's wrong?" the server asked.

"This coffee tastes like crude oil. When did you make it? This morning? It's way too strong for me."

"I'm so sorry, ma'am. Let me take it away and brew a fresh pot for you."

"No, it's just too strong. Bring me a whiskey sour instead."

John raised an eyebrow at me, our secret signal when we were amused. *Like a whiskey sour is a weaker drink than coffee!*

Mrs. White rambled on while we ate. "I've been so busy trying to take care of everything for my move that I haven't even checked on when Melvin's funeral is scheduled. Do you know, Callie?" The waiter had arrived with her whiskey sour, and she took a long swallow.

"No, the services aren't set yet." That's all I really should have said, but I added, "Dr. Melvin's still in Charleston."

"In Charleston? Why?"

"Since he died an unattended death, the coroner had to order an autopsy."

"But surely there's nothing strange about his death." She emptied the whiskey sour and cast a coy look at her fiancé that said *Another one, please.* Mr. Carter caught the server's eye, pointed to Pearl's glass, and nodded. That's always amazed me how men can order without a word, but I usually have to repeat what I want several times to communicate with waiters and waitresses.

"That's just the law," I said and took another bite of my Crab Benedict. I love that dish, could eat it three times a day.

"I guess we all know what probably killed him out there in that Jacuzzi. I warned him that people with hypertension aren't supposed to use hot tubs, but he told me he'd never had high blood pressure." Pearl giggled, knocked back the rest of her drink, and said, "At least he died happy."

George Carter patted her hand and waved to the waiter. I wondered if he thought she needed another drink, but instead he asked for their check. Pearl wasn't ready to leave. She wanted to talk about Dr. Melvin.

"You know, Melvin was my last relative," she said.

"Relative?" I asked.

"Yes, we were cousins on our mothers' side. I was so happy for him when he met Roselle. He'd been so lonely since his first wife died." She sniggered another whiskey sour giggle. "Actually, that's how I met my Georgie." She gave him yet another flirty look and literally batted her eyelashes at him.

"Melvin was so happy after he met Roselle that he insisted I visit the chat room where he'd met her, and that's where I met Georgie." She tipped the empty whiskey sour glass to her lips and flicked her tongue inside the rim. "Online. I met my Georgie online, and now I'm going to live happily ever after."

Mr. Carter stood and gently pulled Mrs. White's chair out. "We'd best be heading back to Beaufort. The weather sounds worse outside."

"You're still staying in Beaufort?" I asked.

Pearl giggled. "Yes, Georgie's such a sweetheart. We're still staying in a bed and breakfast because he doesn't want me to have to cook or clean."

"Good night," George said and tried to nudge her away.

Pearl turned back to me. "Online, Callie. That's what you and Jane should do, find yourselves nice young men on the Internet, like I did." She turned toward George. "Let me use your pen, Georgie." He handed her a pen and she wrote something on the napkin at her place, folded it, and handed it to me. "This is the best place to go on the Internet to meet good people. It's where Melvin met Roselle and where Georgie and I found each other." I shoved the paper into my purse.

When they'd gone, John said, "Little Sister, I'd just as soon you not go online looking for dates. There are plenty of fish in the ocean who aren't hunched up behind their computers."

"Fish in the ocean?" I laughed. "Since when do you talk in clichés?"

"Since I got old."

"Old? You're not *old*!"

"I'll be forty-six next month, and Dad will be sixty-three his next birthday."

"He was only seventeen when you were born?"

"Only sixteen—both him and Mom. They got married at fifteen."

"How'd they do that? Could you get married that young back then?"

"Not supposed to, but nobody checked it. Didn't have to have a birth certificate in South Carolina. People just lied when they got the license."

"I don't think I ever knew that Daddy and our mother married so young. I just never added it up or subtracted it or whatever."

"That's one reason I wanted to talk to you tonight." He refilled our wineglasses.

"About our parents having you when they were sixteen?" I smiled. "I think any worry you may have had about me being an unwed teenaged mother is about fourteen years too late."

"No, about me. I want to talk about *me*, but first, let's celebrate your birthday." John glanced over my shoulder and nodded. More of that silent male communication.

I hadn't noticed, but the waiter was standing behind me. He leaned around and placed on the table a small birthday cake, decorated with pink roses and one flaming candle. I've always loved birthday cakes with pink roses.

At the same time, John pulled a wrapped jewelry box from his pocket and set it by the cake.

"Happy Birthday, Little Sister," he said.

I blew out the candle, wasting my birthday wish on good weather so we could get Jane moved. I knew what the box held. Since I got my ears pierced, John's gifts to me for birthdays and every Christmas have always been earrings. These were pink pearl studs—*real* pearls. John's presents are always nice. I wanted to tell him that I'd lost one of the diamond earrings he'd given me for my twenty-first birthday, but I'd wait and drop that hint closer to Christmas.

Our private birthday celebration turned out fine . . . *until* we finished our cake and John began telling me what he'd come to say.

Chapter Sixteen

"**I**'m not happy, Callie. I'll be forty-six next month. I don't think I want to live out my life working for my father-in-law." He drank the remains from his wine goblet and then drained his water glass. The server hurried over and refilled it. John waited until the young man had moved away before speaking again. "I'm thinking about leaving Miriam. I still love her, but I'm not *in* love with her anymore."

This was John. My perfect brother. The only one of us kids who hadn't already divorced at least one spouse. The successful brother. The stable one.

"Who *is* she?" I asked.

"What do you mean?"

"This sounds like a bunch of caca to me. What did you do? Find some little secretary to make you feel young again? Is she out of her twenties?"

"Callie, it's not that at all. I'm not having an affair. I'd never do that to Miriam."

"But you're going to *leave* her? What about Johnny and Megan? Don't you know what this will do to them?"

"To be honest, I don't know that they'll care. They're

both tied up in so many activities that I hardly ever see them. And Megan is dating now. Did you know that? My little girl is dating. I think fourteen's too young, but Miriam insists that *all* girls date at that age. I know what we'd have done if you wanted to date at fourteen, but my opinion doesn't seem to amount to anything in Atlanta."

"I wish I'd been allowed to date at fourteen. Just think, Daddy and our mother were married and having you at fifteen."

"Yeah, they were having me, so they got married. That's not what I want for my children."

"So you're going to leave them? That doesn't make sense." I hoped my expression didn't show the exasperation I felt toward my favorite brother.

"All I know is that I don't think I can stand living in that big house where I feel invisible." He picked at the icing on the part of the cake we hadn't cut. Licked it off his finger, just like he did when I was a child. "I thought maybe you'd understand. After all, you walked away from a nice house and the prize catch. Donnie's a doctor now. You could have had it all."

"John, you know that there was no choice about staying with Donnie after he did what he did. It's a totally different situation. Are you sure you're not just having the middle-aged blues?"

"I think I've passed middle age."

"You haven't even reached middle age. They say that fifty is the new forty." I smiled and patted his hand.

"I don't know for sure what I'm going to do, but I wanted you to know what I'm thinking and feeling. I don't want you shocked or upset if Miriam and I separate."

"If you leave your family, will you move back to St. Mary?" As much as I hated the thought of John's marriage breaking up, there was just a hint of pleasure in the thought of my favorite brother being back full-time, though I couldn't imagine in a hundred years that he'd move in with Daddy like the others do when they divorce or break up.

"No, I'll go somewhere new. Start over." We sat in silence for several minutes.

Finally, I managed to say, "Thank you for telling me. You know that whatever you do, I love you." That was hard for me to say. I grew up knowing Daddy and The Boys loved me, but we didn't ever say it.

I didn't hear those words until after John married into Miriam's family. Her folks were much more demonstrative than our family. John was the first person to ever actually tell me he loved me, and I still found it hard to say those words to anyone. Where had all the love in my brother's life gone? He said he was invisible in his own home. Was that the truth or just how he perceived things?

My heart hurt for John as he drove me home through the torrential rain and powerful gusts of wind. When he walked me to the door, I asked, "Do you want to spend the night on my couch?"

"No, I'm going to Dad's. The lights are probably back on by now, and if not, we'll play poker by kerosene lamps. It won't be the first time." He gave me a hug. "I'll call you tomorrow."

After he left, I sat on the floor, hugged Big Boy, and did what I'd felt like all day without knowing why. Now I knew.

I wept.

Chapter Seventeen

"Happy birthday to you,
Happy birthday to you,
Happy birthday, dear Callieeee,
Happy birthday to you."

I had to laugh. Jane's singing screeched, and as terrible as the wind and rain sounded from outside, I could still hear her over the telephone.

"Thank you," I said.

"I was hoping we'd be next-door neighbors today," Jane said, "but according to the weatherman, this rain isn't going to let up."

"I thought it would blow over. Are you packed? Want me to come help you get everything ready?"

"Not necessary. Your brother Frank was here last night and finished boxing everything for me."

I laughed. "You *have* figured out he has a crush on you, haven't you?"

"On me?" Jane asked in a little false voice. "Don't tell me Frank's not a good samaritan to everyone like he is with me."

"No, he isn't. When I want him to do something, he always has some excuse. Take advantage of it while you can because Frank is probably the laziest of The Boys."

"You mean his crush might not last very long? Have you no faith in me?" Jane teased.

"I mean you know as well as I do that my brothers don't win any trophies for fidelity."

"Except John," Jane said. I didn't bother to tell her I suspected that he was about to mess up big time and join the same league as my other brothers. Jane had pined for John from our teenaged years until he married Miriam.

When I didn't respond, she changed the subject. "What are you doing today?"

"I'm on standby if Otis or Odell picks up Dr. Melvin," I said. "Otherwise, I don't have to work, and even if MUSC releases Dr. Melvin today, I doubt the Middletons will go for him in all this rain."

"Did you know the electricity's off in parts of town?" she asked.

"It was off at Daddy's last night," I answered. "Probably back on by now."

"I heard on the radio that there are thousands of people without service this morning."

"Did you work last night?"

"Now, what do you think? Do you believe I'd let Roxanne loose while Frank was over here?"

My turn to giggle. "He might like it."

"Call me if you decide to go anywhere, and if you don't get a better offer, I'll cook you a birthday dinner."

"I've already had a birthday dinner. We ate at Blue Crab last night. I even have half of one of those tiny birthday cakes left—one with pink roses just like I always wanted when I was a little girl."

"Who took you? That guy who stood you up at the sub place?"

"No, John's in town. He had them bring the cake to the table."

"Bring it over about six tonight, and we'll have it for dessert. I'll cook something you like." That wouldn't be hard for Jane to do. I love her cooking.

"Sure," I answered before we said our good-byes.

The rest of the day was semimiserable. Lots of phone calls from relatives and friends, most of whom sang "Happy Birthday" a lot better than Jane, but a few from folks who couldn't carry a tune in a bucket any better than Jane.

Puh-leeze. What a miserable day for a birthday. Wind, rain, and a dog whose bladder might pop before he'd be coerced into going out the door in such weather.

The Boys called and wished me happy birthday, but they said Daddy had gone to Beaufort, swearing he was going to buy a generator. I knew they'd waited until he left to call me because Daddy is always mean as a bear on the twenty-second of June. He'd never try to stop them from remembering my birthday, but we learned long ago to steer clear of Daddy on that day. I was a little surprised that none of them mentioned coming over. Guess they thought John taking me out the night before was enough.

Otis telephoned. "Isn't today your birthday?"

"Yes," I answered, expecting him to sing, too.

Instead, he said, "We've got no business and we won't drive to Charleston for Melvin Dawkins until this lets up. Don't try to come out in this awful weather. We'll call you if someone comes in and we need you." That was exactly what Odell had told me the day before.

I agreed and hung up the phone, already chastising myself for the pity party I felt coming on. Pearl earrings, birthday cake with pink roses, and a day off were more than some people receive for their birthdays. But I wasn't some people, I was Callie. I wanted to be special on my birthday.

It wasn't a matter of gifts. I didn't really need anything, and I knew Jane would have something for me. I wanted to be special to someone besides Jane.

What was wrong with me? I've been pretty well happy with myself the past few years, with or without a man in my life. Was the big thirty-three subconsciously bothering me like forty-six seemed to be working on John?

The only recent dates I'd had were an occasional dinner with Dr. Don Walters. I'd been interested in him until I found out he was a bigger womanizer than my brothers. Having divorced a medical student named Donnie, I'd felt anything with a doctor named Don was ill-fated anyway.

The first time Don had taken me out was to Andre's, the most exclusive restaurant in the area. After I refused to take sharing appetizers off the same fork up to a more physical level (or down to a level below the mouth), we'd remained friends, but our occasional nights out were a lot less elegant. Instead of silver forks, we sometimes ate with plastic sporks.

A few months ago, I began to fall pretty hard for a blue-grass performer, Andy Campbell, the Great Pretender, who impersonated Randall Hylton. I hadn't heard from him in over a month. Maybe too busy traveling the bluegrass circuit or probably involved with someone else by now.

The only man I'd even seen recently who attracted me was Dr. Melvin's brother-in-law Levi Pinckney. He'd asked me to meet him and then not shown up, hadn't called to apologize either. What if the flowers weren't from him? They'd come close to my birthday. They could have been from someone else.

I knew I'd have to face Levi at Dr. Melvin's funeral, and I didn't know what to do. If the bouquet had come from him, I should thank him. If he hadn't sent them, I'd make a fool of myself if I tried to express my appreciation. He

isn't even my type. I like tall men. Levi is short. I like blue
eyes and fair hair. Levi has brown hair and dark eyes.

I did some light housework and put a load of black
dresses in the washer before I lay down across the bed to
read. I'd finished *Deadly Advice* and begun reading *Candles
Burning* by Tabitha King and the late Michael McDowell.
It wasn't exactly a mystery. The story was a southern gothic
thriller, but I'd bought it because someone told me the main
character had my name.

Foolish me! I'd thought the girl in the book was named
Calamine Lotion and called Callie, like me. Turned out that
she was named Calliope and called Calley, spelled *e-y* instead of *i-e*. There was mystery involved. Calley's father in
the book was brutally, gruesomely murdered when she was
seven years old, and I hadn't learned who did it yet.

When I got up to go to the bathroom, Big Boy followed
me.

Though the weather was a lot more rain, the winds had
lessened, and there was hardly any thunder, but Big Boy
kept rubbing up against my legs. Buh-leeve me, that's okay
with a cat, but not with a 130-pound dog.

What does a lonely lady do at home on her birthday? If
I'm that lady, my mind cries out for change. The hair color
was still in my medicine cabinet. I couldn't decide between
the Honey Brown and the Sherry Sparkle, so I used both of
them.

Two hours later, I stared at myself in the mirror and
smiled. My hair was back to brown, but not its true mousy
color. The new shade was a warm, golden brown with Sherry
Sparkle auburn accents. I pulled on khaki slacks and a
copper-colored tee that complimented the new shade of hair.

The weather was too bad to drive, but it was my *birthday*,

so I wrapped myself in a raincoat with a slicker over it and held an umbrella over *that*, then dashed through the standing water in the yard. I never lock the car, but for some reason I had the night before. Now I was forced to stand in the pouring rain while I fumbled with the key. Maybe someday I'd buy a new car with those automatic locks that can be opened from a distance. Perhaps I could even have the door locks changed in the Mustang so I could lock and unlock it from my front porch.

It seemed to take forever to reach Jane's because every time the rain became so heavy I couldn't see, I pulled over. When I encountered deep holes filled with water, I slowed down to almost a crawl. Finally I arrived at Jane's yard and even more standing water and mud puddles.

I thought about flash floods I'd seen on television as I searched my pockets for my cell phone to call Jane to open the door. As usual—well, maybe not "as usual," maybe "as frequently"—I'd forgotten to bring the phone. I ran up her steep stairs and pounded on the door.

"Go away!" Jane shouted. "Leave me alone."

"I'm drowning out here," I yelled. "Open up!"

Jane yanked the door back and grabbed me. She was wearing a purple tie-dyed T-shirt with railroad engineer–striped overall cutoffs.

"Come in, Callie," she said. "That woman was here. With all this rain, she demanded I let her in to see the apartment."

"Well, I'm not her. You didn't let her in, did you?"

"No." She handed me some towels and I wiped away the water that seemed to have blown through my rain gear. I was surprised she could even find towels. There were boxes stacked all over, against the walls, on the tables, in the middle of the room—everywhere.

"I don't smell anything," I said. "What are you cooking?"

Jane ignored my words. "Where's that cake you promised

to bring? I don't smell any cake and certainly not any pink icing roses."

"*Dalmation!* I forgot the cake and my cell phone."

"Are you sure you didn't eat all the cake?" Jane frowned.

"No. I colored my hair this afternoon."

"What color?" She reached out and touched my damp hair as though she could identify the color by feeling it.

"Lavender."

"I know better than that."

"How do you know?"

"I might want mine purple one day, but neither of us will ever have light blue or lavender hair like those old ladies at the church."

Just at that moment, a crash of thunder rumbled across the roof. Lightning flashed so bright that it lit up the inside of the apartment even though Jane had the blinds closed.

"I don't think the good Lord liked that comment about the church ladies," I said.

"I won't tempt Him anymore," Jane said. "Dry off. Sit down. I've got coffee to take off the wet chill." I settled into the corner of the love seat with my legs pulled up under me while she poured coffee from a stainless steel thermos into two cups and added cream and three sugars from packets to mine before handing it to me. She plopped down into her recliner, which is her favorite seat. She's as bad as my daddy about not wanting anyone else to sit in her personal chair.

We sat and sipped coffee a few minutes. "Hey," I said, "this is regular coffee, not flavored. Since when did you stop buying the good stuff?"

"Since your brother packed up all my kitchen goods."

"Then how're you going to cook dinner?"

"I'm not. Frank is taking us out. He'll be here soon."

"But where'd you get this coffee?"

"Frank brought it over earlier."

"He's not pestering you, is he?"

"No, he's being really helpful. The only person pestering me is that witch woman Dorcas Lucas. What kind of name is that? Dorcas sounds like that word Odell calls Otis when he's mad with him."

"Doofus?"

"Yes, but even that isn't strong enough for what I think of her."

"Remember—no cussing any stronger than kindergarten. Just say 'dalmation, dalmation, dalmation, a hundred and one dalmations' and you'll feel just as good as you do when you make all those nasty comments."

Jane spieled out a string of words considerably worse than kindergarten cussing.

When she'd finished, I asked, "Feel better?"

"Sure do, but you don't sound so good yourself."

"Just kinda blue. Don't even know why. Maybe it's this weather on my birthday." I handed her my cup for a refill.

Chapter Eighteen

"**Well,** I have the perfect birthday gift for you," Jane said as she handed my refilled cup to me, filled, lightened, and sweetened perfectly.

"What is it? If my birthday present is a cup of coffee, there had better be a cookie to go with it."

"Frank and I ate all the benne wafers, but as soon as I'm moved, I'm going to try some more recipe experiments. I'm definitely entering the Southern Belle Baking Contest." She laughed. "Close your eyes now."

I cheated and kept them open.

Jane pulled a small package wrapped in tissue paper from the pocket of her overalls and held it out to me.

I didn't waste any time opening it. A beautiful red pendant on a silver chain. "I love it!" I said as I fastened the chain around my neck.

"It's garnet," Jane said. I was glad she told me because I'd been thinking it was ruby. In my mind, if it's red, it's ruby; if it's green, it's emerald; and if it's bright, shiny, and clear, it's probably cubic zirconium.

"Garnet will strengthen your aura," she continued.

I laughed and said, "What's wrong with my aura?"

"Dalmation if I know. I can't help it if Mommy taught me all that stuff about gems and minerals. Garnet strengthens your aura. That's what she always said."

"What about diamonds?" I asked.

"Diamonds are a girl's best friend."

"Did your mom tell you that?"

"No, I got it from a movie."

After many thanks and a sisterly hug, I changed the subject. "Did you say that Lucas woman has been here again today?"

"Yes, she said Mrs. White told her I was moving yesterday, and I told *her* it was raining. I didn't let her in. Told her my rent's paid until the end of the month, and if it keeps raining or she keeps harassing me, I'll stay here until then."

"I saw Pearl White and George Carter at Blue Crab last night. I told her that Ms. Lucas is rude to you and she should tell her not to come over here unless Pearl is with her. That's what I said, but I don't know if she'll remember. She was knocking back whiskey sours."

"What?"

"I don't know what she drank with her meal, but she had two whiskey sours at our table and acted like she wanted another one, until *Georgie* got her out of there."

"Pearl doesn't drink," Jane said in a serious tone.

"She sure did last night."

"She's been a 'recovering' alcoholic as long as I've known her. She told me about it when I met her. She made a big deal about alcoholics never being 'cured' and said she would be 'recovering' for the rest of her life. Mrs. White was proud she'd done twenty-four steps, and would never touch alcohol again."

"Twenty-four steps? I thought those programs were twelve steps."

"They are. Mrs. White had a relapse and started the

whole thing over again. That was before I met her, and I've known her since Mommy brought me home from the school and we started going to the Commission for the Blind for special equipment."

Jane spent her early years in an institution for the blind; she calls it "the school." I knew that Mrs. Gray, as she was back then before she married Mr. White, had seen to it that the commission supplied Jane with a new brailler when hers broke, as well as the electronic typewriter she used in high school. More recently, Pearl had been the person who arranged for Jane to receive a computer with the special software that reads her e-mail and research aloud to her.

"Well, she sure was belting down whiskey sours last night," I said. "She looks different, too. She's dressing all young and flirty."

"I didn't realize that, but her voice is different. She's really wrapped up in this George Carter, isn't she?"

"Not George. She calls him *Georgie*." Jane stuck her finger in her mouth and mimed a barf at me when I said that.

"Me, too," I agreed. "I thought if she simpered out *Georgie* one more time, I'd lose my Crab Benedict all over the table."

"Thanks for sharing that pleasant image," Jane said. A pounding sounded over the rain. I jumped up and stomped to the door, ready to give Ms. Lucas a piece of my mind. Not that I usually have any mind to spare, but that's what I felt like doing.

I snatched the door open ready to snarl, but there was no lady there. No gentleman either. Just my brother Frank, holding a dark green garbage bag over his head.

"You gals ready?" he asked. "If you are, I won't track any more of this rain into the house."

"Where are we going?" I asked as I pulled my raincoat and slicker on. Jane wrapped herself in a hooded cape, and we followed Frank out and down the steps.

"Be careful," Frank cautioned. "These steps are slippery as snail snot."

I elbowed him and said, "Don't say that."

Frank was driving the Jeep, so I climbed into the back while Jane sat up front with him. Though Jane couldn't see the way my brother looked at her, I was certain she could feel the vibes.

"Is the electricity back on at Daddy's?" I almost yelled, trying to be heard over the slapping of the windshield wipers and swish-splash of the rain.

"No. Some power company men came by. Said it's not just a transformer. Whole substation's out. Won't be back on before tomorrow."

"Did Daddy buy the generator?"

"Yeah, but it's not really big enough to do much except keep the refrigerator and freezers on." He pulled over to the side of the road.

"What's wrong?" I asked. I hadn't felt the Jeep do anything that would indicate a flat tire or mechanical problem.

Frank laughed. Jane giggled. "Unfasten your seat belt and turn around so your back is to me," Frank said. When I turned, he wrapped a cloth scarf around my face and tied it in the back.

"What's this all about?" I demanded.

"It's your birthday," Frank said.

"That's no reason to blindfold me unless we're playing 'Pin the Tail on the Donkey,' and I don't like it," I complained, but I didn't pull the cloth away from my eyes.

"Don't fuss now, Callie. I spend my whole life like that," Jane said.

"Jane Baker, it won't do you any good to try for sympathy from me. You do more than most sighted people."

"Yes, and you have two eyes that work but you don't bother to look. I 'see' more than you do."

"Just lean back and relax," Frank said as he pulled the

Jeep back onto the road. "It won't be long." I'm sure I had a big silly grin on my face beneath my blindfold. I tried to guess where we were going by the turns but didn't have any luck. I wondered if Frank and Jane were taking me somewhere really nice, like Andre's, but not being able to see, it wasn't long before I couldn't even tell what part of town we were in.

When Frank parked the Jeep, he said, "Now don't move the blindfold or you won't get any dinner." He managed to guide me on one side and Jane on the other. Across pavement, up a few stairs, and about ten steps on what I assumed was a large wooden porch.

Where were we?

Chapter Nineteen

It should have been the surprise of the century, but when Frank opened the door, I knew where we were.

"Amazing Grace" sounded.

I snatched the cloth from my eyes. "You brought me to *work*?"

Jane giggled. "Yes."

Odell came out of Slumber Room A, pulled the door closed behind him, and growled at Frank, "It took you long enough to get her here."

"You told me I didn't have to work today," I mumbled.

"Well, you do, so come on in here," Odell said and turned back toward the door he'd just closed.

I opened the door. The room was dark. I flipped the light switch, and the overhead lights flooded the room. No, there was no shout of "Surprise!" Instead, the crowd of people standing in there yelled, "Happy birthday, Callie!"

My face couldn't have looked more shocked than most of theirs did. The room was full of friends, relatives, and some people I didn't even know, all staring at me. But there was one person there whose presence absolutely stunned me.

My daddy. He stood in front of everyone else.

He came over, hugged me, and said the words I'd never before heard from him. "Happy birthday, Callie." Then, with his arm around my shoulders, he turned to face everyone.

"I want to tell you something before this party gets started," Daddy said. "When I was fourteen years old, I drove my uncle to see a friend of his." He grinned. "And, yeah, back then it was legal to get your driver's license at four-teen in South Carolina. We were setting on the porch, me and my uncle and his friend, when a girl came out on the porch with a tray full of glasses of iced tea. That girl was the prettiest female I'd ever seen and I ain't seen a better-looking woman since then.

"I married her, and we had five sons. When she birthed our only girl, she died, and I've mourned my wife every June twenty-second since then. My grief on that anniversary day of her ma's death kept me from ever telling Calamine here happy birthday, but this past year, I been realizing how lucky I am that my sweet wife left me a little girl."

Daddy coughed and cleared his throat. I couldn't tell if it was his sinuses or emotion when he continued, "Calamine's not a child anymore, and it's time I celebrated her birthday, but this storm ruined my plans for a fish fry and catfish stew over at the house, and Calamine's bosses, Otis and Odell, offered to move the party here since they don't have any dead bodies right now."

I couldn't see Otis or Odell, but I bet they cringed when Daddy said "dead bodies."

He continued, "I want to say happy birthday to Calamine and thank-you to the Middletons. Now, let's celebrate!" Daddy kissed me on the cheek and motioned toward three big washtubs filled with ice. Two of them had beers; the other was full of soft drinks. I thought he'd finished talking, but he added, "And I notice that tonight she's got brown hair again, just like her mama did, except her ma didn't have hers striped red."

That's when I realized what had made everyone look
so surprised when I turned on the lights—my newest hair
color.

The crowd let out cheers and hollering, and a lot of
them made a dash to the beer.

"Do you want a beer?" Frank asked Jane.

"What is there to eat?" she said. "I'm hungry."

That's when I noticed that the back wall of the salon
was lined with cloth-draped tables full of food. Frank took
Jane's hand and led her to the refreshments. I tagged along
as best I could with people stopping me for hugs and con-
gratulations.

Daddy said he'd planned a fish fry and catfish stew. I
knew the electricity had been off at his house, but he usually cooks fish outside on gas. The wind and rain would
have made that impossible. One thing for sure, the food on
the long tables hadn't come from Daddy's house.

Somebody had made a run to Beaufort for food because
we don't have a KFC nor a Pizza Hut in St. Mary. Buckets
and buckets of fried chicken, pizza of every kind, and bags
of chips with opened dip containers beside them covered
the crisp white cloths. There was enough food there to feed
all of St. Mary's residents plus a few extras.

"I smell meatballs," Jane said. "I want meatballs."

"Sorry, no meatballs," Frank answered.

"I know they're here. I smell them," Jane protested.

"Check the pizzas," I suggested. "I've heard of pizzas
with little miniature meatballs on them."

Frank cut me a disgusted look. "I'm who called and ordered the pizzas before Mike went to Beaufort to pick them
up because Domino's in St. Mary has no power," he said.
"I didn't order anything with meatballs."

"But I *smell* meatballs." Jane's tone was becoming argu-
mentative. I wondered if Frank was familiar with this side
of her. Had he seen the stubborn part of Jane yet? "Here

you two have eyes to see and refuse to look. If you did, you'd find the meatballs for me."

I walked the length of the tables and saw no meatballs on anything. I grabbed a paper plate and helped myself to a chicken leg and a slice of pepperoni pizza.

"Did I hear someone ask for meatballs?" I recognized that Charleston accent immediately and turned around to see Levi Pinckney and Tattoo Girl holding l-o-n-g boxes labeled "Nate's Sports and Subs." Levi moved chicken buckets and pizza boxes closer together and made room for the cartons of subs. He flipped one open, and the smell of meatballs permeated the room.

"Meatball party sub for the lady," he said as he slid a portion onto a plate and passed it to Frank to hand to Jane.

"I'll take a piece of that, too," Frank said.

"Let me introduce you," Levi said to me and motioned toward Tattoo Girl. "Callie, this is Denise Sharpe. She works with me at Nate's. With this rain, business was so bad that Nate called and said we could close the shop. We'd had the radio on, listening to the weather, and when we heard about the party on WXZW, we decided to come over. Since we didn't hear about it until too late to buy a gift, we brought along some party subs." He paused. "Denise, meet Callie Parrish, the birthday girl."

Denise grinned and said, "Happy birthday. Aren't you the woman who was in earlier this week? Sat with the sheriff and asked about Levi."

Levi's eyebrows shot up. "Asked about me?" he said.

"Yes," I answered. "The night you told me you'd buy me a sub, but you weren't there."

"Why were you with the sheriff?" Just like a man to ignore what I'd said.

"I wasn't really *with* him. Jane and I ran into him, and we wound up sitting together. What does it matter since you weren't there anyway?"

"Roselle was having a hard time. Sorry I couldn't make it."

I had no reply to his cavalier response. He must have sensed my mood because he turned to Denise. "Let's get a couple of beers and circulate," he said.

Once again, my blue eyes changed color. If that man kept it up, they might turn permanently green. Like when I was little and crossed my eyes. Daddy always told me to stop it or they'd stay that way.

Was Levi dating Denise? She seemed a little young for him, but then, what's age but a number? I couldn't help that the man created little urges in me that I'd tried to keep tamped down for a while. I hoped he didn't know about my personal desires, but I still didn't appreciate his being at my party with a date. Then what he'd said registered in my mind.

"Heard about the party on the radio?" I asked.

"Yeah," Frank said. "When Pa realized there was no way we could have it at home and Odell said move it here, we called DJ Cousin Roger and had him announce that the party would be here. I think Cousin Roger invited anybody shut in with no power tonight to come join the celebration. There are sure people here that I don't think any of us Parrishes invited."

Many of the guests were people I'd never seen before, and they all made a point of expressing their birthday wishes. Close friends were also celebrating with me. Rizzie had even brought her grandmother Maum with her as well as Tyrone, her foster brother.

Maum is a tiny little lady of indeterminate age. I'd met her on Surcie Island when I attended a bluegrass festival there. We'd become friends and I visited her about every two weeks to keep her fingernails and toenails manicured and polished in the newest shades.

"I'm so glad you came!" I said, and hugged Maum.

"Wouldn't want to miss you turning thirty-three. You got me off the island, Callie. Thirty-three. That's almost one-third of a century. I'm a whole lot closer to a century old than that." She nodded toward Tyrone. "Get me another piece of that chicken while I talk to Callie here." He headed toward the table and Maum turned back to me. "I don't really need more chicken. I just sent him away so I could tell you some woman talk."

Rizzie rolled her eyes.

"Callie," Maum went on, "you enjoy your youth while you can. There's gonna come a day that you get up and look in the mirror or into a clear pond of water and you'll see your reflection. And right before your eyes, everything will droop. Your face, your fanny, and your ta-tas."

"Maum!" Rizzie exclaimed.

"She's past thirty," Maum said. "She knows ta-tas will droop one day. I'm just telling her to enjoy her youth while she has it." Tyrone returned with a plate of chicken and a piece of pizza. Rizzie convinced Maum to go sit at one of the side tables. I didn't bother to tell her that my ta-tas would never droop so long as Victoria's Secret kept stocking those inflatable bras.

People of all ages crowded Slumber Room A. Some of my friends from school were there with their children and insisted on showing their offspring to me. Sometimes I think women who do that feel sorry for me that I don't have any children, but I'd rather not ever have any than have one fathered by my ex-husband, Donnie.

Pearl White and George Carter were snuggling over in a corner. Pearl was wearing a lime green sundress. Levi and Denise stood across the room laughing. Jane and Frank were acting like this was a date, and even though people kept talking to me, I felt a little like a fifth wheel until I saw Daddy and my other brothers bring instrument cases from behind the food tables.

John signaled me with his finger. Not the "bad" finger.
The motion was the one that meant *Come here*.

When I managed to move through the crowd to where
Daddy and my brothers stood, Daddy pulled out a case I
recognized and took out the most expensive instrument he
owned—a pristine prewar Gibson banjo. He handed it to me.

"You gonna let me play the Gibson tonight?" I asked
with delight.

"I'm gone let you play it tonight and from now on,"
Daddy said. "I never gave you a birthday present before.
This is my gift to you tonight, and I know it can't make up
for all the years that have passed, but with the rain and our
power off, I haven't had much time to go out and buy you
thirty-two presents to make up for the lost years." His best
Larry the Cable Guy grin crept across his face. "But I did
buy a generator, so the freezers are on and we won't lose
all the frozen fish. We can have us a big fish fry later."

Aside from John, my family is not very demonstrative,
but I reached up and hugged my daddy. He got all
embarrassed-looking, so I kissed him on the cheek and
made him blush redder than a boiled crab.

I said, "Don't worry about the other years. You've made
this one perfect. I love you, Daddy."

"We'd better get busy picking or our guests will think
all we're gone do at this party is eat." Daddy had displayed
as much emotion as he could handle. We formed a circle
and Bill kicked off "Salty Dog." Soon people were dancing
in the middle of Slumber Room A. This was a first for me.
We've had live musicians play at funerals before, but never
any dancing.

Chapter Twenty

Playing music and harmonizing with my brothers and Daddy always makes me happy. I even forgot to watch Levi and Denise until I noticed them dancing together. When we took a break, Odell stood in the middle of the room and announced, "If you'll move to the sides of the room, my brother, Otis, will bring in the cake."

I wondered how far a cake would go with this crowd, but when Otis pushed in a cloth-covered table, it had four large cakes on it, not just one. The biggest had pink sugar roses, "Happy Birthday Callie," and lit candles on it. I looked down at the wheels on the cake table. They were metal, and the table was above waist-high.

That's when I realized that my cakes were displayed on a sheet-covered gurney. I wondered if they'd used a new sheet or if this was one we'd used in the prep rooms. Not that they'd use a dirty one. If it were a used prep sheet, I was sure they'd gotten it from the clean laundry delivery, but it was still a little weird.

The crowd's rendition of "Happy Birthday" was loud and boisterous. I noticed that one of the beer tubs was empty and the other was getting low. Wonderful food, good music, and lots of beer make for a great party and loud singing.

I hadn't expected gifts, but after I blew out the candles, people started handing me packages. For someone who'd never before had a real birthday party, this was fantastic even if the wind was blowing a gale outside and the sound of the rain drowned out some of my thank-yous.

Buh-leeve me, I had never seen so many boxes of candy, bottles of cologne, mystery books, jars of bubble bath, and all kinds of other things, including an assortment of nail polishes from Rizzie and Maum. Tyrone gave me a little sweetgrass basket he'd made himself. Bill's girlfriend, Molly, gave me a crystal dog—a Great Dane like my own pet Big Boy.

After I'd opened all my presents, Frank and Jane began serving cake and we started back playing music. Dennis Sharpe, the Carefree Pet man, came over, carrying a musical instrument case.

"When I heard you folks playing, I just had to go home and get my Dobro. Can I pick with you?"

"Sure," Daddy replied. Most acoustic musicians welcome strangers to play. Sometimes that's bad because not everyone plays very well, but Dennis Sharpe was fantastic on that resophonic guitar. The only thing bad was that every once in a while he'd scoot over to where I was and pat me on the shoulder. His touch made my flesh crawl as I thought about where he obtained cats and dogs for his Carefree Pets.

Otis stacked up all the gifts and told me he was putting them in my workroom. I was watching him take away my birthday loot when it happened.

I heard it before I saw it.

"Leave me alone!" The scream was louder than the music, the wind, and the rain all together.

"You put your finger in my cake. Who would let a blind girl serve food anyway?"

There she was—Dorcas Lucas at the cake table screaming at Jane, with Jane yelling right back at her even louder. Jane uses her fingertips to measure, to gauge, whether it's how full a coffee cup is or how wide a slice of cake is. Of course she'd slightly touched each slice of cake she'd served, and though we've got plenty of gloves at Middleton's, nobody had thought to offer her a pair.

"My hands are clean. If you didn't want cake from me, why didn't you get a piece from someone else?" Jane chuckled and a silly grin crossed her face. Then she continued, "On second thought, if you look like you act, you're probably too ugly to get a piece from anyone." Jane roared with laughter after this comment. I was sure Jane had helped diminish the beer supply.

I carefully put the Gibson back into its case and moved over to Jane. I put my hand on her arm. She jerked away, screeching, "Don't you touch me, you . . ." She shouted a whole lot of names that I won't even repeat.

That crazy Dorcas Lucas began bouncing: up, down, left, right. As she moved, she reached around me, tapping Jane at different places on her shoulders. Jane flipped out, trying to strike at where the woman seemed to be. I pulled Jane away, but she couldn't tell who had her and fought against my restraint.

Frank grabbed her from me and said, "Jane, Jane, it's me, Frank. Come on. Let's get out of here."

"Oh, no!" I didn't mean to yell as loud as I did. "Jane's my best friend. She's not leaving. This witch is!" Okay, I confess, I didn't say "witch."

Daddy stepped up to Ms. Lucas. She gave him a look that showed how low she thought he was, and said, "Stay out of this. You people are nothing but trash."

Now, I admit that Daddy and The Boys are rednecks, but *nobody* calls my daddy "trash." Jane might not have been able to grasp exactly where Dorcas Lucas was, but I could see her, and I did something I should not have done. I, Calamine Lotion Parrish, am a calm, polite person (most of the time) and a former kindergarten teacher, trained to behave in a civilized manner. That didn't stop me.

I slapped Dorcas Lucas smack across the face.

Instead of hitting me back, kicking me, or screaming like I expected her to, she burst into tears before shrieking, "How dare you?"

"It's time for you to leave." Me.

"I'll stay if I want to." Lucas.

"Oh, no, you won't." Otis, as he stepped into the fracas with Odell right behind him. "This is a private party in my place of business, and you're not welcome."

"How can it be private when it was announced on the radio?" Ms. Lucas still sounded belligerent.

"Stay out of this, Doofus," Odell said to Otis before turning to Ms. Lucas. "Lady, this is a mortuary. Unless you want us to be measuring you for one of the caskets in the storage room, I suggest you get out of here. We don't take kindly to prejudiced people picking on a handicapped person."

I looked around for Jane. If she heard Odell call her "handicapped," we'd have a bigger fight on our hands. I didn't see her. Bill leaned over me. "Jane wanted to go home. Frank took her."

After Ms. Lucas left, I was afraid the party would die, but we got back to music and dancing. I saw Levi refilling the beer tubs. My first-ever real birthday party lasted far past midnight before the crowd thinned out, and we were left to clean up.

As we packed up presents and leftover food, I realized

that Frank hadn't returned. He'd been my ride, so I'd have to ask another brother or Daddy to take me home.

"A little bit of a spitfire, aren't you?" I looked up to see Levi putting empty food containers in a big black trash bag near me.

"Not all the time," I mumbled and thrust several bare pizza boxes into my own trash bag.

"Might be a good thing the sheriff wasn't here tonight. He could have arrested you for assault." Those dark brown eyes twinkled at me.

"Don't say that. Sheriff Harmon's a friend of my family, and I don't think he'd want to arrest me, but that Lucas woman might swear out a warrant, sure enough."

"I was just teasing you." He stopped working and looked me in the face with those deep, dark, sensuous eyes. *Whoa, Callie,* I thought. Don't go thinking *sensuous.* "Could I take you home?" Levi asked.

"I can get a ride with . . ." I stopped midsentence. "Yes, yes, if you don't mind, I'd like for you to give me a ride home. I came with Jane and Frank, but they left early. Where's Denise?"

"Her brother has to go right by her house, so she left with him. You know her brother, the bearded guy with the Dobro. Mullet Man." He grinned. "You didn't think Denise and I came together as dates, did you?"

"I hadn't really thought about it," I fibbed.

"We work together, and I feel protective toward her, but I'm too old for her. I wouldn't be dating Denise even if she didn't have that big brother."

"Dennis Sharpe with Carefree Pets is her brother?"

"That's the one. Denise said everyone used to call him Mullet Man because he wore his hair like that years after it went out of style."

"I don't know that it's any kind of style now," I said.

"Wonder what he looks like with his hat off and ponytail loose around his shoulders."

"Don't know. He's always got some scheme how to make a fortune. Meanwhile, his sister waits tables to pay her bills instead of going to college."

"Does she live with her brother?"

"No, she says she couldn't stand to live out there with Dennis and all those animals. She lives in a rooming house."

Levi turned back toward Daddy, Bill, and Mike. "Hey, nice party. I'm going to give Callie a ride home."

"Fine, see you later," Mike called.

"Wait here while I get the car," Levi said when we got to the side door. He drove a dark blue PT Cruiser, which he pulled up under the awning, close to the door. Rain still poured, and thunder rumbled as lightning streaked across the sky. We rode silently to my apartment, and Levi parked off the drive so that my car door was close to the porch steps. I started to open the door, and he said, "No, no. I'm old-fashioned. Let me get that for you."

He ran around to the passenger side, held the car door for me, and helped me up the steps. When I found my house key, he took it from me and opened the door.

"Umm," I said, "I hope I didn't mislead you. I accepted your ride, but I'm not sure I want you to come in."

"You don't like me?"

"I might like you just a little too much for you to come in," I said, expecting him to plead his case or even get huffy about it. Instead, he leaned over and said, "I understand, but can I please give you a birthday kiss?"

Not a word came from my mouth, but my eyes and expression must have said yes, because he gave me a gentle kiss. He had the softest lips I'd ever felt. The kiss deepened and my weakness heightened. I was considering telling him he could come in for one cup of coffee when he broke the kiss and whispered, "Happy birthday, Callie."

I closed the door as he said, "Lock everything," from the other side of the door. I don't know why every man I know thinks he has to tell me to lock my doors. What kind of stupid do they think I am? Besides, as soon as he left, I had to try to make Big Boy go outside and tinkle before the poor dog exploded.

Chapter Twenty-one

Rays of sunshine slanting through the window blinds woke me. Big Boy sat by the bed with his leash in his mouth. I pulled on a pair of Keds and khaki shorts with the tee I'd slept in and took him outside. When he finished, he ran up to me with what I swear was a big grin on his face. Water still stood in the yard, but the sky was clear. We walked about a mile, then turned back.

In the apartment, I poured Big Boy a bowl of Kibbles 'n Bits, started a pot of coffee, and called Jane.

"Hello-o-o-o-o," Jane answered in her sexy Roxanne voice.

"Hey, Jane. Wrong phone. This is Callie," I said.

"Oh, you woke me up."

"How long did my brother Frank stay?" I questioned.

"Don't ask," Jane said.

"I'm treating myself to breakfast at the Pancake House, and I want you to come with me. I'll pick you up in twenty minutes."

"How do you know the Pancake House is open?"

"If it's not, we'll drive on to Beaufort and eat there."

"I thought I'd sleep in today. I drank a lot of beer last night."

"Come on. The sun is out. The Boys will probably want to move you today, and Daddy's started going to early church service. They'll be over there and underfoot all day. I want to talk."

"I'm not answering questions. I told you that."

"Well, after the two of you left without me, Levi Pinckney brought me home."

"Oh. Okay, but I'll treat since I didn't have a present for you at the party."

"You gave me the garnet before we went."

"I'll treat anyway. See you soon."

I play-wrestled with Big Boy for a few minutes, got a quick shower, and headed over to Jane's.

When I turned into her driveway, I noticed that she still had more puddles in her yard than I did. I pulled up close to the steps so Jane wouldn't have to walk through all that water and mud. My first thought was that someone had splashed mud all up on the stairway. Then I saw what looked like a pile of rags at the bottom.

I promise, I had no idea that I was screaming. The sound escaped my mouth with no conscious thought. I was vaguely aware of the sound of the door opening and Jane calling from the top of the stairs, "What's wrong, Callie?"

"Stop!" I screamed at her. "Stay at the top and call 911."

"Why? What's wrong?"

"There's blood all over down here and about halfway up the steps. Don't try to come down. You'll step in it."

"Blood?"

"Yes, I think it's blood and the pile of clothes here might be a body."

"You're kidding. You haven't found *another* corpse have you, Callie?"

"I'm afraid so."

"She's upset. Can't I go up and sit with her?" I pleaded with Sheriff Harmon. The cloth at the foot of the stairs had been Dorcas Lucas's raincoat, and now the whole yard was crawling with forensics technicians, sheriff's deputies, and state police officers. The coroner had given me a strange look when he arrived and saw me there. I would imagine he's drawn a few strange looks himself with his tall, skinny body and an Adam's apple that beats any other I've ever seen.

"No, Callie," the sheriff said, "for the last time, Jane can't come down those steps and you can't go up them until we've finished here." They'd already shot about a million photographs. Well, it seemed like a million, probably not more than a thousand. Maybe only a few hundred. I'm inclined toward hyperbolism. They'd measured distances and marked distances, and they'd finally moved the raincoat and turned the body. Her head was broken. I know that's not a medical term, but I'm not a medical person.

The back of the woman's head exhibited more than a fractured skull. Her skull was shattered, with bits of bone showing in the bloody brain matter exposed by the hole in her head. I hate, positively hate, the fact that when a body is exposed for a while, whether undiscovered or while waiting for the authorities to complete their tasks, flies can't stay away. The sun shining on the wings of flies around the body made them look iridescent, a spot of beauty in the otherwise ugliness of insects swarming over a corpse. The coppery smell of blood made me feel nauseous.

"I asked you a question." Sheriff Harmon said.

"I'm sorry," I said. "What did you say?"

"A deputy took a report from you about Dorcas Lucas harassing Jane. I've been told they had words at your party last night also." A flash of embarrassment crossed his face. "By the way, I'd planned to be at your party, but we've had more than our share of traffic accidents with all this rain. Matter of fact, Cousin Roger had been announcing for people to stay off the roads at the same time he was inviting them to your party."

"I still haven't heard your question," I said in an almost, but not quite, smart-alecky tone. I've known Sheriff Harmon my whole life and sometimes I treat him like one of my brothers.

"I want to know if Jane called you to come over here to try to get her out of this mess after she shoved Ms. Lucas down the steps."

"What?"

"Did Jane call you over here this morning?"

"No, I called her and told her I'd pick her up to go to the Pancake House."

"They're closed. Still no power."

"I didn't know that. When we got there and they weren't open, we would have driven on to Beaufort. Their power's been restored, hasn't it?"

"So far as I know, Beaufort didn't have any long-term outages."

"Sheriff Harmon," one of the state officers called.

"I'll get Jane out of there as soon as I can," Harmon said as he turned away from me and headed toward the officer.

"Can't I just go up and sit with her?" I called.

"No, but you can call her on the cell and talk to her." He shook his head and looked disgusted. "What am I thinking? You're both persons of interest. I can't let you talk to her until we get a statement from each of you."

He turned toward a deputy and said, "We're going to need a search warrant for Miss Baker's apartment."

"Everything in there is boxed up," I said. "My brothers are moving Jane today."

"Not until my men have been through everything, including looking in packed boxes. I want to see if Jane has bloody clothes hidden before we release her belongings."

"Do you think we can move her this afternoon?"

Harmon didn't bother to answer. He just gave me an official reprimand look and left me standing while he went to talk to the state officials.

I sat in the Mustang and pulled out my cell phone. I don't know why I hadn't made my first call before, probably too surprised and upset to think. I flipped the phone open and hit the automatic dial for "Daddy."

The hello that answered was too low and sleepy for me to tell which Parrish man it was. "I need to talk to Frank," I said.

"This *is* Frank," the voice responded.

"I'm at Jane's."

"Yeah, we'll be over there, but not yet, Callie. It's too early to start moving her."

"That's not why I called. Ms. Lucas is lying at the foot of Jane's steps."

"Then call an ambulance, not me."

"She's dead, and Jane's upstairs, and Harmon won't let Jane come down or me go up. He seems to think Jane pushed her down the steps, and he's getting a search warrant for Jane's apartment. He's sure to want to talk to you, too."

"I'm on my way."

I clicked the phone off and started to call Jane when a deputy rapped his knuckles on my window.

"You've got to get out," he said.

"Why? The sheriff told me to stay out of the way."

"We're taping off the crime scene, and you're in it."

"What?"

"Your car is parked so close to the body that it's part of the crime scene."

"I'll move it," I said, as I turned the key in the ignition.

"No, don't move the car. It's part of the scene. Just get out and walk away."

I'm proud that I limited myself to kindergarten cussing as I stomped across the yard. I had my purse and my phone with me. I knew from experience that once a vehicle becomes part of a crime scene, it could be impounded and held for ages. My brother John's Winnebago camper—excuuze me, motor home—was still impounded from April. I also knew that once that yellow tape encircled anything, authorities wouldn't let me get back in for any belongings.

I leaned against Mrs. White's house and called Jane. Yes, I know the sheriff said for me not to talk to her, but I didn't call to discuss our statements.

"Sheriff Harmon says he'll get you down as soon as possible," I said. "Stuff your toothbrush and some clean undies and bras in your clothing. He's not going to let you bring anything out, and you know we still haven't got our clothes from the Winnebago."

As inappropriate as it was, I laughed. "I'll lend you clothes, but you know my underwear won't work for you." The thought of Jane wearing my inflated bras and padded panties was funny. Jane was blessed with an abundance of bosom and a pert little behind that needed no help.

After Jane and I disconnected the call, I looked around to see if George Carter's Continental was in the garage. Surely if he and Pearl were in the house, all the commotion would have brought them out by now. The garage was empty. That led to another thought. Where was the gray Lincoln Town Car that Ms. Lucas always drove? It wasn't parked in the yard.

By the time Frank arrived, accompanied by John driving Dad's truck, yellow crime scene tape had been looped around my car and the front of Jane's apartment, but not the back wall. Frank and John solved the problem of getting Jane across the crime scene with a tall ladder they'd brought from Daddy's. They propped it against a rear window. Frank climbed while John steadied the ladder. Frank carried Jane down the ladder like a hero fireman. I noticed that Jane looked a lot pudgier than usual.

John and the sheriff were best friends all through school, and that's probably why John was able to convince Harmon to let us go over to my apartment until he was ready to talk to us.

"Don't discuss this at all until after I take your statements," Sheriff Harmon cautioned. "And you'd all *better* be there when I arrive."

The four of us piled into the truck with me in the passenger seat beside John. Frank was in the backseat, apparently thinking Jane would need comforting, but Jane was not upset and crying. She was mad. Rip-roaring, college-level-cussing mad!

"How *dare* that old woman fall down my stairs and cause me all this grief!" After that statement, Jane proceeded to call Ms. Lucas every bad name she could think of and some she made up on the spot.

John rode through McDonald's drive-through and ordered a lot of sausage and pancakes. It wouldn't be like going to the Pancake House, but it would be better than eating my cooking. No hope of Jane cooking. She was in no mood to do anything but fuss and cuss.

Chapter Twenty-two

Bored and irritated. My brothers, my best friend, and I were beginning to get on each other's nerves. By four o'clock that afternoon, we'd watched two movies on the DVD player and Big Boy had finished off our McDonald's leftovers before Harmon got there. Daddy had called and told us the electricity was back on out at the farm. Frank and John were having a heated discussion about which sports show to watch on television.

When the sheriff arrived, he questioned Frank and me quickly. He accepted that Jane hadn't called me to go over to her house and that it had been my idea. I'd arrived at Jane's about 8:30 a.m. Frank assured him there'd been nothing at the bottom of the stairway when he left at 3:00 a.m.

I wanted Harmon to ask Frank and Jane what they'd been doing all that time, but he didn't. He concluded that Ms. Lucas had fallen down the steps during the five-and-a-half-hour time span between when Frank left and I arrived. The sheriff would obtain a closer time of death from the medical examiner.

When Sheriff Harmon was ready to take Jane's statement, he asked if he could speak to her privately. I wanted to listen, but I knew he'd only *asked* to be polite. If we'd said no, he would have *demanded*. John, Frank, and I took Big Boy outside for a long walk. When we got back, John knocked, but the sheriff called out for us to wait. John had a Frisbee in the trunk of his car, so we all played with Big Boy until the sheriff stuck his head out the door.

"Okay," Harmon called, "you can come back in now. I doubt I'll have any more questions, but I need to ask that none of you leave town without checking with me."

"Not even to Beaufort?" Frank asked.

"Nope, not even to Beaufort," the sheriff said in an official tone.

Big Boy followed John to the Mercedes and watched as John opened the trunk. The dog sniffed a back tire as John tossed the Frisbee into the car. I was absolutely positive he was going to hike his leg and tee-tee like a male. Big Boy, not John. I would assume all my brothers have used the bathroom in masculine fashion for many years, and I have no interest in knowing for sure. Big Boy sniffed the tire, then squatted. I rolled my eyes as we went back into the apartment.

"I'm not kidding," Sheriff Harmon said, passing us. "Stay in St. Mary unless you talk to me first."

He pulled the door closed behind him, then opened it again. I expected him to tell me to be sure to lock it. Instead, he said, "By the way, Callie, Otis called you."

"I can't believe he answered my phone," I commented when I heard the sheriff's cruiser leave my driveway.

"He didn't," Jane said. "Otis left a message on the answering machine. He wants you to call him."

I picked up the phone, then put it down without calling. "Jane, are you okay?" I asked.

"Yes, I'm upset that the sheriff would even consider that I'd kill that woman, but he wasn't mean about it."

"He'd better not be mean to you," Frank said and swaggered over to Jane. He put his arm around her.

"Don't cop an attitude," John cautioned. "Wayne does his job well, and I've never known him to be mean to anyone who didn't deserve it."

"I don't think I'd test him by going out of town either," I said as I dialed the funeral home.

"Middleton's Mortuary. Otis Middleton speaking. How may I help you?"

"Otis, this is Callie. Did you just call me?"

"Yes, can you come over here? Odell has gone to take Ms. Lucas to Charleston for her postmortem exam, and I've got a pickup call at the nursing home."

"I can do either. Stay there or make the pickup for you."

"Just come on over and answer the phone. Bring a book. You won't have anything to do except take calls." He sighed that mournful sound that meant he was worried about the business.

John agreed to drive me over to Middleton's Mortuary. Frank and Jane stayed at the apartment so Frank could watch the televised ball game he'd chosen.

Otis chatted with John a few minutes, then left in the funeral coach. I noticed that Odell had taken the older one and left the new one for Otis. I doubted the average person could tell one from the other anyway because they're both always polished to a high shine.

John and I peeked into Slumber Room A. It looked just like it always did. No signs of a party the night before. Not even the smell of pizza. We sat down.

"I'm going to head back to Atlanta this evening," John said.

"Have you decided what to do?" I asked, hoping he'd changed his mind since our dinner at Blue Crab.

"No, I don't know, but pulling Johnny's Frisbee out of

the car made me think that I do want to see my children regularly, so if Miriam and I separate, I'll probably stay near Atlanta instead of going somewhere totally new."

He stood, leaned over, and kissed me on the forehead. "I love you, Little Sister, and I hope I didn't ruin your birthday by dumping my problems on you."

"Oh, no," I said, "this was my best birthday ever and I'm glad you can talk to me about how you feel."

When he left, I confess that I had to pull a few of our expensive aloe-imbued tissues from their fancy container and shed a few tears.

I went back to my office and booted up the computer. I was checking to be sure that I hadn't left any outdated info on our pages when "Immortal, Invisible, God Only Wise" sounded. I headed for the front door, hoping that it wasn't a relative of the nursing home pickup. Sometimes the bereaved arrive at the funeral home before the deceased.

Dennis Sharpe stood in the entry hall with a gift-wrapped box in his hands and the usual unlit cigar in his mouth. He thrust the package toward me before I was within reaching distance.

"I didn't know anything about your party last night 'til I heard about it on the radio, so I didn't have a present for you then. I've brought you something."

He put the box in my hand, and I placed it on the shelf of the mahogany hall tree beside the door.

"No," he protested, "don't do that. I want you to open it now."

I followed his directions and opened the package. No appropriate words came to mind when I pulled out a stuffed squirrel. I don't mean like the Squiggy the Squirrel puppet we'd had in my kindergarten class. This was a real squirrel with real squirrel fur and a real squirrel tail. He was mounted on a branch. Then I noticed it wasn't a "he" squirrel because it had a stuffed baby squirrel in a suckling position.

Dennis looked at it with such pride that I knew he thought he'd given me something special. On the other hand, I don't like squirrels. I don't like what they do to gardens, and I don't like their rattiness, and I'd rather eat barbecued possum than squirrel stew. That's saying a lot because I'm not fond of possum either.

"Thank you," I managed to say, "but this is too nice. You hardly know me. I'm sure you can sell it."

"No, it's for you. If you don't want to take it home, I thought you might put it on display here at the funeral home."

I promise, I tried not to laugh at the thought of using a couple of dead squirrels to decorate a funeral home. I grinned and hoped Dennis thought it was in appreciation of his gift.

"It's been so hot today after all that rain, I was wondering if ya'll might have Cokes for sale or even some leftover beer from last night. I'd be happy to treat us both to something to drink." He shot a shy smile at me and I realized that he was not just interested in taxidermy and freeze-drying and embalming. Dennis Sharpe was interested in Callie Parrish.

"The only beverage I have available is bottled water, and there's no charge for that. Would you like one to take with you?" I was trying to be nice and not hurt his feelings, but I didn't want to be here with him and his creepy dead squirrels.

"Oh, I didn't stop to think. You're probably busy doing mortuary work. I didn't mean to interrupt you."

"Don't worry about it. Let me get you a water to go, and thank you again for the present."

"I don't need anything to drink. I'll just be going now. Maybe I'll see you later," he said as he backed out the door and "The Old Rugged Cross" sounded.

Chapter Twenty-three

Riiiinnnng. I grabbed the phone and almost said "hello" before I realized that I was at work and had been sleeping at my desk.

"Middleton's Mortuary. Callie Parrish speaking. How may I help you?"

Someone was crying. Sobbing with great wretched gasps.

"Just take your time and catch your breath," I said. "I'm right here when you're able to talk." I'd had calls like this before.

A few more sobs and some long sniffles later, an elderly female voice said, "Can you help me?"

"What do you need?"

"It's Amos. They won't keep him."

"Yes, ma'am," I said in what I hoped was an encouraging voice, urging her to continue.

"I said they won't keep Amos."

"Who won't keep Amos?"

"Those people at the medical university. He had willed his body for research because after he was laid off and got sick, we couldn't afford to keep paying his life insurance. Now those people say they won't take him."

"I'm sure you can make other arrangements. Perhaps you and Amos can come in tomorrow and speak with Mr. Middleton about prearrangements. You can finance services if they're prearranged." As I spoke, I realized that I really needed to go to the bathroom.

"You don't understand. It's too late for prearrangements. Amos died this morning. The university people came and got him, but now they've called and said they don't want him. They said I have to hire a funeral home to fetch him from them. I want to know if Middleton's will do that."

"Yes, ma'am. We can take care of it for you. I'll need some information. Give me Amos's full name, date of birth, and the name and number of who called and told you to get a funeral home to pick up Amos."

I squeezed my legs together and picked up a ballpoint pen. The lady was spelling, "B-a-l," when I realized I couldn't wait.

"Ma'am," I interrupted, "please hold. I'll be back to you in just a moment." I pressed the button and dashed to the bathroom. When I returned, the light wasn't blinking.

More than one time I'd suggested to Otis and Odell that we have caller ID put on the office phones, but no, they didn't want to spend the money. Now I'd lost a customer, but I didn't have to worry long. The phone rang and I answered on the first ring.

"Middleton's Mortuary. Callie Parrish speaking. How may I help you?"

Little old lady voice: "Did you hang up on me because I don't have any money?"

"Is this Mrs. Ballentine?"

"No," she said.

"Was I just speaking with you?"

"Yes, we were talking about Amos, but our name is Valentine, just like those little cards with hearts on 'em."

"Oh, I misunderstood." I scratched out the B on my notepad. "I didn't mean to hang up on you. The phone's acting up. You know, with all that rain we've had."

She was crying again. Sobs so harsh that she couldn't catch her breath. Finally, she said, "I'm so glad. I was afraid you'd hung up on me, and I don't know what to do about Amos. They said they won't bring him back. I *have* to send someone to pick him up. I've got a station wagon, but I just don't think I could manage going for him. I'm sure I'd wreck the car."

"No, ma'am. I didn't hang up on you." I knew I was repeating myself, but I thought she needed to hear it again. Besides, I wondered if I *did* hang up on her. Maybe in my rush to tinkle, I'd pushed the wrong button.

"Now tell me again how to spell the last name," I said.

"I already told you. It's just like February fourteenth."

"And can you give me the phone number and name of the person who called you?"

"Wait a minute. I wrote it down, but I'll have to find it."

Ten minutes later, I had all the information I needed to pick up Amos, but my natural nosiness made me ask, "Mrs. Valentine, did Amos die of a communicable disease?"

"What do you mean?"

"Did Amos die of something that's catching? Did he have tuberculosis or AIDS or something like that? I was just wondering why the medical school can't use his body." Thank heaven my bosses weren't there. They might have fired me for that last question and the word "body." Technically, deceased who are donated for research are called "cadavers," but that sounds worse than "bodies" to me. Otis and Odell would solve the entire issue by calling him "Mr. Valentine."

"Amos had emphysema for years. I don't think that's catching."

"No, ma'am. Let me write down your phone number, and I'll call you when we have Mr. Valentine here. You can come in then to make arrangements."

She gave me the telephone number and was sobbing again when we said good-bye.

This was a first for me, but I doubted seriously that it would be for Otis or Odell. Everytime something strange happened at work, one of them would say, "Yeah, like So-and-So," back in some year before my time.

Otis returned before Odell.

"A lady called and said that her husband donated his body to the medical university and they picked him up, but now they don't want him. I've filled out the info on a pickup form." I'd thought it probably wasn't a new situation for him, and I was right.

"Yes, that happens. I'll take care of it," Otis answered. He made three telephone calls. One to the medical university, one to Odell to tell him to pick up Amos, and the last one to Mrs. Valentine to assure her that Middleton's would take care of everything. She agreed to come in the next morning.

Otis brought in the lady from the nursing home and put her in his prep room, where he'd embalm her—pardon me, *prepare her*—before going home for the night. I followed him in there.

"You don't have to wait here, Callie," he said. "Her family will be in tomorrow with a photo and clothing. You can go on home now."

"Um, well, I have a problem," I told him.

"What's that?"

"The reason John was with me when I came in is that he brought me to work. Sheriff Harmon has my car."

"Oh." He transferred the body bag from the portable gurney to his worktable. "I need to get started here. Just drive one of the family cars home and be back tomorrow by nine."

He didn't have to tell me twice. I *love* driving those elegant vehicles. As I drove home, I thought about what a relief it was not to have to drive through rain. Then I remembered my birthday gift from Dennis Sharpe. I'd left those two squirrels sitting in the entry hall at the mortuary.

What would Otis say about *that*?

Chapter Twenty-four

The wreath on my door was even larger than the bouquet of flowers had been. I couldn't miss it when I pulled into my drive—a tremendous wreath, as big as a casket spray. Who'd sent that? Had John come back by with it before he left for Atlanta? If he'd gone back. I didn't know if Harmon had let him. Standing on the porch, I realized it wasn't a gift from anyone who cared about me.

The flowers weren't just wilted. They were disintegrating and decaying. The ribbon was mildewed. It looked like a wreath a few weeks after a funeral if the cemetery doesn't remove it. I snatched it off the hanger and threw it in the Herbie Curby on the side of the building. *What kinda jerk thinks sending dead funeral flowers to a woman is funny?*

Jane was asleep on the couch, but Big Boy met me with a grin on his face, his tail wagging, and his leash in his mouth. When we came back in, Jane was stretching and yawning. "Hey," she said, "guess what I learned?"

"No telling," I replied.

"I was watching one of those court programs on television, and they had a woman who does the same job as Roxanne. She calls herself a 'fantasy phone actress.' I think I'm going to start using that instead of 'conversationalist.' Don't you think it sounds better?"

Jane went to the kitchen and got a glass of water. She was learning her way around with no trouble.

"Maybe. When are you going to tell Frank what you do? It seems you two are mighty interested in each other. Don't you believe he should know?"

I walked to the bedroom to change clothes, leaving the door open as I dropped my black dress and panty hose in the clothes hamper and pulled on shorts and a shirt. Big Boy came loping into the bedroom and barked at the window.

"I've been thinking about that. Please don't tell him. Let me do it," Jane said, trying to talk louder than Big Boy's howling.

"Sure, but don't wait too long. I'm not the only one who knows your occupation, and you don't want Frank to hear it from someone else. He'll probably be all right with it, but if you get serious, he'll want you to give it up."

"I figured that, and I thought I'd see if we develop a relationship before I risk quitting my job. It's the best money I've ever made." She turned toward Big Boy. "Why is that dog howling and barking like that?"

"I don't know. There must be a squirrel outside near the window." I stepped over to Big Boy and scratched behind his ears. He began to settle down.

Jane rubbed her stomach. "I'm starving. Are you cooking?"

"No, I'm going to pick up something. Wanna ride?"

"How are you going? Did you get the Mustang back from the sheriff?"

"No, Otis lent me a family car to drive."

"Limousine?"

"No, a smaller one. A Lincoln Town Car like Ms. Lucas had, except ours are all black, not gray." That reminded me. I wondered if the sheriff had determined where Ms. Lucas's car was and how she'd gotten out to Jane's place.

"Do you mind if I don't go? Frank said he'd call."

"Not at all," I said, thinking we might just have subs again. Maybe Levi Pinckney would be working.

Big Boy stopped barking. He seemed to sense I was going somewhere and wanted to go with me, but I didn't dare let him ride in a mortuary vehicle. He'd get excited and drool everywhere.

I felt better than I had in days as I drove toward Nate's Sports and Subs. I fooled around with the radio and got a station of oldies but goodies. Growing up in a family of six left me a fan of all kinds of music, from the sixties tunes Daddy loves through the disco and eighties of my brothers' youths to nineties and current cuts Jane and I like. Everything from eight-track to audiocassettes to CDs and back to some old LPs and even some 78s and 45s Daddy had saved.

The Beatles were singing "I wanna be a paperback writer," and I sang right along with them, occasionally glancing in the rearview mirror. A black Tahoe with dark tinted windows pulled up behind me. I looked out my front windshield at the road in front of me and then back into the rearview mirror again.

Dalmation! The Tahoe was bearing down on me, gaining speed. I slammed my foot on the accelerator to get away from him. The engine chugged as though it would stall from the sudden surge, then leaped ahead. The front of the Tahoe looked like it was in the backseat when I checked the mirror again, but I still couldn't see the driver. Even the windshield looked opaque from the outside.

I *knew* that Tahoe would hit me. I've been in fender benders, but I'd never before known that I was going to be hit. Going to be struck, careened into on purpose. I jerked the steering wheel to the right. Desperate to move off to the shoulder of the road and let the Tahoe pass me.

Had I done something to trigger road rage in the driver? I didn't think so. I yanked the steering wheel to the right as hard as I could. My foot floored the accelerator, but it wasn't fast enough.

The Tahoe smashed into my left rear fender with a loud *bam*, knocking me forward. Only my seat belt kept me from going through the windshield. My head banged against it, causing the glass to explode into a creepy web pattern.

For a moment, I though I'd pass out. My head swam as I hit the brakes trying to stop the car. Through the crackled safety glass, I saw the Tahoe make a three-point turn and head back toward me, speed increasing every second. Its impact on the front of the Lincoln threw me back against the seat.

The Tahoe pulled around me, then revved up and slammed into the rear of the Lincoln again. I felt my car leave the ground, go airborne, then slam into a tree. I heard the Tahoe speed away at the same time I heard the screech of an eighteen-wheeler's airbrakes.

"Are you okay?" a young male voice asked as he looked through the smashed side window.

"I'm banged up, but I don't think I'm hurt bad," I answered, though my chest and head were agonizing.

"Why didn't your airbags go off?" he asked.

"I don't know," I said, though I did. Odell had disconnected them after he read about an airbag going off unexpectedly when the car wasn't involved in an accident. Odell claimed that as slow as funeral vehicles are driven, the airbags would never be needed.

The young man yanked and yanked on each door in turn, but the sides of the Town Car were crushed and wrinkled.

"Don't worry," he said. "I called 911 the minute I came over the hill and saw what was happening. I've got the tag number of whoever hit you, too. Wrote it down as he sped away."

Just my luck that when the law showed up, there was no one I knew on patrol. Same with the EMTs. I felt like I must be getting old at thirty-three. Everyone looked about fourteen or fifteen. A medical technician crawled through the broken window and said, "Be still. Stop moving. I want to stabilize your head until we get you out of here. It won't be long. I called for the hearse."

"The *hearse*? I'm not dead." I tried to shout it, but my words came out a whisper.

"The *Hurst*. It's one of those car can openers, like the Jaws of Life. We'll have you out of here in no time." As he talked, he wrapped my head in some kind of swaddling that held it still against a hard surface.

When the man arrived with the machine, the EMT in the car with me laid a cloth over my face, explaining, "This is just to keep any glass that rattles loose from getting into your face."

For some reason, when I'd seen them use equipment like this on television, I'd always thought of it as gentle. It wasn't. The car rocked back and forth violently as they tried to open it. I caught a faint whiff of something unpleasant.

"Gas! Get her out of there before this thing explodes," another voice called. The next thing I knew I was being pulled from the car onto a body board and wrapped snugly to it. I glanced around and saw two fire trucks, several Jade County Sheriff Department cruisers, and two ambulances—all of them a pretty far distance from the Lincoln.

The guys carrying me on my body board slid me into the back of an ambulance, which drove off just as I heard the *boom* of Middleton Mortuary's best family car explode.

Inside the ambulance, a young technician unwound enough wrappings to take my left arm out and stabilize it on a smaller board. He took my blood pressure, then patted the inside of my elbow. He muttered, "Her veins are rolling like crazy," but after several jabs, he succeeded in getting a needle in and hung an IV over me.

"Can you call someone for me?" I asked.

"Yes," he said, "who do you want me to call?"

"Middleton's Mortuary."

"Honey, you're going to be okay. You don't need a funeral home," he answered.

"You don't understand. I work there."

"Don't worry about your job right now," he consoled.

"You still don't understand." Tears filled my eyes. "The car that just exploded belonged to my bosses."

Chapter Twenty-five

Déjà **vu.** Back in the ER with handsome, smooth-talking Dr. Don Walters leaning over me, pointing his little flashlight into my eyes.

"Callie," he said, "the waiting room is full of Parrish men, the sheriff, your friend Jane, and some trucker who just wants to know you're going to be okay before he gets back on his route." He shined the light up my nose. I was glad I didn't have a cold.

"Of course," he continued, "there are two undertakers waiting to hear about you, too. The bald-headed one is cussing, and I think the spiffy one is praying. They all want to see you, but I need tests before I let them. Scans of your head, chest, and back." He straightened up.

"Can you tell me how you feel?" he asked.

"I hurt, but not unbearably."

"Where?"

"Everywhere."

"Can you stand it until we get the scans? I had the nurse give you a little something for pain through your IV, but I'd rather hold off on anything stronger until after the scans. If we need to call in a neurosurgeon, I'd like for you to be able to answer her questions."

I grinned.

"Yes," he said, "I said *her*. The best in this area is a female, and if you need one, we'll get the best."

Don hadn't said what he was looking for, but I knew. Damage to my brain or spine. He hadn't unbound me from the board. The transport personnel put me on the gurney still wrapped to the body board to go to X-ray.

Up or down? I was too spacey to feel which direction we moved on the elevator or where we went when we got off. They lifted me onto a table similar to the ones we use in the prep room at the mortuary.

"Take off her earrings," the attendant said. I saw and felt hands remove my birthday pearl studs from my ears. Vaguely aware of being left in the room alone, I heard the mechanical voice say, "Breathe in and hold it."

What felt like eternity.

"You may breathe out."

This occurred over and over as the equipment moved me backward and forward through an opening in the gigantic machine that seemed to groan and moan when not telling me how to breathe.

The transporters had me back to the elevator before I remembered.

"My earrings. They took them off, and I didn't get them back."

"Are you sure?"

"Yes, they're pink pearl studs."

"I'll go check."

They wheeled me off the elevator, down the hall, and into a private room before the young man returned with my earrings. He put them back into my ears "so they won't get lost." He didn't say stolen, but I thought it.

* * *

I heard voices. Frank and Jane were talking to Don. I wondered if all the other people he'd named were there, but when I opened my eyes, only the three of them were in the room.

"Callie?" Don leaned over me. I swear that man winds up over me every time I get hurt. Notice I didn't say on top of me, just leaning over me. "I gave you some pain medicine after the scans were negative.

"You have a couple of cracked ribs, but other than that, you're fine except for bruises, some small cuts, and probably two black eyes," he continued. "I've been letting your friends and family come in to see you two at a time. Now that you're awake, they can speak to you for a few moments, then I want them to go home and let you sleep through the night. Your body needs rest."

Jane and Frank had little to say. Just, "We're so sorry you were hit, but so glad that you aren't hurt worse." I could hear in Jane's voice that she'd been crying.

The trucker came in next. He'd been waiting to get back on the road. "Miss," he said, "I'm glad you're going to be okay. I gave the sheriff the license number for the Tahoe that hit you. I'll check on you next time I'm through St. Mary." I thanked him again and again until Don sent him away, saying there were others waiting.

Don Walters lied to me again. He said two at a time, but Daddy came in with Bill and Mike. Even as drugged up as I felt, I knew that was three people, not two. They didn't have much to say except that if they found whoever was driving that Tahoe, all of them might go to jail. Before they left, Daddy kissed me on the cheek.

I lay there, drifting off, enjoying the sensation of my daddy showing me the feelings I'd always known he had but he'd never before been able to express.

"They said she was awake." I heard Odell's raspy voice complain.

"Well, she's asleep, so don't wake her," Otis answered.

"I'm awake," I mumbled. "I'm sorry, so sorry."

"Sorry for what?" Odell.

"Your Lincoln. It has to have been totaled, as many times as it was hit, but then it burned."

"Don't worry. It's insured," Otis said. "The important thing is that you're okay. Lord knows, if you'd been in your Mustang, you'd probably be dead now."

"Don't even think of Callie getting killed, Doofus," Odell scolded. "Let her go back to sleep." Danged if Odell didn't kiss me on one cheek and Otis on the other.

I'd been kissed more in the past few days than in a year, but they were all just affectionate family-type kisses. Except for that one sweet kiss from Levi. What did it matter? I felt so sore that if Levi Pinckney himself crawled in bed with me, I'd probably push him away, roll over, and go to sleep.

"Wake up, sunshine, your breakfast is here." The attendant was pleasant and smiling. She pulled a side table across my bed and placed a covered tray on it. "Do you need help with eating or can you do it by yourself?" she asked.

"I'll be fine," I said, then added, "thank you," as she left.

Sometimes I react to situations like a child. I was hungry and the covered tray delighted me. I'd almost been killed, could even have burned to death, but here I was ecstatic over a breakfast tray.

I hoped that removing the lid would reveal pancakes. I grinned and snatched the top off the plate. No such luck. Grits, scrambled eggs, and two slices of bacon. Not so good as pancakes, but as hungry as I was, I dug in.

A saucer beside my plate had two slices of buttered

toast and little plastic packets of strawberry preserves. I slathered the toast with jelly and put the bacon inside. One of my favorites—a bacon and jam sandwich. I ate that first with the little carton of milk, then stirred the grits and eggs together. I was finishing them off and ready for my coffee when Dr. Don Walters came in.

I glanced down at my chest. Well, actually at my lack of a chest. Like the first time I'd ever met Donald Walters, I wore one of those little cotton thingies that hospitals use instead of gowns and pajamas.

Oh, well, Don was a doctor. He wasn't supposed to be aware of such things when acting professionally, was he? I wondered if he ever thought about why I looked and felt so round except when in the hospital.

"Callie Parrish, you're a lucky young woman. From what that trucker and Sheriff Harmon said, it's almost unbelievable that your injuries are so minimal. I didn't tape your cracked ribs last night because they'll heal the same without it. If you want them wrapped, I can do it, but most patients say the taping is more painful than letting them mend by themselves."

"Don't do anything that's going to hurt more," I said. I finished the last swallow of coffee. "When can I go home?"

"As soon as someone comes for you. Who do you want the nurse to call to pick you up?"

I didn't answer because I wasn't sure who to request. I didn't want anyone making a fuss over me and reminding me that, from what everyone said, I should have been dead. I didn't want to think about it.

Didn't want to remember that black Tahoe aiming at me, trying to kill me. I didn't want to think about the flashing lights and sirens of the ambulances, fire trucks, and law enforcement vehicles the night before.

"Tell you what," Don said. "I'm off right now anyway— why don't I drive you home? Where do you want to go?

Maybe your dad's? I'm letting you leave the hospital, but I'd really rather you not be alone for a day or so."

"I can go to my place. Jane's staying with me for a few days."

"She's blind."

"Yes, but Jane sees more than most sighted people."

Chapter Twenty-six

"**I'm** never going to marry or have kids because I'm not the nurturing kind."

Jane used to say that all the time, but she'd certainly been a tremendous supportive help when I divorced. Now she was overdoing it.

"Do you want another pillow? Can you reach the remote control? Do you like this program or should I change it? Are you too hot? Do you feel chilled?" A thousand questions, one after the other, then she'd start over and add, "What do you want for lunch? Shall I make some tuna salad? How about homemade beef stew or vegetable soup?"

"Nothing!" I finally screamed. "I just want to be left alone."

Normally, if I'd said those words in that tone, she would have reacted in the same mode. Now she just said, "I'm sorry," and sounded hurt. Big Boy whimpered from the side of my bed.

"I'm sorry, too," I apologized. "It's not you, Jane. I just feel irritable, and I hurt all over. Why don't you bring me a glass of water? I'll take one of those pain pills and try to sleep for a while."

I awoke from my nap to Jane's voice saying that she didn't need a ride to the hospital. "Okay, Frank," she said before I heard the telephone disconnect. She came in to check on me and fluffed my pillows—again.

"The doctor said you need to drink lots of fluids. I'll get you a Coke."

She came back with a tall glass full of iced Coca-Cola. I usually drink soda from a chilled can and will, given no other choice, drink it at room temperature, but my favorite way is over ice. She'd even put a straw in it.

"You've had lots of calls," she said as she handed me the glass and sat on the edge of the bed. "Frank is coming over, and the sheriff needs to talk to you. I told everyone else to wait a while because the doctor advised you to rest and sleep today."

I laughed. "So Frank can come to see you, but no one can come see me?"

She giggled. "He's *your* brother!"

"Yes, but he's coming to see *you*. Don't go breaking my brother's heart, Jane."

"I think I care as much about him as he does about me." She smoothed out the rumpled bedcovers beside her. "But what if he wanders away from me like he's done the others?"

"Are you worried Frank's going to hurt you?"

"Well, I have feelings, too."

I grabbed her and gave her a little hug though it hurt like crazy.

"You always tell me to enjoy the moment. Live for the day. Why don't you do the same thing?" I said.

"I'll try. Anyway, Frank is bringing lunch. I told him sick people need mild, bland food, but no telling what it will be. Knowing men, he'll bring pizza or tacos."

My youngest brother surprised both of us. He brought homemade chicken and rice soup with bits of slivered celery and carrots. He insisted on spoon-feeding me and was slopping soup all over me until I convinced him I could do it myself and explained that I'd fed myself breakfast. Not to hurt his feelings, I refrained from telling him that I thought Jane would spill less on me and she couldn't even see to aim the spoon.

Sheriff Harmon showed up before we'd finished eating and ate two bowls of soup. When we'd all finished, Jane and Frank went to the kitchen to do the dishes while the sheriff and I talked.

"Callie, do you have any idea who might want to hurt you?"

"No, I haven't done anything to anyone, and I haven't been snooping around about Ms. Lucas or her death either."

"Well, the Tahoe that hit you was stolen from a textile salesman in Beaufort. We learned that from the tag number the trucker wrote down, but we've found the vehicle abandoned now. Forensics is checking it out, but they've already told me it appears that whoever took it wore latex gloves. The only fingerprints belong to the salesman and his family."

"I don't know a salesman from Beaufort."

"We know the salesman wasn't driving the Tahoe when you were struck. His alibi is solid. He was at a meeting with a dozen other salespeople." The sheriff patted my hand. "I want you to let me know if you think of any reason someone would try to k—I mean, hurt you."

"Can I ask you a question?"

"Sure. I don't promise to answer, but ask away."

"Do you know where Ms. Lucas's car is? I noticed it wasn't over at Jane's when we found the body. How'd she get there?"

"Her car was parked at the motel in Beaufort where she'd been staying. We don't know how she got to Mrs. White's property."

"Oh," I murmured. "I just wondered."

"Callie," the sheriff said authoritatively, "don't go sticking your nose where it doesn't belong. Let us take care of it." He cleared his throat. "And be careful, Callie, be careful."

I slept most of the rest of the day, ate some more chicken and rice soup, then slept through the night. Frank and Jane teased me about sharing my pain pills with them. The medicine not only eased the pain, it relaxed me. They were joking, but I put the pill bottle under my pillow. I didn't want to tempt them, and I didn't want to share or run out of the medicine either.

Miraculously, the next morning, I felt better, even when I realized that Frank had spent the night at the apartment. Since my spare bedroom has no bed in it, just junk and boxes of mystery books, I assumed that my friend and my brother spent the night together on my couch.

I showered carefully and almost went into shock when I saw my face in the mirror for the first time. No way would my personal cosmetics cover the black-and-blue bruises on my forehead, cheeks, and neck. Nor the dark purple eyes. I dressed in a black work dress and talked Frank into driving me to the mortuary.

The shock on Odell's face when he looked at me as Frank and I walked in was something I'd never seen before. He's usually not emotionally involved in even the worst scenarios. "We can get along without you today," he rasped. "Otis picked up Melvin Dawkins yesterday and he's been prepared, dressed, and casketed. He's in Slumber Room A already."

"I'd really like to stay for a while, if you don't mind."

Odell grumbled, mumbled, and finally said, "I don't want you in the front rooms if clients come in."

I gave him a puzzled look, then realized he was talking about my face. "I may look like a walking wreck now, but

I've beautified walking wrecks before." I thought about it. "Well, I guess not walking. Just give me some time in my workroom."

"Okay, call us if you feel weak or anything," Frank said to me, then turned to Odell. "I'd like to pay my respects to Melvin if he's ready."

I slipped into my workroom and took out my full makeup kit, the heavy-duty stuff I used for really bad cases. It took almost an hour, but when I returned to the hall, there were no signs of bruises or black eyes. My skin did feel a little stiff though. I'd laid it on pretty thick. I wondered if that was how Botox felt.

Frank and Odell had been joined by Otis in the kitchen area, and they were drinking coffee from the mugs we use in the back.

"You look great!" Frank said.

"She's good at makeup," Odell said, "the best I've ever seen and she hasn't even been trained in mortuary cosmetics."

"Have plans been set for Dr. Melvin?" I asked.

"Yes," Otis said. "Visitation is one to two this afternoon and services are here at two in our chapel."

"Where's Roselle burying him?"

"That seemed to give her some problems. Since Melvin never had children, he bought only two plots. The new Mrs. Dawkins had the secretary at the cemetery look up who owned the sites beside Melvin's first wife and bought two more. She's putting Melvin between his first wife and a plot she swears is for herself. That brother of hers tried to talk her out of it, telling her she'd probably remarry, but she was determined."

"Mr. Pinckney," I suggested.

"Yep, that's his name. Mrs. Dawkins says Mel, as she calls him, was the love of her life. Her brother told her you can have more than one love of your life, and she threw a crying hissy fit about how she'd found the right man and wouldn't ever want another."

"Will food be served at the visitation?" I asked.

"Yes, but it's just catered cookies and punch. I'll set up the coffee service," Odell said. "You look pretty good now, but I really think you should go home and rest another day."

"I'd rather stay here. Did one of you post Dr. Melvin's plans on the web page?"

"No," Otis said, "I tried to, but I didn't have much success. We got everything into the newspapers though."

"I'll update the web page, and then I might spend some time on the Internet," I said to the Middletons before turning to Frank. "Are you coming to Dr. Melvin's service?"

"I'm bringing Jane, and I think Pa will be here with the rest of the family."

"Is John here?" I confess I brightened at the thought of seeing my oldest brother.

"No, I meant Pa and Bill and Mike."

That upset me. Normally, John comes to St. Mary when anyone in our family is sick or hurt. He hadn't come to see me after I'd been in a horrible wreck. That wasn't like him and probably meant he was still having a hard time with his personal life.

"I really want to stay here until after the service. You or Daddy can give me a ride home."

I left my brother talking to my employers and went to my office. I quickly brought the web page up to date, then began surfing the Internet. I'd never searched for a person online before, but I'd read about it in mystery books. Kinsey Millhone does it all the time.

My first search was Levi Pinckney. It appeared that everything he'd told me was true. At least, the parts that were documented. His full name was Levi Halsey Pinckney,

Jr., son of Levi Halsey Pinckney, Sr., who'd made a bundle in the meatpacking industry.

Levi had grown up an only child in Charleston, South Carolina, graduated from high school and from the Citadel. Now, that was surprising. A lot of Citadel graduates went into the military. Levi was a Citadel graduate working at a sub shop.

I didn't find any evidence that Levi had ever been married or in legal trouble other than a couple of speeding tickets when he was a teenager.

Usual searches told me nothing about Roselle Dawkins. When I realized that Dawkins was her married name, I got off the Internet long enough to call the Bureau of Vital Statistics. Under normal circumstances, I couldn't have gotten any info from them, but an old school friend of mine works there.

Roselle's full maiden name was Roselle Annalee Farmer; she was twenty-seven years old; and she came from Valdosta, Georgia. Dr. Melvin had been seventy-three, which I already knew from his obituary.

Back on the Internet, I discovered that Roselle had worked in a small drugstore after graduating from high school. I found no record of her ever having been married before she wed Dr. Melvin.

I'd just typed in "George Carter" when my door opened. Levi Pinckney stood there. "Hi," he said. "I heard you were in an accident and I asked Mr. Middleton if I could speak to you. He showed me to your office."

My mind went blank. I couldn't even think to say hello. I just sat there like a zit on a chin.

"How are you feeling?" Levi asked.

"Better, much better," I answered, still clueless as to anything else to say.

"I'm here for Mel's services, but I wondered if I could

take you to dinner tonight. Kind of make up for the other night when I wasn't at Nate's."

"What about your sister? Won't Roselle need you?"

"Her mom and half brothers and half sisters from Georgia are all here. They don't seem to like me much, especially her mother. I think they'd all just as soon I stay away tonight. Roselle may need me more when all of them go home."

"I can't meet you at the sub shop. I don't have a car. One of my brothers was going to give me a ride home."

"You're probably feeling a little weak from that accident. Why don't we make it an early supper? You can just leave with me after the funeral, and I'll take you home after dinner."

If I'd thought about it, I might have said no, but I didn't give myself time to consider anything. Jane says "Live for the day," and that Tahoe had convinced me that there might come a time when there was no tomorrow. I accepted his invitation and told him to look for me at the cemetery. Levi stepped out.

Chapter Twenty-seven

"**W**as that someone you wanted to see?" I looked up to see Otis had come in. "I told him where you were, but I had second thoughts about it and came back here to check on you," he said. "Odell and I think you need to be careful, but we want to watch out for you, too."

"It was fine," I said.

"Sheriff Harmon suggested that everyone should keep an eye on you. While we were waiting at the hospital, that trucker told Odell and me that someone ran you off the road intentionally, then turned around and came back to hit you over and over."

"That's what happened, and I'm so sorry about the Lincoln."

"Forget it, Callie. We're fully insured and even if we weren't, you're more important than a car." He laughed and added, "You're even more important than a funeral coach, but I'm glad you weren't driving the new one."

"What about Amos Valentine? You know, the man whose wife called because he'd donated his body to MUSC for scientific research and they called and told her to come pick him up?"

For some reason, that just seemed so awful to me.

When I was a student at USC in Columbia, I had a friend who was thrown out of the Waffle House after a football game. There's rejection and insult; then there's total rejection and insult. To me, having your body refused to be accepted as a cadaver for medical students to practice on was even more rejecting and insulting than being put out of the Waffle House at three in the morning. Note that the clubs in Columbia close at two in the morning, so the majority of the Waffle House customers were wasted and feeling no pain. In other words, you had to be pretty far gone to be put out.

"Oh," Otis answered. "That was a really special case. We picked him up and sent him off for cremation. When the cremains are returned, we'll take them to her and Odell said to give her one of the display containers that isn't often selected. We'll let her pay for the cremation a little along and along."

I wondered if my mouth had dropped open in shock. During the years I'd been working for the Middletons, all services provided had to be paid in advance if there wasn't adequate insurance.

Wanting a few moments with Dr. Melvin, and, to be truthful, to see if he was cosmetized well since I didn't do it, I went to Slumber Room A. In the mortuary business, we try to make each person look as good as possible. Dr. Melvin looked at least ten years younger than he had in the hot tub.

Roselle had selected a tan-colored summer suit, cream shirt, and brown striped tie for her husband. Otis or Odell had combed Dr. Melvin's hair exactly the way he'd always worn it, and his lips were set in a very, very slight smile. His skin and features looked healthy, but not painted. I couldn't have done a better job myself.

Otis was setting up tables in the back of the room for the caterer, who was new to me. I saw her bringing in boxes and boxes, stacking them on the floor in front of the tables. This lady was barely five feet tall and not over a hundred pounds max. Her auburn hair was wrapped and pinned up on the back of her head in a way that made my bun at the nape of my neck look anemic.

"Callie," Otis called. I walked over to them.

"This is Phyllis Counts with Counts Cookies and Catering. She'll be setting up refreshments for the Dawkins family." He turned to the petite lady and said, "Mrs. Counts, this is Callie Parrish. She can assist you in any way you wish."

"I'll take you up on that," she said, and her voice was twice as big as her body. Not loud, just commanding, yet still feminine. "I hired a couple of teenagers to assist me, and they haven't shown up. I do all my baking myself, but I could use some help setting up."

"What should I do first?" I asked. "Is there more to bring in?"

"Oh, yes, there's a lot more."

I followed her out to her van. The lettering, "Counts Cookies and Catering," was surrounded with so many drawings of cookies that the vehicle looked polka-dotted. We hauled boxes inside for what seemed like forever, but probably wasn't over fifteen minutes.

Mrs. Counts spread the tables with pale green cloths, then began arranging silver and cut-glass trays on them. I helped. When she opened the first box that actually contained food, I almost passed out. The cookies smelled better than anything I've ever eaten. I realized I hadn't had lunch. The woman looked at me.

"Would you like a sample?" she asked.

"Definitely, but they all look so good, I don't know which to try."

She held a tray out to me with cookies rolled in confectioners' sugar. "Try this," she said. "These are my son's favorite."

It was the best cookie I'd ever put into my mouth. I reached for another one. The kind, but authoritative, voice said, "Not now. Later. And if there are any left over, I'll give you some to take home." She laughed. "And I won't charge the Dawkins family for what I give you either."

By the time Otis had the silver urn of coffee made, Mrs. Counts and I had the tables spread with gorgeous trays of cookies, immaculately arranged in concentric circles. Otis looked over everything approvingly and set up the silver punch bowl set. Mrs. Counts filled it with a beverage just slightly darker green than the pale cloths.

Odell arrived just as we finished putting the empty boxes out of the way in the kitchen area. He smiled at the display of food and reached for a cookie. "Oh, no," Mrs. Counts said, "not until one o'clock." I took Odell into the kitchen and snitched a cookie for him from a backup box that was there.

Roselle Dawkins showed up just before one o'clock with a whole gaggle of relatives from Georgia. Funerals in their part of Georgia must still be formal occasions. All the men wore suits, and the women were in brown, navy, and black. Roselle wore a simple black crepe dress that reached her ankles. A black hat with a veil, black gloves, black stockings, and black patent leather shoes completed her ensemble. Only the white tissues clutched in her hand varied from her black monochrome. I'd bet that if the Kmart sold black Kleenex, Roselle would have been carrying them.

The salon was packed. Daddy, Jane, and The Boys were already wandering around speaking to folks. Almost everyone had known Dr. Melvin. He'd filled their prescriptions and recommended over-the-counter remedies for those who couldn't afford doctors, for many years.

Levi Pinckney was circulating, too. I noticed that Tattoo Girl seemed to stay close to him, moving wherever he was. George Carter stood beside Pearl White. She had changed the tennis balls on her walker to pink and wore a bright hot pink sundress that didn't do a whole lot for her upper arms. Pearl wasn't overweight, but buh-leeve me, time and gravity have their effect on even the slimmest old arms.

Mrs. Counts and I kept busy replacing almost empty trays with freshly filled ones from the kitchen. Good grief! I wanted two o'clock to hurry and arrive so the people would go into the chapel before they ate all the cookies. Standing by Mrs. Counts, I asked her, "Have you heard about the Southern Belle Baking Contest? You should enter some of your cookie recipes."

"Afraid I can't do that," she said. "I didn't create my cookies. I gathered the best recipes I could find and adjusted them to my taste. I think that contest is for original items." I didn't see why she couldn't enter them if she'd changed some ingredients, but I kept my mouth shut. For a change.

Finally, at two o'clock, Otis and Odell ushered Roselle and her family, along with Melvin's cousin, Pearl, and her fiancé, George, into the chapel. The others would follow them before Otis or Odell closed and locked the casket. Then the morticians would roll the bier into the chapel for the service.

"Who's that?" asked Mrs. Counts and motioned toward the family at the front of the crowd moving toward the chapel.

"The young red-haired woman with the black veil is the widow. I don't know a lot of the people with her. They're her relatives from Georgia."

"No, I mean the older lady with the walker. The one wearing the pink dress."

"That's Pearl White. The man with her is George Carter."

"I've never heard of a George Carter, but I've seen that man before."

Since no food would be served after the funeral service,

I began bringing boxes from the kitchen to help Mrs. Counts pack up. Sure enough, she filled a box with assorted cookies for me to take home, then stuck on a gummed seal that had her company's name, address, and phone number on it. I was putting the box on my desk when I heard Mrs. Counts demand, "Aren't you going to speak to me, Sean?"

"I have no idea what you're talking about." George Carter's voice was irate, but an angry whisper, not so loud as Mrs. Counts's had been. The talking was coming from the hall outside the public restrooms. I could hear singing in the chapel.

"Don't pretend you don't know me. Listen, bub, your name is Sean, and you know it." She reached up, grabbed his lapel, and tugged his head down to her level. He pulled from her, but she held on, clutching his coat.

"Or at least, that's one of the names you go by," she scolded.

George Carter snatched his lapel from her grip and went back into the chapel, peeking over his shoulder to see if the tiny woman was following him.

"What was that about?" I asked.

"I could be wrong, but I doubt it. Last Christmas, I went to a family reunion in Summerville. My aunt Edna, who's in her seventies, was there with her new boyfriend. She introduced him as Sean somebody. Her kids were at their wits' end because she planned to marry him."

My eyes bugged and my heart fell to the pit of my stomach. "Tell me more," I said.

"Her daughter told me Edna met this man on the Internet and invited him to her house. It's a gorgeous place with a swimming pool, and her husband had left her a bundle of money. The first thing Sean told Edna was that she needed a privacy fence around that pool. Her son was afraid Sean planned to marry her and drown her like it was an accident."

"Did she marry him?"

"No, before New Year's Day, he was out of the picture, and nobody's mentioned him since then. But that man with the woman with the walker is the person I met in Summerville a year ago as Sean."

"Do you know his last name?"

"No, but I'll call one of Edna's children. They'll probably remember."

Mrs. Counts gave me a little shoulder hug. "Thanks for your help. I'll call here when I find out Sean's last name."

"Thank you for the cookies, and I'll recommend you for refreshments."

The little woman walked away, and I wondered if her memory was half as good as her cookies.

Chapter Twenty-eight

"**A**shes to ashes, dust to dust."

The graveside service ended with the immediate family shaking dirt on the casket from a silver shaker that looked like a great big fancy saltshaker. Personally, I prefer when the bereaved simply pick up a clod of earth and drop it on the casket, but Otis pushes people to use the shaker. He ordered it from a funeral catalog.

Other than that silver shaker, the service had been simple. Dr. Melvin's instructions had been followed, and they'd been very suitable for someone as beloved as he had been.

I'd ridden to the cemetery with Frank and Jane and told them that I had a date and would be home whenever I got there. During the brief service, I'd also noticed that Tattoo Girl, or Denise to be more polite, hadn't come to the cemetery.

Levi spoke to Roselle, then headed toward me.

"Are you ready?" Levi asked when he reached me.

"Just a minute," I said. "I want to speak to Roselle." I joined the line and moved slowly toward the widow. Levi stood beside me.

"I'm so sorry for your loss," I said when we stood in

front of Dr. Melvin's wife-turned-widow. I still wondered about his death. The sheriff hadn't shared any more information about the autopsy and toxicology reports.

"Thank you," Roselle said. "I'm sorry if I was rude to you that night. I was really upset. I was so happy with Mel. I can't imagine my life without him now." She was shaking. "I'm so upset. My heart's just pounding." She looked at Levi. "Are you coming back to the house tonight?"

"Not unless you need me," Levi said, and I found myself hoping she wouldn't say she needed him.

"No, Mama and everyone else are planning to stay until tomorrow."

"Okay, I'll see you later."

In only a few moments, we were driving away from the cemetery in Levi's Cruiser. "You look really good to have been in that wreck," he said, as he pulled out onto the highway.

"It's makeup," I said. "You don't want to see me without it."

"Oh, I bet I'd love to see you with no makeup and your hair all loose and wild."

I shuddered at the thought. "Why?"

"Because it would mean we'd given in to the chemistry I feel between us."

Not knowing how to respond to that, I asked, "May I?" and reached out to the radio controls. He nodded yes, and I pushed the power button. The radio was set on the jazz station—nice, easy instrumentals. I leaned back and rested for a few minutes. Then I remembered.

"Dalmation!" I said.

"What's that?" he said.

"Kindergarten cussing. I used to teach five-year-olds."

"What's got you using profanity, even if it is a dog, not an earthen barrier or a mother horse."

"Mother horse?"

"Also called a dam; a father horse is called a sire."

"How do you know that?"

"I have horses. They're stabled in Aiken where my dad and I used to play polo."

Yeah, like I believe a deliveryman for a small-town sub shop stables his polo ponies in Aiken!

"What's got me kindergarten-cussing?" I said. "Mrs. Counts gave me a tray of cookies. I left them in my brother's Jeep when we rode to the cemetery, and I'll bet he and Jane eat them all before I get home."

"Are you saying that you want to go home for cookies instead of going out to dinner with me?" His tone was serious, but his face smiled.

"No, I'm just hoping they don't eat them all. Did you try them? The ones rolled in confectioners' sugar were the best cookies I've ever had."

"I didn't taste them because Roselle's husband left a ton of baked goods in their kitchen. I don't think I want any more homemade cookies, cakes, pies, or bread for a long time. She said he was trying to develop a recipe for a contest."

"Yes, the Southern Belle Baking Contest."

"Well, he'd baked a lot of good things, but Roselle has no idea what he did with his recipes."

My antennae went up. Could someone have killed Dr. Melvin for a recipe? I didn't think so.

"Do you have anything special you'd like to eat?" Levi asked.

"Not really."

"I've found this little place that has great food. It's fairly new and they specialize in Gullah dishes. Do you like Gullah food?"

"Sure do," I answered, thinking I knew where we were headed.

Before long, Levi pulled into the parking lot at Rizzie's

Gastric Gullah. He walked around to open the door for me. "The lady who runs this place is totally amazing," he said.

"I know," I answered.

"You mean you've been here before?"

"Rizzie Profit is a friend of mine."

"Good. I called her on my cell from the cemetery to be sure she's open, and she's promised a special meal."

The screened door slapped closed behind us as Rizzie called out a Gullah greeting. Suddenly, she stopped the Gullah and said, "I can't believe it. Levi said he'd met someone extraordinary and wanted a special meal. I never dreamed it was you, Callie."

"You don't think I'm worth a special meal?" I snapped. Ex-cuuze me. I knew I was being rude, but I felt tired and irritable.

"Of course you're special," Rizzie said as she led Levi and me to a corner table. She patted my hand. People always do that when they think you've been hurt or insulted. Like that's going to make you feel better.

"I heard about your accident," Rizzie continued.

"It wasn't an accident," I snapped. "It was intentional. Someone stole a Tahoe and tried to run me off the road and hit me three or four times. The car exploded, but I was already in the ambulance when that happened."

Why was I sounding so nasty? "I'm sorry," I said. "Maybe it wasn't a good idea to come out today. I'm still feeling out of sorts, and I'm sore."

"Oh, no," Rizzie protested. "I understand you don't feel well, but I've cooked shrimp gumbo for you with the biggest, tastiest shrimps you've ever seen and tiny little fresh okra."

Still feeling foul, I said, "You didn't cook it for me. You didn't know I was who Levi was bringing."

"Maybe a beer or glass of wine will make you feel better," Levi suggested.

"Can't drink alcohol with my pain medicine." I picked up my purse. "This really isn't a good idea. Please let me take a rain check. We'll eat here another time." I stood. "Pardon me. I'm going to the powder room."

Rizzie followed me. "What's wrong with you?" she asked.

"I feel awful and I really like this guy and I'm making a fool of myself," I said, and then tears flooded my face. I hate, absolutely hate to cry in front of anyone, even a friend like Rizzie.

"Stop that," Rizzie said. "You'll ruin your makeup."

"No way," I said. "Without remover to dissolve it, I couldn't get this stuff off with a trowel."

"Well, you're going to make your eyes all red and puffy. Levi was so happy when he called and said he was bringing someone special in for an early dinner. Why are you acting this way?"

"I don't know. I just don't know." I started to cry again, but Rizzie patted my face dry with a paper towel.

When we went back to the dining room, Levi looked like I'd slapped him. "If you really want to go, I'll take you home," he said.

"No, I'm sorry. It's just been a rough few days. We should eat before we go. Rizzie's a fantastic cook."

"I know. I've been eating here since I moved to St. Mary."

Rizzie brought steaming bowls of rice and gumbo to the table. She set them in front of us and said, "I'm surprised the two of you didn't meet in here. You're both among my best customers."

She went back to the kitchen and returned with a basket of hot corn bread, a beer for Levi, and a Coke on ice for me.

"Enjoy!" she said and moved on to another table of customers.

"I love this food," Levi said, spooning gumbo from his bowl.

"Have you ever eaten Rizzie's tomato pie?"

"No, I haven't had that."

"Get her to make it for you. It's delicious. Fresh tomatoes, onion, and seasonings in a pie shell. She tops it with a cheese crust that's wonderful. Rizzie's is a little different from other people's tomato pie because she adds tarragon."

By the time we'd both finished our gumbo, I felt better. Perhaps part of my irritability had been because I'd skipped breakfast and had eaten only a few cookies since yesterday.

Levi paid the bill and escorted me to the PT Cruiser. I almost said "car," but those things just don't look like cars to me. Once again, he held doors for me and treated me like a lady. Now, I'm as modern as most southern women, and I expect to earn the same pay as a man for the same work, and I go by Ms., not Miss or Mrs., but gee whiz, I do like for men to treat me special.

"Do you feel like driving to a movie or club in Beaufort?" Levi asked.

"Not really." Then I thought about how I'd been behaving. There are lots of kinds of rejection, and surely I'd hurt his feelings too much already. "I'd invite you back to my place to watch television or listen to music, but I've got company. They'd ask you a thousand questions and want to play some loud game. Could we just ride around a little?"

Levi grinned, and those dark eyes sparkled. He'd taken off his suit jacket, and his biceps showed through the sleeves of his white shirt. He obviously worked out, but he wasn't ropey muscle-bound.

"How about we ride to the beach and watch the ocean? That could be relaxing."

"Sounds good," I answered. On the ride, I remembered

my younger years. When I was in college in Columbia, we used to ride up to big ole Lake Murray to "watch the submarine races." Another euphemism—this time for grubbing or, as my brothers said, making out. *Cool down, Callie,* I thought.

Levi headed toward Hunting Island, and I expected to stop there. He didn't turn in, though, and continued to Fripp Island.

"We can't go here," I said. "Fripp is private. You have to have a membership to go on the island."

"I know."

Levi pulled up to the gate guard and showed him a card. We drove through the beautiful entrance onto the divided road that runs from one side of the island to the other. On our left, an alligator lay on the bank of a small pond. A little farther down, two deer stood on the bicycle path. We passed large, elegant homes. At the end of the pavement, we reached the golf club and private restaurants.

Fripp Island is the home and vacation spot for people far more wealthy than my family. I'd been there before on a field trip when I was in high school, but my family and Fripp Islanders weren't in the same social league. The houses aren't McMansions. They're *real* mansions. The island is home for alligators in their own pools and free-roaming deer, along with birds and other animals that are protected by the rules of the island. As a matter of fact, Fripp Island is a sanctuary—everything protected—except me.

Having chosen celibacy over sex for sport, I'd stopped my birth control over a year ago. *What's wrong with me? Why am I thinking about this? We're here to look at the ocean, not to seduce each other. I've never boinked anybody on a first date. Well, I guess this is a second date if I count the time he stood me up.*

One end of Fripp Island is bordered by large rock formations, while on the other end, the beaches are wide and sandy. Levi drove to an elegant house straight out of *Southern Living*. He parked in the driveway facing the ocean. "Would you like to sit here in the car or go around to the back of the house and sit on the deck?" he asked.

"Outside sounds nice, but will we be trespassing?" I answered his question with one of my own.

"We won't be trespassing."

"Do you know the folks who own this place?"

"My dad owned it, so now it's mine. This is where I'm living since I came down from Charleston."

"Then let's sit on the patio."

We sat on deck chairs. Levi's home was oceanfront but built far enough back that even at high tide, there was a lot of landscaped yard before the sand began. I watched the waves lap against the manicured lawn between the house and the ocean. Sea oats and other coastal plants accented the walk down to the beach.

Though the sun didn't set over the ocean, we enjoyed that lovely effect of dusk descending over the sand and water. Soon stars danced out into the night sky. Levi went inside and came out with glasses of sweetened tea with sprigs of fresh mint.

We sipped our drinks and talked about the things most people do on first dates. He said he'd never been married and had no children. I told him I'd been married and divorced one time, but I didn't go into any details about Donnie.

"This is a first for me," he said. "I've never dated a teacher."

I almost replied that I'd never dated a delivery boy, but this house indicated that Levi might actually be working there to learn about the business. I confess I'd really figured that was just a line to excuse having a low-paying job when he was obviously in his mid thirties.

The thought even crossed my mind that instead of owning

this property and living here, perhaps he was a hired house-sitter. When the mosquitoes started biting, he invited me inside.

The house was big, modern, and exquisitely furnished. I'd always considered beach houses informal, but this place had both a formal living room and dining room that could be seen through the door of the room we entered. Those areas had massive furniture made of deep polished wood and brocade upholstery.

We stood in what I would call a den. Three huge leather couches created a conversation area facing a gigantic fireplace. I wondered how often a fire had been lit there. It's pretty warm around here most of the year. Behind the couches had been designated a recreational area, with pool table, foosball, brass and glass octagonal table with several decks of cards on it, and a bookcase filled with boxed games. I wondered where the GameCube was.

I sat on a couch and looked around. Quite a comfy setup. Levi picked up a remote control and the wall beside the fireplace disappeared, revealing a gigantic plasma-screen television.

Monk.

"Do you like this show?" he asked and sat beside me. Close, but not touching.

"Yes," I said and sipped my tea while Monk neurotically solved the mystery.

When the program ended, Levi pressed a few more buttons, and soft, shimmery colors played across the screen like those old lava lamps my brothers used to have. Soft jazz filled the room. Levi moved closer and I knew he was going to kiss me.

No doubt about the chemistry between us. His kiss was tender but it shot flames. He took his time—sweet and gentle—and the longer his kisses lasted, the more sense Jane's advice to live for the moment made.

Levi leaned back and pulled me over onto him.

My mind remained focused on his kisses. And his hands. He'd been stroking my behind. Problem was I couldn't feel it. He stopped kissing and moved his mouth and tongue to my neck and throat. He nibbled my ears. I loved every minute of it. Then I realized that he was touching my breast. Not really. He was cuddling my inflated bra. I couldn't feel a thing.

I'd thought the heat of the moment and gentleness of his touch were keeping his hands from hurting my bruises, but no. The padded and inflated garments beneath my dress were protecting me from feeling pain. Would it hurt to be touched when my clothing came off?

Chapter Twenty-nine

*O*h, *my heavens!!!*
    Holy moly!!!
  Good grief!!!
  Dalmation!!!

If I took my clothes off—or let him remove them—Levi would know that the body he saw when he looked at me in my black dress wasn't mine. My chest was, in reality, as flat as a pancake, and my bottom was even flatter.

I gently put my hands over his and removed them from my bosom. I sat up straight and adjusted my dress. Levi had gotten a glance at a lot of leg. At least my legs are my own and not padded or inflated.

"Not yet," I said.

"Oh, I'm sorry. I wasn't even thinking. Let me look in the bedroom. Surely, there's something in there."

"No, that's not what I mean. You're right. The chemistry's great, but I'm not ready." How many men had I told that to in the past year or so? I'd been determined to be in a real relationship, possibly even married again, before allowing such closeness.

Now I wanted to forget all my lofty ideals. I really wanted the comfort of this man's arms. The pleasure of his touch. I wanted all that, but I couldn't let myself.

I could be self-righteous and say I came to my senses, but that wasn't it at all. I simply couldn't bear to think of seeing the look on Levi's face when I took off my clothes. It would be a whole lot worse than that song about the man marrying the woman who took out her glass eye and her false teeth, then pulled off her wig when she went to bed on the first night of their honeymoon.

Levi did the gentlemanly thing. He got us each another glass of tea and found a good movie on TV. He sat close with his arm around me but didn't touch any personal spaces again. He took me home before it got too late, kissed me gently at the door, and told me he'd call me at work the next day.

Standing for a moment in the open door, I watched Levi walk back to his car and drive away. I really liked that man, and *not* because he was from a wealthy family. In fact, that could be an obstacle. Opposites attract, but our attraction had nothing to do with our social standings, and I'd already been in a relationship with a guy from a higher socioeconomic standing than mine. Donnie's family had money, but that had actually almost prejudiced me *against* the so-called upper classes.

Frank's Jeep hadn't been there when Levi pulled up. I wondered if he'd gone to pick up a pizza or something, and if so, was Jane with him or waiting for me inside?

"Jane," I called as I turned around and stepped into the apartment. Good grief! The place was a shambles. Couch cushions lay on the floor beside overturned end tables. The splintered glass top of the coffee table reminded me of the family car's windshield.

"Big Boy! Big Boy!" I shouted frantically and ran to the bathroom, hoping that Jane and Frank had locked the dog in there before leaving. I looked in the bedroom, dreading finding Jane or the dog injured or—let's be truthful—dead. There were no signs of life or death in the apartment. Just trashed furniture and clothes. The closets and drawers had been emptied and everything thrown all over the floor.

In books, villains sometimes leave messages written in lipstick on mirrors. I always thought that was kind of hokey, but now it happened for real.

"Callie, I know what you're doing" was lettered across the mirror above my dresser.

After searching the closets and under the beds, I called Sheriff Harmon and put on a pot of coffee. Like caffeine would calm me down. I knew the sheriff would ask what was missing, first thing, but I didn't feel like looking. He'd want to see the place like I'd found it anyway, and I couldn't know if anything had been stolen until things were back in order.

"Whew! Looks like that storm turned into a hurricane and went through here," the sheriff said when I opened the door for him. "Do you have any idea who might have done this?"

"No idea at all, but there have been some strange happenings lately."

"What kind of events?"

"I think I hear someone at the windows, but when I look, no one is there."

"Which windows? The bathroom?"

"No, generally it's a side window. By the bedroom."

"Could be a Peeping Tom, but they generally try to watch women shower."

"I haven't noticed it when I've showered, but the curtains overlap on the bathroom window. It would be hard to see in there." *I'd better check my bedroom drapes. Big Boy was barking at the window when I changed clothes. Had someone been outside, looking in at me? I'd thought there might be a squirrel outside. Maybe it was a rat instead. A human rat.*

"What's missing?" Sheriff Harmon stared all around the room, as though he could see beneath the clutter.

"I don't know. I haven't moved anything since I came in except I made a pot of coffee. Do you want a cup?"

"Sure, since you've already touched the pot, I might as well." His gaze darted around the room again. "If you have any disposable cups, use them."

Personally, I felt that if the intruder had bothered the cups in my kitchen cabinet, they would be broken and scattered across the floor like everything else. That's what I thought, but I was too tired to argue, and my pain medicine had worn off. I didn't complain, just poured two cups of coffee and handed him one before loading mine with sugar and cream. I confess. I was upset, needed comfort. I put four spoons of sugar into my cup.

"I see that your electronics are here," he said. "Television, DVD player. What about your computer?"

"I don't have a computer." I didn't bother to explain that my dog kept eating up my savings.

"What about your guns?"

Should have checked them first thing, I thought. If burglary was the intruder's intent, guns don't even have to go to pawn shops. They can be sold on the street.

"Let's go see," I answered and led him to my bedroom. I opened the drawer of the bedside table and pulled out the .38.

"This one's here," I said and put the weapon back. Sheriff Harmon knew all about my firearms. I once shot an intruder with the revolver. In the knee. Didn't kill him or I'd probably never have seen that one again. Sheriff Harmon is quick to impound evidence. *Like my Mustang.*

Opening the closet door, I stretched to the highest shelf and pulled down the double-barreled shotgun and rifle my daddy lent me. Daddy keeps all weapons in a gun safe, and I'd thought about buying one, but I kept thinking I'd give all three or at least the shotgun and rifle back to him.

"How about Jane?" the sheriff asked as I stood on tiptoe to return the guns to their place at the back of the shelf.

"I hope that Frank took her and Big Boy off."

Sheriff Harmon sat down and flipped open his cell phone. "First, let's call your dad's house and see if Frank is there."

That's when I realized there was a possibility that whoever had trashed the house had taken Jane and my dog. Jane had been kidnapped once before. The thought of her being at the mercy of some psycho again made me tremble.

"Hey, Bill," Sheriff Harmon said into the telephone, "I'm trying to locate Frank to see if Jane Baker is with him. Is he home right now?"

The sheriff listened silently.

"Okay, well, there's been a little problem here at Callie's apartment. We just wanted to make sure everyone's okay. No, Callie isn't hurt. Just a bit upset, that's all." He put his hand over the receiver. "Frank took Jane and Big Boy over to your dad's for supper, and they're watching television. Do you want them to come back here or do you want me to take you over there?"

"Neither. Tell them to spend the night. I'll be fine."

Sheriff Harmon frowned at me, but told them to stay at Dad's. He'd call back if we needed them.

I sat and drank coffee while the deputies photographed the apartment and bagged some items like the lipstick tube on the dresser. It appeared to be the color that was used to write the message. They fingerprinted a lot of surfaces, leaving fine black dust for me to clean up after they left.

When everyone had gone except the sheriff, he insisted that I let him take me over to Daddy's. I refused, and he couldn't legally make me.

After several more tries, he finally gave up and went to

the door. "Okay, but call me if you hear anything or even if you just get the heebie-jeebies. I'll be right here."

As I closed the door behind him, the sheriff said, "Now be sure this door is locked." Is there *anyone* in my life who thinks I have enough sense to lock my doors without being told what to do?

Chapter Thirty

Two hours later, most of the clutter was reorganized. Belongings were back in the proper drawers and cabinets except for what was broken. The glass-topped coffee table and end tables were a lost cause. It would probably be as expensive to replace their tops as to buy new ones.

Just looking at the broken furniture and knickknacks made me jittery. I gathered the smaller items and shattered glass into trash bags and took them to the Herbie Curby at the side of the building. Then I dragged the wooden and wrought-iron parts of my tables out the front door to cart them around there, too.

I heard what sounded like a cat or other small animal rummaging around in the shrubbery at the rear.

Dropping the armful of furniture pieces, I picked up a wooden table leg and ran around to the back of the house, eager to chase away the raccoon or whatever was there. I didn't stop to think that it might not be a four-legged animal.

What if the noise was from a big two-legged creature? I pictured him bolting from my backyard as I turned and took off around to the front door. I slammed the door behind me and locked the deadbolt without anyone telling me what to do.

If I'd had a car, I would have jumped in it and driven away. I hadn't really seen whatever made the noise out back. I wasn't even sure that I'd heard anything, but what if it had been a person? What if he came back? I went into the bedroom and took my .38 from the bedside table.

I looked in the closet. Both my shotgun and rifle were on the top shelf where I'd put them back while the sheriff was there. To think I'd considered taking them back to my daddy. No, sirree. The way I felt right then, I wanted a loaded piece in every room.

Strange that someone tossed the apartment and didn't seem to have stolen anything, not even guns, which could easily be sold on the street. Nothing appeared to be missing. Was I overlooking what had been taken or had the place been ransacked looking for something I didn't have? Or was all this just to frighten me? Or to scare Jane, since she lived with me for the time being?

With the shotgun on the floor beside the bed, the rifle on the other side, and the .38 on top of the bedside table, I tried to go to sleep. Wide awake, I read, but my mind kept wandering to who might have been here. I kept *thinking* I heard something. I got up and walked through the apartment with the shotgun in one hand and revolver in the other. The next three times I checked out the door and windows, I left the revolver by the bed. I'd realized it would take both hands to fire the shotgun, but the scattered pellets were more likely to hit someone than a bullet from the .38 with my hands shaking like they were.

When my alarm clock chimed eight o'clock, I got out of bed without a minute's sleep all night. I was glad Big Boy had spent the night at Daddy's. I would have been scared to take him outside for his morning walk.

I set a cup of last night's coffee in the microwave to heat and went to shower. The night before, I'd removed the makeup but had been too scared to shower. Afraid the noise of the splashing water might cover the sound of someone creeping around or breaking into the apartment.

After blow-drying my hair and finishing my coffee, I called the funeral home.

"Middleton's Mortuary. Odell Middleton speaking. How may I help you?"

"Odell, I want to come to work, but I don't have a way."

"Otis is here and I'm going to Shoney's for breakfast. I'll swing by and pick you up. Have you eaten?"

"Not yet."

"Good, you can have breakfast with me. I'll be there in twenty minutes."

Since I was dressed and had cleaned up the apartment the night before, I tried to read. Neither my eyes nor my mind would focus. I dropped the book onto the floor where my coffee table had been before last night.

My apartment had always suited me, felt like home. No more. My eyes darted around as though I'd never been there before. I kept thinking I heard something outside. Maybe a branch brushing against a window. Then I thought I heard someone in the apartment with me. I went into the spare room and looked at the books stacked everywhere. No one could possibly walk around in that room.

The kitchen and living room are visible from each other. I opened both bedroom doors and the bathroom door. By sitting at exactly the right place on the couch, it was possible to see every room in the apartment from one position. Maybe I'd start sleeping on the couch and let Jane have my room if she agreed to keep all the interior doors open when we were home.

Too much. Too much. Dr. Melvin dead with no known

cause. Ms. Lucas murdered on Jane's steps. My one dependable brother about to abandon his wife and family. My best friend dating my brother. The good Lord only knew what that could turn into. I wanted them both to be happy, but if that relationship soured, I'd be torn between the two of them.

All of that was bad enough, but worst of all was that someone had tried to kill me, had been peeping in my windows, and had gone through everything I owned. Was it all being done by the same someone? It had to be.

To top it off, Jane and Frank had taken my cookies and *someone* had gone into my car and stolen Jane's thongs. Sure, I'd told myself a possum or squirrel had taken them, but that was ridiculous. A small animal might have carried off one or two pair, but not that whole pile.

Someone. Someone. Someone. Someone was out to get me.

The thought made me so frightened that by the time Odell arrived, I was nauseated.

Chapter Thirty-one

Shoney's clientele looked like a rerun from Dr. Melvin's funeral the day before. Roselle and several tables of the people who'd been introduced as her relatives from Georgia filled half of the dining area. Odell and I sat in a booth toward the rear of the restaurant.

The line for the breakfast buffet was l-o-n-g, but I knew Odell would be willing to wait. We both ordered the bar.

My nausea had subsided, and I fixed myself a plate that looked like a typical southern breakfast—grits, scrambled eggs, a biscuit, and a small slice of country ham. Odell brought two plates back to the table from his first trip. One plate was filled with grits and eggs topped with sausage gravy; the other, several biscuits and servings of every meat on the bar. Bacon, sausage links, sausage patties, country ham, chicken nuggets, and fried fatback. I'm sure he was disappointed that barbecue wasn't available for breakfast.

Roselle and her family kept staring at me. When they started to leave, Roselle went to the register and paid. She turned and came over to our booth.

"Hi, Ms. Parrish, I heard about your accident, but your

injuries weren't as obvious yesterday. I guess it took some time for the bruises to surface."

Makeup. I should at least have tried to cover the discoloration on my face with my own cosmetics before going into a public place.

"I think it looks even worse than it feels," I said.

"I sure hope so." She looked around at her relatives standing in a group at the door. "My folks are heading back to Georgia this morning, and I figured it'd be easier to treat them to breakfast here than try to cook for this crowd at Mel's house."

A look of dismay crossed her face. "You know, Mel and I'd planned to go to Georgia so Mel could meet my family, but we hadn't gotten there yet. Most of these people never even had the chance to meet him, much less get to know what a sweetheart he was. Even with all these people in the house last night, I just missed him so much."

A tear glistened in her eye, and she wiped it away with the back of her hand. "I just wanted to thank you and to tell you I'm glad you weren't killed in that wreck. From what I heard, you were lucky."

"Thank you," I said, thinking, *Yeah, I'm sure lucky that someone tried to kill me, destroyed the Middletons' family car, then came back and trashed my home.*

"You take care now, and do what the doctors tell you to," Roselle added. "My Gran-Mee-Maw had this medicine. I think it was called nitrogen, and the doctor told her to put it under her tongue whenever her heart hurt. She didn't pay him any attention. She wound up dying because of her heart because she had vagina and didn't do what the doctor said."

When Roselle and her family left, Odell slowed his eating enough to ask me, "Did she say what I heard?"

"Yes, she meant angina. I've heard her mix up words before. The night Dr. Melvin died, she went to get a warmer wrap so she wouldn't catch 'ammonia.' She must have meant pneumonia."

"Let's talk about you instead of the Dawkins family. How do you feel? You don't have to work today, you know."

"I'd rather be at work than stay home." I told him about the night before—about the apartment and my fear that someone had been outside my house, not about my time with Levi—and it did me good to talk about it.

"Wish you'd called me if you were scared. I could have come over and stayed with you or taken you to your dad's house. Sometimes you don't make the wisest choices, Callie. I worry about you."

"Callie," a familiar voice said.

The voice repeated, "Callie." I looked up to those deep, molten eyes and dark hair. Levi stood beside our booth.

"Excuse me," Odell said, standing. "I'm gonna get some pancakes for dessert."

"May I join you?" Levi asked.

"Sure." I slid over and let him sit beside me.

He motioned to the waitress. When she came, he told her he'd like a cup of coffee, but nothing to eat.

"I wouldn't want to hurt your feelings," he said, "but that makeup you were wearing yesterday should be marketed. It hid a lot of damage."

I laughed. "It is marketed. For use on corpses."

"Oh." He accepted his coffee from the server and took a sip.

"I came by to tell Roselle's family good-bye. They don't much like me. In fact, I overheard one of them encouraging Roselle to try to break my father's will. If she's his side child, and I believe she is, they think she should have some of what I inherited."

"How do you feel about that?" I pushed my plate to the edge of the table so the waitress would know to take it away.

"Like most people, part of me is selfish and would like

to keep it all. I could justify to myself that my father must have wanted me to have everything or he would have made some other provisions in his will." He drained his cup and refilled it from the carafe on the table.

"On the other hand," he continued, "I can understand why she would feel entitled. Of course, her husband wasn't hurting for money. She's a lot better off now than the rest of her family, from what I heard."

"I won't ever have to worry about that. All Daddy has is the farm and the equipment to run it." I laughed. "I've got five brothers. It wouldn't be a whole lot if everything was sold and divided, but we wouldn't do that anyway because usually at least one of them is living at the home place."

"What about all those musical instruments your family played at your birthday party?"

That's when it hit me! I didn't even check to see if my banjos were safe after the intrusion last night. I'd glanced in the closet and seen both cases, but I hadn't opened them to make sure the instruments were there. I turned my attention back to the conversation.

"Daddy had a banjo that he claims is worth more than his house, but he gave it to me for my birthday," I said. "The other instruments my brothers play are their own. They wouldn't be a part of Daddy's estate." I shuddered. "Let's talk about something else. I'm sorry you lost your dad and I don't even want to *think* about something happening to mine."

Odell returned with a plate piled high with pancakes, strawberries, and whipped cream. He'd hardly had time to set the plate on the table when his cell phone chirped.

It was impossible not to overhear what he said. "Yes, she's with me. Unh-hunh. We'll come right now." He stood and took his wallet from his pocket. I opened my purse.

"No, I'll treat, but we have to go straight to the mortuary."

"Who died?" I asked.

"It's not that. Something else." He shot a look of remorse at his plate and went to the cash register.

"Sorry," I said to Levi, "gotta go."

"May I take you to dinner again?"

"I don't know. There's a lot going on right now with Jane moving in with me."

"We have great chemistry," he said.

"I know," I answered. "I don't believe I'm ready for chemistry in my life."

"We can go out as friends, and . . ."

Levi didn't have time to say any more. Odell had finished with the cashier and gestured toward me to follow him.

Chapter Thirty-two

The trip from Shoney's to the funeral home was silent and uneventful. Odell seemed to be concentrating. I couldn't imagine what had happened that would upset him enough to leave that plate of pancakes and strawberries untouched.

Otis met us at the back door. He looked shocked at my face, though he'd seen it before makeup yesterday. He led me back to my office.

"What's going on?" I said.

"Mrs. Counts called here and asked for you. I told her you'd be in later, but she refused to leave a number. Said she has to talk to you and that it's a matter of your health, maybe even your life. She's supposed to call you back." He looked at his wristwatch. "Should be soon now."

"I don't know anything about that woman except she makes great cookies. Why would she want to talk to me?" I said.

The phone rang before anyone responded.

"Middleton's Mortuary. Callie Parrish. How may I help you?" I pushed the button for speakerphone so Otis and Odell could listen.

"Oh, Callie, I'm so glad I reached you. This is Phyllis Counts."

"Yes, ma'am, I remember you."

"I talked to my aunt Edna's son. He said he hired a private investigator to check out the man Edna was seeing. The man's name was Sean Gunderson. He'd been married seven times, divorced once, and widowed *six* times."

She'd been talking so fast that she had to breathe loud and deep before saying, "All of those wives died by accident not very long after marrying him and making wills leaving everything to Gunderson and him leaving everything to her. Of course, it didn't matter that he'd willed all his possessions to his wives because they never survived him."

"And you think the man we know as George Carter is actually Sean Gunderson?"

"I don't think it. I *know* it." She coughed. "I believe he changed his name after the investigator unearthed all this and reported it to Aunt Edna's family. According to the detective, law enforcement has been suspicious of him several times and places, but there's never been enough evidence to prove anything." She coughed again. I wondered if she had a summer cold.

"My cousin said he threatened Sean, accused him of what the report said," Mrs. Counts said. "He told Sean to stay away from Edna or he'd be sorry. The next day Sean was gone. Can you believe Edna still says she loves him even after her son told her all about him?"

"Well, George *is* very charming."

"Oh, yeah, he's had a lot of practice. He charmed those wives right into their graves."

"I really appreciate your calling me," I said. "That explains why I couldn't locate any information about Pearl's *Georgie*." I said the name just the way Pearl said it.

"Oh, I could have called to tell you this stuff later, but

I'm worried. Concerned enough that I'm leaving Beaufort. I had to talk to you this morning before I go because you could be in danger."

Could be?

"Leaving? Where are you going?" I said.

"I'm not going to tell you where I'll be," Mrs. Counts said. "Last night, someone broke into my home and destroyed almost everything I own. I think it could have been Sean Gunderson."

She gasped. "Thank goodness I'd gone to a church ladies' meeting and wasn't here. When I came in and found the mess, I called the police, but I doubt they'll find him. I fully believe this man I know as Sean and you know as George has killed his wives and wouldn't hesitate to kill me. You were there when I confronted him. I wanted to warn you."

"But do you have somewhere safe to go?"

"Yes." She chuckled. "I spent the night at Sister Care. I've worked as a volunteer there. I know how to disappear."

"I wish you luck," I said. "Will you be in touch?"

"Yes, I'll call you occasionally. I want to know what happens and when it's safe to come home. You really need to warn the woman with the walker, but if she's like Edna, she won't believe you." She paused.

"There's something else I need to tell you," Mrs. Counts said. "I saw Sean Gunderson going into the Beaufort Best Bed and Breakfast. I called there and got the room number for George Carter. I talked to that Pearl White woman and told her everything I've told you, but she didn't believe me. That's why I think you need to talk to her. Warn her."

"You were right to tell her, whether she believes you or not."

"That's not all, though." She sighed. "Callie, I was afraid to tell her who I was." Another longer, louder sigh. "I told her I was you."

A click. She'd disconnected the line.

Odell let loose a string of cusswords that were way beyond kindergarten cussing, positively graduate level.

Otis said, "I didn't like that man the first time I saw him. You need to call Wayne Harmon and tell him what that woman told you."

"I should have asked how to contact her cousin and the investigator he hired," I said.

"Call her house," Odell growled.

I found her telephone information on the Counts catering invoice and called, but a recording informed me that this was no longer a working number. Otis rang the sheriff's office, where he was told that Sheriff Harmon wasn't available, but he could speak with a deputy. Otis left word for the sheriff to contact the mortuary.

Odell gave me a quizzical look.

"Doofus, bring some coffee for all of us to my office. We need to talk." I followed Odell and sat down opposite him. Otis was right behind us with three mugs of coffee on a tray. He dispensed cups, then sat down beside me. Each person's java was sweetened and lightened perfectly to that individual's taste. He and Jane are the only two people I know who can consistently do that for me.

"We all heard what Mrs. Counts said, and we need to get that news to Harmon as soon as possible. What you don't know, Otis, is that someone trashed Callie's apartment last night."

They both frowned at me before Odell continued, "We need to be taking better care of our cosmetitian or we might be stuck with painting and powdering clients ourselves again."

Otis turned toward me with a look of astonishment on his face. "You stayed home alone after someone invaded your home?"

There were no good words to explain, so I just nodded.

"What would you have done if he'd come back?" Otis said.

"Doofus, she'da shot him," Odell rasped.

"What I think we need to . . ." Otis didn't finish. His words were interrupted by "Old Rugged Cross."

It only takes one of us to go to the foyer when a hymn or gospel song signals the door has been opened, but all three of us walked to the front.

"Speak of the devil," Odell mumbled.

"Hello, Sheriff Harmon," Otis said.

"Man! I am so glad to see you," I gushed.

"Come on back to the consulting room." Otis waved his arm to encompass all of us.

"I was headed over here when I got the message from dispatch to call you," the sheriff said as we all sat around the conference table. He pulled a small notebook from his shirt pocket.

"You talk first, then," I said. "Why were you headed over here?"

"The autopsy report on Dorcas Lucas doesn't look like an accident. It's the same thing I thought at the scene. There was too much blood, and the spatter patterns weren't consistent with a fall, even down those steep steps. It appears to be BFT."

"What's that?" Otis said.

"Blunt force trauma. Someone beat her over the head with a weapon, perhaps even a two-by-four. They found wood splinters in her head wounds, and the injuries are the correct size and shape for a board that size."

"Couldn't that be from the wooden steps or banisters?" I asked.

"Nope, newer wood than the stairway." He smiled. "But I have some good news for you, Callie. I spoke with your dad this morning. He's picking up two tires and rims for your car. I'm releasing your Mustang, but we'll need to keep the two front tires. You drove onto the blood at the foot of the steps. There's no blood on the car except there, so you'll get your car back, but we're keeping the two front wheels. Your father is sending Bill and Mike to have the new tires installed and pick up your car. They should have it here before the end of the day."

The sheriff grinned like he'd done something wonderful.

I exploded.

"How *dare* you call Daddy about my car? In case you haven't noticed, I am an *adult*! Don't tell me if the Mustang belonged to Otis, you would have called a parent to see about the tires," I screeched.

"Couldn't call my parents," Otis muttered. "They're both dead."

"Shut up, Doofus," Odell growled.

"Well, maybe what I mean is that if Otis owned the car, you wouldn't have called Odell to take care of it. You'd call the owner and treat him like an adult, instead of treating me like a little girl!"

"I'm not quite sure I understood that first sentence," the sheriff said. "I thought you'd be glad to get the car back, and after last night, I didn't want to stress you more by making you deal with the tires."

"Yeah," Odell mumbled, "he was thinking about you, Callie. You might try being grateful instead of angry."

"Yes," Harmon mumbled. "I thought I'd make you happy. Even thought you were probably calling me to complain about the Mustang."

"I called to tell you what Mrs. Counts said."

"Who's Mrs. Counts?"

"The cookie lady." I paused. "I need to be excused. Otis and Odell both listened to her on speakerphone. Let them tell you about it."

I went to the restroom and almost jumped out of my skin. The face staring at me was hideous. Even evil. At second glance, I realized I was looking at my own reflection in the mirror. A bump had risen on my forehead. The bruises on the rest of my face were changing from blackish blue to purple to hideous brownish yellow, with different spots in various stages. The discoloration around my eyes remained dark violet while the bags beneath them were black.

No way. No way did I want to see anyone or have anyone see me again looking like that. I slipped from the restroom to my workroom and began working the magic of mortuary makeup.

"Callie! Callie!" Sheriff Harmon's voice sounded high and stressed.

"I'm in here," I called.

Otis, Odell, and the sheriff piled into my workroom.

"You scared us," Otis said. "We were afraid you'd run off."

"Or someone had snatched you," growled Odell.

Sheriff Harmon looked at me with a puzzled expression. "You changed yourself that much with makeup?"

"Not regular makeup from the drugstore. This is professional makeup we use here at work."

"Amazing." He shuffled back and forth on his feet for a moment. "Are you finished?"

"Not quite."

"That is just unbelievable. I do want to talk to you some more, but perhaps Otis and Odell can round us up some more coffee while you complete what you're doing. We'll wait for you in Odell's office."

I rapidly smoothed out the cosmetics on my face. My reflection in the mirror was gratifying. I looked normal except for the slightly swollen knot on my forehead. Dealing with that on a corpse, I could have used a needle to draw out fluid and reduce the swelling. Instead, I contoured with concealers, both lighter and darker than my natural complexion, to trick the eye into not seeing the lump on my noggin.

When I returned to Odell's office, I found the three men sitting around, drinking coffee and talking.

"Well?" I said.

"Have a seat." Odell.

"You look great." Otis.

"What are we going to do about George Carter?" Harmon asked.

"That's your problem, not mine," I said. "You're always telling me to stay out of law enforcement business."

"Indeed, but what are you going to do to stay safe while I'm taking care of department business? If Carter/Gunderson has pegged you as dangerous to him and broken into both your and Mrs. Counts's homes, I don't want you staying at your apartment alone until this is settled."

"May I remind you that I am an adult, fully capable of defending myself, as I've proven in the past?" I revved up my sassiest tone.

"May I remind you that I can call your dad and all your brothers to back me on this?" The sheriff's tone was every bit as ugly as mine.

"Whatcha gonna call me about?" Daddy stood at the door. Must have come in through the back because no hymn had announced his arrival.

"Callie wants to ignore that someone broke into her apartment last night," Sheriff Harmon said. "This morning, we've been told that Pearl White's boyfriend might be a serial killer and that the woman who fingered him has left town because her place was trashed last night, too."

"George Carter?" The gasp came from Jane, who had stepped up behind Daddy with Frank.

"Yes," the sheriff replied. "George Carter. On top of that, the woman who died at the foot of Jane's steps didn't fall, and probably wasn't pushed. The autopsy indicates she was beaten to death with a weapon, maybe a two-by-four."

Jane spluttered. "I knew that Lucas woman was bad news the minute she showed up at my place. She deserves everything she got."

"Did *you* do it?" the sheriff asked her. "I admit, I've wondered if you shoved her down the stairs by accident or maybe even on purpose."

"Now wait a minute," Frank broke in. "Jane wouldn't have done anything like that."

"Oh, yeah?" the sheriff said. "You have no idea what Jane Baker is capable of. You don't know her like I do."

"I can guarantee I know her better than you do," Frank argued.

"Perhaps in the biblical sense, but you've never read her arrest record, and I'll bet you don't even know what she does for a living," Harmon spat back.

"Of course I do; she's an evening telemarketer." Frank.

"Drop it," I said to both of them.

"And what product does she telemarket?" Harmon ignored me.

"I don't know," Frank mumbled before turning to Jane. "What do you sell?"

"Fantasy and magic," Jane said, with her head hanging so that her chin rested on her chest. Then she straightened up. "I didn't want you to learn about it this way, Frank, but I'm a conversationalist, a fantasy telephone actress."

"What in the four-letter-word is that?" Daddy demanded.

"A 900 phone sex operator," Jane said, loud and clear. "And nobody ever touches me or knows where I am. It's the best money I ever made, and I'm not ashamed of it."

"What?"

I'd known Frank would react like that when he found out. I'd even cautioned Jane to tell him before he found out some other way. True enough, he'd heard it from Jane's own lips, but not the way I meant.

Frank stormed out. Daddy handed me the Mustang keys, which I could identify by the SpongeBob SquarePants key ring, and followed Frank out the back door.

"Well, what good did that do?" I asked the sheriff.

Chapter Thirty-three

Jane cried.

Sheriff Harmon apologized because it wasn't his place to force Jane into announcing her occupation. It wasn't like being a "conversationalist" is against the law. He then took off, saying he was going to the bed and breakfast to talk to Pearl White and George Carter.

Otis and Odell got around to telling me what was scheduled for the day.

"Will we be preparing Ms. Lucas?" I asked. I'd never liked the woman, and though I'm never glad when anyone dies, I didn't want to work on her.

"No, she's going directly from MUSC to a local funeral home in her hometown, but we do have a job this afternoon."

"What's that? Is it a pickup?"

"Kind of," Otis said.

Odell ignored us and asked Jane if she'd like to go out for lunch.

"No, thank you," Jane said in her sweetest, though not Roxanne, voice. "If it's all right, I want to stay here with Callie in case Frank comes back or calls."

"Give him time to cool off," Odell consoled. "If he really cares about you, he'll be back regardless of what you've done in the past."

"Well, it's not exactly the past. I haven't really quit the job," Jane said. "I haven't worked much lately because I've been with Frank, but I can go back if I need to. I don't know what I'll do if I have to quit. It's easy and it pays well."

"Something to think about," Odell said. "I'm going for lunch. I'll bring everyone back a sandwich because Otis and I need to get out of here early this afternoon. You ladies need to decide where to stay tonight. I know the sheriff, and I know Callie's dad. The two of you won't be sleeping in that apartment unless there's someone there with you."

When a person passes away, which I've always thought was a pleasant if unnecessary euphemism, the mortician doesn't hang around waiting several hours to go fetch the body. The sooner the person is removed from the place of death, the better, whether death occurred at home, in a hospital or nursing home, or at the scene of an accident. Once the deceased is pronounced dead, we try to move the person as quickly as possible. What was this about a job for early afternoon?

It's impossible to schedule a pickup ahead of time, too. Even if the person has been on a respirator and the decision is made to cut it off, sometimes death is immediate, but sometimes the person manages to hang on a lot longer than expected.

Jane settled in the chair in front of my desk with a bottle of water. She was still sniffling over Frank. I didn't say, "I told you so."

I brought the web page and online obituaries up to date. Wasn't much to do except change some verbs. We leave the obits up for a week or so after burial, so I deleted future tense verbs, like "Mrs. So-and-So *will* be laid to rest" and converted them to past tense, like "Mrs. So-and-So *was* laid to rest," and make all the other appropriate changes.

Otis stuck his head through the open doorway. "I'm going outside and put some tarps, cloths, and drapes into the oldest funeral coach. Call me if you need me."

"Cloths and drapes?" Jane turned toward me. "You told me that you move corpses in body bags."

"We usually do. Let me go ask him what's going on."

I followed Otis to the garage where the funeral coaches were parked, and asked, "What's happening?"

"Remember I told you we're doing an exhumation? Mrs. Whitaker finally got all of her paperwork in order. We're going to disinter her grandmother at two this afternoon."

"Are you taking the body directly to the perpetual care cemetery?"

"Now, Callie, we don't call anyone a body, even if they have been buried for several years. The grandmother's name is Mrs. Bristow."

"Well, are you taking Mrs. Bristow straight to the new graveyard?"

"No, remember I told you that we will be recasketing her? Depending upon Mrs. Bristow's condition, we may change her clothing also."

"How long has Mrs. Bristow been dead?"

"A little over ten years."

I didn't say another word. Just turned and walked back into the huge, two-story white house that had become as comfortable to me as my kindergarten classroom had been in Columbia. My feelings could change if they put a ten-year-old corpse on the table in my workroom.

Recently deceased people are my job. I enjoy making them as attractive as possible for their loved ones. My mental pictures of a body ten years after burial were based on scary movies and the occasional horror book I've read when I didn't have a good mystery available.

In Stephen King's *Pet Sematary,* the little boy Gage's face was covered with mold when his dad dug him up before he'd been buried a week. And the child had been embalmed, too. Ex-cuuze me. He'd been "prepared."

I'll never forget that book. The scene where the daddy gets into a fight with his father-in-law and they knock the casket down at the funeral home was horrifying to me. I've always been very conscientious that the coffin is stabilized on the bier at Middleton's because I used to have nightmares about that scene from the movie.

"Callie?" Jane called when I entered my office.

"Yes."

"I called Frank on my cell phone. He's coming to get me. We need to talk. Is that okay with you? He said you've got keys and your car's in the lot."

"That's fine. Will you be at the apartment tonight?"

"Not only will I be at the apartment, Roxanne will be working tonight."

"What are you going to tell Frank?"

"I'm telling him that my job really is acting and it's only talk, but I need to work to survive. If we get truly serious, I'll consider changing, but Roxanne isn't stopping until I'm into something committed that means sharing expenses, and we're not there right now."

"Makes sense to me. I thought you were just sitting here. You must have been thinking."

"That's right, and I'll have supper cooked for you when you get home." She leaned over and cocked her head toward the window. "I hear the Jeep. Please walk me to the door, so he doesn't come in. This needs to be private."

I guided Jane to the door with my fingers gently touching her arm. We reached the loading dock the same time

Frank parked. He jumped out and climbed the steps, took Jane by the hand, and in just a few minutes, they were gone.

Just as Frank's Jeep drove away, Odell pulled his Buick in.

"Was Jane in there with Frank?" he asked.

"Yes, they've gone to talk things over."

"Well, I brought her a sandwich along with some for you and Otis. Come on in, and we'll eat."

"You didn't eat at the restaurant?"

"I did, but there's no point in letting Jane's lunch go to waste."

Otis joined us and we pigged out on great big barbecue sandwiches and potato salad, with sodas, not bottled water.

"Do you want to go with us?" Odell asked.

"To the old graveyard to get Mrs. Bristow?" I said.

"Yes, we've got authorities and workers meeting us there. I can call Jake in to catch the telephone or we can just lock up and forward all calls to my cell phone," Odell continued.

"I don't know. I don't think I want to see it."

"It's up to you, but in all the years Doofus and I've run the mortuary, this is the first time we've done a reinterment. Our father handled one years ago when a body had to be disinterred for an autopsy after evidence changed the manner of death from natural to homicide, but I don't remember it too well. I was just a chap back then."

I closed my eyes and thought of Gage in *Pet Sematary*. I could hear Jane's frequent advice: "Live for the day." Sometimes Jane took her own advice too literally, but I needed to take it myself sometimes.

"Will I have to dig?" I asked.

"No, not at all," Otis said.

Against my better judgment, I agreed to go. A note went

on the front door advising anyone who needed us to call on the telephone. The business lines were forwarded to Odell's cell phone. Odell took his car; Otis and I rode in the "oldest" funeral coach, which is only three years old and just as shiny and bright as the new one.

Chapter Thirty-four

Taylors Cemetery was less than an hour's drive from the funeral home. I was surprised at how many people were standing around when we drove into the fenced yard. A Middleton's Mortuary canvas awning stood over the grave site. Two bright yellow backhoes sat on the edge of the road, and several of our part-timers were there, each holding a pick or shovel.

A middle-aged lady wearing a navy blue dress, white shoes, and a white hat stood beside a Beaufort County sheriff's deputy. We'd crossed out of Jade County about five miles ago. The lady in blue smiled at me. I realized that until we arrived, she'd been the only female there. I walked over to her and said, "Hello, I'm Callie Parrish. I work with Middleton's."

"Yes, I'm so glad you came. I'm Kitty Whitaker. I was afraid I'd be the only woman."

"I'm glad to be here for you, but I can assure you that my employers would take excellent care of you anytime, anywhere."

Otis spoke with the deputy and gave him a handful of legal-looking papers. The officer nodded.

Odell approached the digging equipment and spoke with one of the drivers, who started the smaller backhoe and slowly drove it to a grave with a very small gray granite marker bearing the name "Catherine Margaret Bristow" and dates showing she was eighty when she died ten years ago.

"I understand Mrs. Bristow was your grandmother," I said.

"Yes, but when she died, there was no insurance, and we didn't have much money. Grandmama had the cheapest funeral we could get."

"Is your grandfather here, too?"

"No, he was MIA during the war."

I didn't ask which war. He would probably have been in his nineties now, so I assumed she was talking about World War II.

"The first thing I thought when I found out I'd won the lottery was that now Grandmama can have a nicer funeral." She watched silently for a few minutes. "I'm her only survivor. I want her where someone will keep her grave clean when I'm gone, and I want to be buried beside her."

We watched as men swung picks to chip an outline of the grave in front of the tiny marker. After the picks, they used shovels to dig around the edges. Then the backhoe dug into the earth, throwing each load of dirt on a pile.

Odell stood by the deepening hole. He threw up his hand and yelled, "Stop!" A lot of people think that six feet under means that the top of the casket or vault is six feet beneath the surface of the ground. Actually, the bottom of the burial container is six feet below the surface, with the top sometimes barely two feet down. In front of the backhoe, in the same area that the workers had outlined with picks and shovels, parts of two caskets were visible. There was no vault around either of them, not even the concrete blocks some cemeteries use. The coffins lay side by side at about a sixty-degree angle across the grave.

"What's happened?" I asked Odell.

"They've shifted. Sometimes it happens, especially in these older graveyards. If there are no name plates on the caskets, and I doubt that there are, we're going to have to open them to find Mrs. Bristow. Then we rebury the other one and take Mrs. Bristow back to St. Mary with us."

Mrs. Whitaker approached us. Otis walked by her side.

"Is there a problem?" she asked, then looked down into the grave. "Oh, no, how could this happen?"

"Very minor underground shifts of earth," Otis said.

"Like an earthquake?"

"Not anything big enough to be felt on the earth's surface, but kind of like small earthquakes. Heavy rains cause underground shifting, too," Odell responded.

"What do we do now?" Mrs. Whitaker's voice quivered. Like me, she probably dreaded watching them open two caskets. One with her grandmother buried ten years previously; the other, perhaps dead and buried long before.

"I've read about this, but I haven't actually encountered it before," Otis said. "I think perhaps you and Callie should go sit in Odell's car while we sort this out."

"You don't happen to remember what your grandmother was buried in?" Odell asked Mrs. Whitaker as he handed me his car keys.

"Yes, I do. We buried her in her favorite church dress. It was burgundy with a white lace collar."

"What about the casket? Do you remember what kind she had?"

"It was metal, not expensive, but metal. We couldn't afford a vault for the grave, so we didn't want wood. Besides, the metal one we chose was cheaper than the available wooden ones."

That wasn't surprising. Some of the most expensive coffins are highly polished woods like mahogany, oak, or teak. A few years back, Middleton's buried a lady in a cherrywood casket that was more beautiful than any piece of furniture I've ever seen.

"I'd really like to see Grandmama," Mrs. Whitaker added.

"We agreed that you'd let us do what's necessary first," Otis said.

"Okay, but I want you to be sure that the right body is moved."

"I assure you we shall treat this as though Mrs. Bristow were our own grandmother."

Personally, I hadn't wanted to be here anyway, but now that I was, I breathed a sigh of relief that I wouldn't have to watch openings of the two old coffins. I led Mrs. Whitaker to Odell's car. I held the passenger door open for her and then slid in the other side under the steering wheel, cranked the car, and turned on the air-conditioning.

The Buick faced away from the grave, and I didn't want to see, but I glanced in the rearview mirror to see what was going on anyway. The men were excavating around both caskets with picks and shovels. The backhoe had been driven over to the road. I realized I should be talking to Mrs. Whitaker, distracting her, but I couldn't stop watching the scene behind us.

"What do you do at the funeral home?" the lady beside me asked.

"My title is cosmetitian, which is the name for a mortuary cosmetologist, but I'm kind of like a girl Friday. I do the obituaries and a lot of paperwork, too."

"Well, I hope you'll be able to make Grandmama look good. If so, I'm going to invite some of her old neighbors to her new service."

My mouth flies open too quickly and when it does, I often insert my foot into it. For once, I was speechless. Did this woman think I could make a ten-year-old corpse pretty enough for an open-casket service? I wondered if Otis and Odell knew about her expectations.

Trying to make small talk with Mrs. Whitaker was almost impossible because I couldn't keep my eyes off the rearview mirror. After more digging and manhandling, the two coffins lay side by side on the ground beside the expanded hole.

From where we were parked, they both looked reddish brown, not a common color for a metal casket, especially one of the thinner, basic models. Odell began wiping the sides of one of the coffins with a cloth. The color changed from brown to a light gray. He must have been removing mud. After that, he opened a small case and took out several tools. He attempted to release the lid with various implements, then pried it open with a crowbar.

Otis moved to bend over beside his brother. I could see they were talking, but of course, I couldn't hear a thing.

As it often does, my mind traveled back to a book I'd read. *The Adventures of Huckleberry Finn* by Mark Twain is one of my favorite books. I've read it numerous times and just skip over the *n* word—verbally, visually, and mentally. I also think of Jim as Huck's "friend" instead of using the word "slave."

Having read the book the first time over twenty years before, I could still remember my reaction when the townspeople dug up the casket and found the bag of gold on the chest of the corpse. Mark Twain milked the scene for all it was worth. They were out in a graveyard after dark with only the light of a lantern because the clouds and thunder blocked off the moon's illumination. The first time I read that scene, it had several results. I felt scared, excited, and horrified all at the same time.

The scene here in Taylors Cemetery should not have made me think of that wind-torn night with lightning and thunder in Mark Twain's book. This was a bright, sunny June afternoon.

Mrs. Whitaker turned around and looked over her

shoulder. "They've opened one of the caskets. Do you think it's Grandmama? I'm going over there and find out."

"No, no," I quickly said. "I'll go check. Sit tight until I'm back."

I slipped out of the car and walked to the open coffin. I didn't walk quickly, more at a snail's pace. The thought actually crossed my mind that perhaps there was a bag of gold in the coffin.

"Mrs. Whitaker wants to know what you see," I said when I reached Otis and Odell.

"Look for yourself," Odell said and stepped back.

No doubt in my mind that the open casket held Grandmama Bristow's remains. There were some worn spots on the thin metal casket, but none were corroded completely through. The satin-type fabric interior had probably been cream or a light pink ten years earlier. Now it was a muddy rusty color. Even waterproof caskets leak, and this one had never claimed to be sealed against seepage.

Mud or rust had changed Mrs. Bristow's burgundy dress beyond recognition, and the lace collar Mrs. Whitaker had described was now almost brown. Mrs. Bristow's face and hands looked dried to the bones, with a fairly heavy growth of yellowish mold, but I thought the features remained natural enough for recognition if I'd known her in life. Otis leaned over the body and gently wiped the mold away with a soft cloth. A few patches of brownish gray hair were detached from the head, and the lady's plastic pearl earrings had dropped from her ears and lay on the shoulders of her dress. I couldn't call it a pretty picture, but it definitely wasn't half as horrible as I'd expected.

"Well?" said Otis when he'd cleaned off most of the mold.

"Well what?" I answered.

"Do you think Mrs. Whitaker should see this?"

"She has to," Odell said. "This appears to be Mrs. Bristow, but unless Mrs. Whitaker identifies her, we can't be positive that two women in lace-collared dresses weren't buried beside each other and we got the wrong one. Either she identifies her grandmother or we open the other one and hope there's a man inside. Both caskets were partially in Mrs. Bristow's grave. We need positive identification."

The deputy had come over. "You're right," he said. "You need to know for certain that you have the right casket when you leave. Could be a whole lot of legal hassle if you take an unauthorized body out of here."

"If we have to break open that other casket, we'll have to recasket or repair the lock. I think we should just bury the other coffin and take this one back with us," Otis said and gestured toward the body we assumed was Mrs. Bristow.

"Didn't you hear what the officer just said, Doofus?" Odell grimaced. "We either open both or see if Mrs. Whitaker can positively identify this one as her grandmother."

"I'll go get Mrs. Whitaker," I said, but when I turned to head toward the Buick, Mrs. Whitaker was approaching the grave.

I put my hand out and touched her arm. "This isn't pretty, Mrs. Whitaker," I said. "There's water damage, and of course, time changes appearances even after embalming." I didn't comment that the stains on Mrs. Bristow's clothing and the lining of the casket could as easily be from body purge as from water and mud.

"None of that's news to me. I just want Grandmama moved to Eternity Perpetual Care Gardens in Adam's Creek. I'd want to do this even if there were nothing in that box but a pile of bones."

"No, she hasn't completely skeletonized," I answered,

remembering that a few of her fingers did have exposed bone.

"I want to see," Mrs. Whitaker insisted.

Suited me. I'd been sent over to talk her into taking a look.

For all her talk of not feeling different even if nothing more was left than a pile of bones, Mrs. Whitaker fell apart at the casket.

She wailed; she moaned; she rocked back and forth. I patted her shoulders and back, helping stabilize her physically if not emotionally. We certainly didn't want her to fall into the open grave. Otis offered tissues, and Mrs. Whitaker wiped away her tears.

When she appeared to be under control, Otis asked, "Can you positively identify Mrs. Bristow?"

"Oh, yes, that's Grandmama. She's shriveled up, but she still looks like herself." She leaned over and looked closer. "I even remember those earrings."

"You drove yourself here?" Otis asked.

"Yes."

"Do you feel up to driving yourself home?"

"I thought I'd go back to the mortuary with you," she said.

"No, we have the clothes you brought." Otis was using that Mortuary 101 soothing voice he's perfected. "I'd prefer that you wait and see Mrs. Bristow again after we've finished our preparation. Why don't you plan to come by tomorrow morning? Perhaps around ten."

Preparation! Are they planning to try to embalm the woman again?

Otis stepped up. "I think Callie should drive Mrs. Whitaker home, and we'll have Jake pick Callie up there."

Mrs. Whitaker's eyes widened. "Oh, no, I don't want Callie to drive me home. I'm okay to drive."

Odell grimaced. "See, Mrs. Whitaker, I'm afraid that if

we let you drive away from here after being so upset, we might be liable. Like a bartender who lets a customer drive home who's had too much to drink."

"You don't understand," Mrs. Whitaker said. "I've heard about Ms. Parrish's accident. I know about your car burning. The rumor is that someone tried to run her off the road intentionally. I don't want her driving my car."

For the second time that day, I was speechless. Otis and Odell solved the problem by calling the deputy over. He thought Mrs. Whitaker was calm enough to drive and assured Otis and Odell that they weren't legally obligated to keep her there.

I sat in the driver's seat of the funeral coach and listened to the radio while the workers cleaned more mud off Mrs. Bristow's casket. After Mrs. Whitaker drove away, they closed the lid and loaded the coffin onto the tarps in the back. I didn't watch. I really wished I hadn't come. I heard the thud of the back being closed.

Chapter Thirty-five

ap, tap, tap. Otis rapped on the window beside me. "Move over to the passenger side. I'll drive."

"Don't we have to wait until that other casket is back in the ground and covered?"

"No, Odell will see to that. You and I need to get Mrs. Bristow to the mortuary and get started."

I moved over to the passenger side of the seat and managed to stay silent until we were out of the cemetery.

"Otis," I said, "I don't understand. The rust and mud indicate that water has been in the coffin, but the body looks almost dried out."

"Don't say 'body.' Call her by her name. Mrs. Bristow."

I've heard that so many times that I didn't bother to give my usual explanation, which is "I forgot" or "I slipped."

When Otis realized I wasn't going to answer him, he continued, "Even unsealed caskets might stay waterproof for a while. Until then, the body might deteriorate to bone or become adipocere. You know what that means, don't you?"

"Yes, grave wax."

"That's the common name, or 'mortuary wax.' It's

actually the conversion of tissue, primarily fatty tissue, to a soaplike substance that could even be used as soap."

I couldn't help it. I shivered at the thought of bathing with the remains of a corpse.

"In Mrs. Bristow's case," Otis continued, "I doubt there's much adipocere. I'd bet she was very slim, and that even her low end coffin stayed dry for a period of time. Mummification is an alternative to formation of adipocere, but really, there's no way to predict exactly what might be found years after burial. The kind of embalming used plays a big part, too."

Most of the time I have little to say when Otis begins one of his lectures about the mortuary business and related issues, but I had a comment this time.

"I've read that Abraham Lincoln's coffin has been moved seventeen times and opened five times."

"Yes, Callie, I read a lot about that as a young boy. When they opened his coffin in 1901, Lincoln was recognizable. His beard and the wart on his cheek were the same, but he had no eyebrows. His suit was covered with yellow mold, maybe even the same kind I removed from Mrs. Bristow. I read about it in one of my father's books, but I'll bet you could look it up on the Internet."

Oh, joy! Just what I wanted to look up. There might even be a picture.

"The thing is," Otis said, "there's 'wet' and 'dry' adipocere as well as mummification and just plain deterioration. Do you know who Lee Harvey Oswald was?"

"Yes, I went to school," I smarted. "He was the accused assassin of President John F. Kennedy."

"Well, he was exhumed for a new autopsy almost eighteen years after burial. The vault had cracked and the casket was filled with putrid water. That's the most common finding. Groundwater seeps in and does its damage."

I turned on the radio, and we rode silently. When we were almost back to the mortuary, Otis added to our delightful previous discussion.

"We really should go to the Mutter Museum. It's in Philadelphia and has amazing medical exhibits, including 'the Soap Lady.' She's the most famous example of adipocere, died during the yellow fever epidemic in the late 1800s. She was exhumed about eighty years later during redevelopment of the old graveyard."

I didn't know if Otis meant the Mutter Museum would be a good vacation or a mortuary field trip, but if the Middletons would pay, I'd be willing to see it.

Maybe.

Chapter Thirty-six

Screams woke me. Terrified, horrified screeches. I wouldn't have known the sounds were coming from me if Jane and Frank hadn't been shaking me and shouting, "Wake up, Callie! Wake up!"

I sat up in bed and shook my head back and forth, trying to clear away the images.

Otis had sent me home in the Mustang when we reached the mortuary. Told me he'd take care of Mrs. Bristow and made me take home the squirrels Dennis Sharpe had given me.

"Just go on and get some rest," he'd said. "You haven't had time to get over that car wreck. I'll see you tomorrow morning."

"Will we have to try to make up Mrs. Bristow?" I'd asked.

"No, just clean her up, change her clothes, and put her in a new gasket-sealed casket. I'll take care of it. You go on home."

I hadn't exactly followed his instructions. Instead, I'd stopped by the used book store. Not that I need any more books at my place. The reason Jane was sleeping on the couch was because instead of a bed, I had boxes and boxes, as well as bookcases, filled with books in my second bedroom.

My conversation with Otis hadn't made me seek out a book on grave wax and decay of the deceased. I'd just as soon not think about those things. Instead, I wanted to read more about Abraham Lincoln. My favorite books are mysteries, seconded by true crime and thrillers, but our talk had pulled up memories about some eerie events concerning President Lincoln.

I bought a few paperbacks—a life of Lincoln as well as a book about strange events surrounding and following his assassination.

Jane wasn't at the apartment. I considered driving to Daddy's, but I was tired, so I lay down to read until Jane came home. She'd said she would cook dinner.

Abe Lincoln's log cabin and walking to school didn't intrigue me, but the other book did. I read about strange events like some towns supposedly hearing that Lincoln had been assassinated *before* he even went to the theater that night. I read about the recurring incidence of mental breakdowns of those associated with Lincoln and his assassin. Then I read about the eerie hauntings and ghost stories.

I, Calamine Lotion Parrish, do *not* believe in ghosts. I believe that the soul or whatever someone wants to call the part of a person that makes him or her unique leaves the body at the time of death. I enjoy working to make the remaining shell an attractive memory for those who loved the deceased. I've said it before, and I'll say it again, if ghosts were real, there'd be no room for patients in hospitals nor for funerals at mortuaries.

That's what I was thinking when I drifted off to sleep. What I was dreaming when I awoke was that Lincoln's ghost was in the room with me. He looked pretty much like he did in my history books in school except that he was growing some mold on his face and part of his hair was missing. He wanted to sit on the side of the bed and talk to me. In my semiconscious state, I was wondering what makeup and tools I would need to restore his looks. When Lincoln's features turned into Mrs. Bristow's face, I screamed.

"Wake up, Callie," Jane repeated. "You must be having a bad dream."

I opened my eyes. "I had a nightmare," I said.

"No kidding," said Frank. "I'll get you something to drink."

"Coke," I said. "Coke with ice."

While Frank went to the kitchen, I excused myself and went to the bathroom. I washed my face. Looking in the mirror, I realized that the makeup wouldn't come off without remover. Thank heaven I had some in the medicine cabinet. I sponged it on and gently revealed the true state of my skin underneath. In addition to the bruises, there was now a red rash on my face. Probably an indication that the makeup might be hiding what I looked like, but it wasn't speeding up the healing process, and I might even be allergic to it. I cleaned my face and left my skin bare.

A knock on the bathroom door.

"I'm okay, Jane," I said.

"It's not Jane; it's me," said Frank.

I opened the door and he handed me the glass of Coca-Cola. The expression on his face was enough to convince me that I now *looked* like a nightmare.

"What did you do?" he asked.

"I took off my makeup. Apparently, I'm having a reaction to it as well as the remains of bruises from the accident."

"Accident? From what I've heard, it was an *attack*."

"Yes, I guess so," I agreed.

"Come on in the living room. Sheriff Harmon is here to talk to us."

The sheriff gave me a shocked look, but didn't comment on my face. He was sitting on the couch scratching Big Boy's ears.

"I went to the B and B in Beaufort to see Mrs. White and talk to Mr. Carter. She was intoxicated and couldn't tell me where he is. The most I got from her was that her fiancé had to leave town 'on business.' She really wasn't making much sense other than that you had started some trouble for George. Do you know what she's talking about? You didn't confront him, did you?"

"No. I told you what the cookie lady said about him, but I haven't talked to him. Don't you remember? Mrs. Counts said she told Pearl that she was me. George saw us together at Dr. Melvin's funeral, and Mrs. Counts tried to get him to admit that he's Sean Gunderson. She thinks he's after Pearl's money. She also thinks he killed some of his other wives and that he came after her last night while she was at church."

"Callie, you know that could have been who tossed your apartment."

"What about Pearl?" Jane interrupted. "Her last living relative was Melvin Dawkins. You can't just leave her drunk in a rented room in Beaufort. What if he thinks of something that will make her a threat to him? Or what if he comes back for her and marries her while she's drinking? Then he could kill her and inherit. She never had any children."

"That's not going to happen," Sheriff Harmon said. "She seemed dehydrated, so I called an ambulance and had her transported to the hospital. After a talk with the Beaufort sheriff, Pearl White is not only hospitalized, she's under protective observation."

"Whew! I just don't want anything bad to happen to her," Jane said. "She's been really good to me until that Lucas woman tried to buy her out."

"I don't want anything to happen to any of you," said the sheriff, "and I'd just as soon you ladies not stay here by yourselves until we've located Sean Gunderson, aka George Carter."

Frank grinned. "I can stay here with them."

"I think it would be better if all of you go over to your father's place."

If looks could kill, Jade County would have had a dead sheriff.

"You know how I feel about that," I said.

"Look what I'm dealing with here," Sheriff Harmon said. "I still don't know if Melvin Dawkins died a natural death or someone helped him along. I've got a lot going on. Someone beat Dorcas Lucas to death. I'd been afraid that Jane pushed her off the steps. That could have been an accident, but beating someone is homicide." Jane frowned at him.

"You know Jane couldn't beat anyone to death," Frank said.

"I could if I wanted to!" Jane protested.

"Are you admitting you beat Ms. Lucas to death?" the sheriff asked.

"No, just saying I could if I wanted to. I'll bet there have been blind murderers. I'm just not one of them."

I had never seen it before. I roll my eyes sometimes when I'm not thinking, but I'd never seen a man do it. Sheriff Harmon rolled his eyes as well as any woman I've ever known. "I have no doubt," he said, "that you can do anything you put your mind to, Jane.

"The point I'm trying to make here," he continued, "is that I've got all of that plus a possible serial killer loose in this town, and I don't want to have to worry about Callie Parrish sticking her nose somewhere it doesn't belong and getting herself hurt or in trouble."

To the affronted look on my face, he responded, "Pearl

White said George Carter was all upset about *you*. He thinks you and Mrs. Counts talked to me about him. Mrs. Counts has disappeared, and I suspect Carter will come after you unless he's skipped town."

He grimaced. "Add to that the facts that someone tried to kill you on the road, someone was in your apartment, and someone's been sneaking around in your yard, probably playing Peeping Tom." He paused. "I think that's enough, don't you?"

"Enough for me," Frank said. "I suggest we pack up some clothes for you gals and head back to Pa's. He'll welcome both of you."

"How about supper?" Jane said. "I was going to make spaghetti. We bought groceries."

"We'll take them with us," Frank said. "Big Boy can come, too. He loves playing at the farm."

I didn't like the idea at all, but I was clearly outnumbered. Frank and Jane packed the food into the Jeep. They wanted me to ride with them, but I insisted Big Boy and I would follow in the Mustang. Sheriff Harmon helped me get Big Boy locked into his special seat belt. As I drove off, I saw the sheriff back at the front door, double-checking that I'd left it locked.

Chapter Thirty-seven

"**B**ig Boy," I said, "do you ever wonder how we wind up in all these situations?"

He didn't answer, not even a bark, but I could imagine what he would tell me if he could. "Callie," he'd say, "you need to get a life."

If I had a real life, lived for the day as Jane said, I wouldn't have time to get mixed up in everything that happened in St. Mary. If I had a real life, if I lived for the day, I'd find myself a job that didn't throw me right into the middle of every death in town, especially the ones that weren't natural. A job that didn't send me to a graveyard to watch a ten-year-old coffin come out of the ground and give me nightmares.

I looked over at my dog again. His tongue was hanging out of his mouth, flopping around, but his ears stood straight up like they should on a purebred Great Dane. It had cost a small fortune—in my budget anyway—but cropping his ears had given him a much better look.

"Want to ride convertible, Big Boy?" I asked.

I didn't wait for an answer, just pulled over to the side of the road and put the ragtop down.

Big Boy grinned. Well, maybe not everyone would know his expression was a grin, but I did. I was still frightened, scared, and curious. What was going on? Why so many mysterious deaths at one time in a town the size of St. Mary?

Both Dr. Melvin and Pearl White thought they'd found true love on the Internet.

"Do you think I should try looking for love online?" I asked Big Boy.

He gave me a *What kind of fool are you?* look and rolled his eyes. I know it sounds impossible, but it's the truth. I promise. My dog rolled his eyes at me!

"I guess not," I said. "Neither of those turned out too well. Dr. Melvin's dead, and we don't know why or if his wife did away with him to inherit from him. Pearl White's gotten herself involved with a man who might be a serial killer, and she's started back drinking."

Vanessa crossed my mind. I had submitted the profile, but no one could ever trace that back to me. Or could they? Computer geeks can do all kinds of things. What if someone traced it? I laughed out loud. If they traced my entry, it would lead back to a mortuary. I didn't think anyone would be eager to come looking there.

Since Big Boy was now gazing around, not paying any attention to me, I stopped talking to him and thought to myself, *Thank heaven Pearl hadn't yet sold all of her property and given the proceeds to charity, thinking Georgie would take care of her the rest of her life!*

Ms. Dorcas Lucas had been the biggest witch with a *b* that I'd ever encountered my whole life. Bad enough the sheriff had thought Jane pushed her down the steps. Now he was convinced from the autopsy that someone had beaten her to death. I couldn't swear—well, I try not to swear anyway—that Jane wouldn't push someone away and that person couldn't fall down the steps. But I was positive that

Jane wouldn't have beaten even Ms. Lucas to death with a two-by-four.

I really didn't have anything to do with those events, so why was I being harassed? Why did someone try to kill me on the road? Why break into my apartment? Why peek in my windows and leave notes for me? It was too much, just too much, to all be coincidental. There had to be a connection.

Big Boy was looking at me like, "Why'd you stop talking to me?"

"Don't you agree?" I asked him. "There has to be a connection. Dr. Melvin and Pearl were cousins and both found romance on the Internet." I stopped talking again.

Romance could have come to me through the Internet, too. Indirectly. The Internet had enabled Roselle to find her half brother Levi. Then the Internet had led her to Melvin here in St. Mary, and Levi had followed her. If I hadn't run Levi Pinckney off, I may have had a relationship from online. Jane and I hadn't had a chance to really talk, but I'm sure she would think I was crazy to tell Levi I wasn't interested in chemistry.

I could tell from their actions that Jane and Frank had worked their problems out. I wondered if Jane had convinced him she needed her job, or if he'd convinced her she needed him more than she needed the work.

Someone, I think it was Sherlock Holmes, said something like, "When you rule out all the impossibles, what's left is the solution." That wasn't doing me much good since I couldn't identify the impossibles. I decided to think about probables instead of possibles.

From what Mrs. Counts said and from what the sheriff told us, it was more than probable that George Carter was an alias for one of those men who marry and murder over and over for profit. If that were the case, he'd never loved Pearl White. He would have married her, moved her to

Florida, and seen to it that she met with an accident that left him rich.

If. There was a big *if* involved. He'd told Pearl that they didn't need her money. She'd taken him at his word and put everything on the market, planning to donate the proceeds to her favorite charities to help people with vision or hearing impairments. George Carter wouldn't inherit a thing if Pearl liquidized and donated her proceeds to charity before he married her.

That was the connection!

Dorcas Lucas wasn't killed for personal reasons. She hadn't been murdered because she was such a horrible person, though she truly was an awful being. She'd died because of her job. Because if she negotiated the sale of Pearl's property and Pearl donated the proceeds to charity before her wedding, there'd be nothing left for George Carter to inherit after he killed his new bride.

From what I'd read, blunt force trauma was a much more masculine than feminine way of murder anyway. Females were more inclined to kill by poison, smothering, or some other less combative means. Of course, Jane said she could beat someone to death if she had to. I didn't believe her, but I feared Sheriff Harmon did. I wondered if he'd figured out the motive for Ms. Lucas's death. If he'd figured out that George Carter had beaten her to death.

Good grief! George Carter could have killed Dr. Melvin, too. Maybe he feared that Pearl would leave some money or property to him since he was her only relative. If the toxicology reports showed something had been slipped into food or drink to cause Dr. Melvin's death, I'd put my money on Carter as the culprit.

But why would Carter try to run me off the road? And why would he be peeking through my windows and plundering through my apartment? Those questions would take more thought, but I felt like I was on the right track. I reached for the cell phone to call Sheriff Harmon.

Dalmation! I'd left it home again. I know sometimes I give Big Boy credit for more human-type intelligence than he can possibly have, but when I turned toward him, I promise he gave me a *What now?* look.

When we reached the apartment, I opened the door and let the dog in, then remembered I'd left my purse on the seat. I went back for it, then returned and entered.

Chapter Thirty-eight

George Carter stood at my kitchen sink with Big Boy sitting on the floor right beside him, the dog looking up like he was Scooby-Doo and Carter was Shaggy. I could see them from my front door.

"What are you doing?" I demanded. "How did you get in here?"

"I'm running fresh water for your dog. You shouldn't leave his bowl empty, even when you take him off with you. You might forget to fill it when you come home." He reached down and patted Big Boy on the head.

"He's a friendly fellow, especially to people who bring him hamburger." George set Big Boy's water bowl on the floor. "I came in through the bathroom window. Someone will have to replace the glass, but it won't be you." George walked from the kitchen area into the living room. "Your face looks terrible," he said, "but it won't matter."

"Why are you here?" I backed against the door.

"So you can tell me exactly what you told Pearl. You've upset her tremendously. As a matter of fact, Pearl was so disturbed that she's drunk. I left her passed out on our bed. She kept saying your name and crying. What did you do to her?"

"I didn't *do* anything. She just knows what I learned about you."

"How'd you learn anything about me?"

"Surely you know that it's as easy to check a person's background on the Internet as it is to create a new persona and scam poor widow ladies out of their property and life's savings."

"You don't understand. I really love Pearl." His tone was sincere, but the smile on his face wasn't.

"If you love Pearl so much, why'd you beat Ms. Lucas to death to stop the sale of Pearl's home and beachfront property?"

"What makes you think I killed Ms. Lucas?"

"It's pretty obvious. You're strong enough, no one knows where you were that morning, and you telling Pearl you didn't want her money was nothing but lies. You never counted on her deciding to liquidate everything and give the money to charity. When you couldn't stop Pearl from selling, you stopped Ms. Lucas from buying."

"And now I have to stop you from talking. I have to stop you and convince Pearl that nothing you told her was true." George had gradually walked over to me, close enough that we were so face-to-face that I could feel and smell his breath as he spoke. "I'm lucky my lady love has a taste for alcohol. It makes her easier to manipulate and makes a future possible accident more believable. I felt blessed when she acknowledged her alcoholism and I convinced her that her drinking problem had been due to unhappiness. She could have a little drink now that she was going to live happily ever after. It didn't take but one to knock her slap off the wagon." He grinned. "But you know too much. I have to silence you."

"What if my brother knows what I learned?"

"Then I'll have to stop him, too."

I realized then that bringing Frank into the picture

wouldn't save me. It was more likely to end up with both of us dead.

"I haven't really told him anything, and I don't have to let anyone else know about you," I lied. "I can deny to Pearl that I ever said anything. She was drinking. You're right. She can be convinced that it never happened."

He laughed. Not the pleasant, charming sound I'd heard from him before. This was maniacal. "All I have to do is decide how to make your death look like an accident."

George looked around. Big Boy finished lapping up water, walked to me, and lay down on the floor beside me in front of the door.

"Put your dog outside unless you want him dead, too."

"He never goes out without his leash. I leave him in the bathroom sometimes. Can I put him there?"

"Just do it. I don't want that big hound jumping me. I don't have any more hamburger in my pocket." That previously charming man looked and sounded meaner than anyone I'd ever encountered. More than mean. Wicked and evil.

I took Big Boy by his collar and led him to the bathroom. There's something weird about me. Well, some folks would say I have lots of strange characteristics. The one that took over right then was my habit of throwing up when I'm frightened. Puh-leeze. If I could control it, I would.

It seemed a better idea to heave in the bathroom instead of all over my kitchen or living room. I was hugged over the toilet like a college freshman at a frat party when two strong hands pulled me upright.

"What are you doing? Why are you making yourself do that? I didn't poison you."

"You just scare me. I barf when I'm frightened."

"Oh." He wet a washcloth and wiped my face. That sounds gentle, but it wasn't. He hurt my bruises then pulled my hair as he grabbed it and dragged me backward to the living room.

"Why'd you come poking around, watching me? Why'd you try to run me off the road?" I asked.

"I haven't had time to follow you and watch you. Between Pearl and Dorcas Lucas, I've had my hands full. I was lucky to run into Dorcas and get her to agree to go with me to your friend's place. I'm still expecting that local yokel sheriff to blame Dorcas's death on your blind buddy."

He jerked me tighter against him with one arm and used his other hand to pull a gun from his pocket. A tiny snub-nosed revolver.

"No one will believe I died accidentally of a gunshot wound," I said. "I've been around guns my whole life."

"Then it will have to be suicide." He pointed the weapon at me and said, "Get some paper and a pen."

He followed me into the kitchen, where I took down my magnet grocery list pad and pencil that hung on the refrigerator. We sat at the table, and he moved in closer, pressing the gun against my cheek. He dictated. I wrote:

I am too ashamed of the lies I've told Pearl White and of pushing Ms. Lucas down the steps and hitting her. I can't go on, so I am ending it all.

Callie Parrish

"Is that your legal name?" George asked.

"Not really."

"Then sign it with your legal name."

That didn't make a whole lot of sense to me. It's not like the note was a will or anything legal, but I was in no position to argue. I drew a line through the signature and signed "Calamine Lotion Parrish" beneath it.

That suicide note was as bad as the original part of the perfect country song. The song that didn't say anything about rain or trains or Mama. That note didn't say anything about love or caring. Nothing about Jane, Daddy, or my brothers, and it didn't say who would take care of Big Boy with me gone. Anyone who knew me well would know those weren't my words when they read it. *Duh.* What difference did that make after I was already dead?

That little snub-nosed H&R revolver might be a sissy gun, but with nine shots of .22 bullets at close range, I was sure it would work. But then, who could empty nine shots into their own skull? Would Carter shoot and wait to see if it killed me before firing again?

Forensics can tell everything nowadays, including what shot was fired first and what shot killed the victim. Couldn't be suicide if all nine shots were fired and the second one was deadly. My family would never believe I'd committed suicide anyway, and even if they did, they definitely wouldn't think I'd used that gun instead of one of my own. Well, actually one I'd borrowed from Daddy.

All these thoughts of not only dying, but suffering between shots made my stomach rumble again. To be polite about it, I regurgitated on my suicide note.

"What the . . . ?" Carter said and jumped back. He yanked me into a headlock and a little bit of vomit dribbled onto his sleeve. He looked at it and scowled in disgust, then he placed the gun against my temple. My heart pounded. I closed my eyes.

The gun went off.

Amazing!

I didn't feel a thing.

I opened my eyes. George had been yanked away from me. The bullet smashed through my kitchen window. The gun clattered to the floor. George and another man struggled from the kitchen into the living room. I dared not follow and wished again that I had a door to the outside from the kitchen. I complained about that every time I had to take my trash out the front door. Now I needed another exit not for trash, but to let me escape the apartment without going through that fight.

Picking up the revolver, I peeked around the kitchen door. For an instant, I'd imagined that Levi Pinckney had rescued me, but George's assailant was much bigger than Levi. The ponytail and beard identified Dennis Sharpe. I wanted to get a clear shot at George, but I didn't want to kill him or harm Dennis.

I had the gun sighted, waiting for the perfect opportunity, when Dennis pulled out a great big hunting knife. He rammed it into George's belly and yanked it straight up to his chin. I turned away and dropped the revolver.

George Carter was scum. He'd killed women before. Preyed on older, widowed ladies, the loneliest people in society. He would have murdered both Pearl and me. I see corpses every day at work, but I couldn't look at George Carter's gutted body lying on the floor with a pool of dark red soaking through my old avocado green shag carpet. The coppery smell of blood seeped through the other death odors.

Chapter Thirty-nine

"I was just in time," Dennis Sharpe said, wiping the blade of his hunting knife with a tea towel he'd pulled from a rack over the kitchen sink. "That man would have killed you, ruined that pretty face and your perfect body." He put the knife into the holder attached to the belt loop on his brown cargo pants. He wasn't wearing a belt, just those leather suspenders over a gray T-shirt.

"He was going to murder me!" I gasped.

"I heard him," Dennis said and tossed the dishcloth into the sink. "Looks like you got banged up pretty bad in that car wreck."

"I did."

"You're still beautiful and got that great body."

Reaching for the telephone, I said, "I'll dial 911."

"No!" His tone wasn't pleasant now.

"You stabbed him in defense of me. I'll tell them what happened."

"No, I don't want the law over here. Just leave him where he is. I'll take you to my place. You'll be safe."

"I'm safe here now. You stopped George from hurting

me." The man had saved my life, but deep inside, instead of appreciation, I felt fear.

"You run around getting into too much trouble. I liked your looks when I saw you at the beach with your red-haired friend. I shot your watermelon just to scare the two of you and watch you jump around like you did. When I went to talk to Mr. Middleton about freeze-drying and recognized you as the beautiful blonde from the beach, I knew you'd be perfect for me. I wanted you to be mine, but you barely even glanced at me."

He smiled, but it was a crazy, wicked expression. "I still want you forever even if you did change your hair. I want to protect you from getting into trouble again, but I have to make a living, can't spend my days and nights following you around to take care of you."

Gut instinct took over. Dennis Sharpe was a few crayons short of a pack, missing the red in his Crayolas. He'd just saved my life, but I had no intention of going over to his place. At that moment, I wanted Daddy, all my brothers, and Sheriff Harmon to rush in and protect me. The wish didn't come true. I tried talking my way out of what I knew was a bad situation. Maybe even a deadly one.

"I didn't know you felt that way about me," I said in as sweet a tone as I could muster. "Why don't we go out sometime? Maybe see a movie." If I hadn't been so scared, I'd have gagged at the sugary sweetness of my voice. My stomach was already retching with fear.

"That won't solve anything. I think about you all the time. Why do you think I showed up when I did? I've been following you, watching you. I was looking through the side window when Carter threatened you. If he killed Ms. Lucas like you said, he would have killed you, too."

"I know. That's why we need to call the sheriff and let him know you saved me. You're a hero." I swear that last word was as close as I've ever gotten to being a Magnolia Mouth.

"No, I'm taking you with me. When they find Carter in here and you gone, they'll never think of me."

I stepped away from him, easing closer to the front door, but he snatched my arm and yanked me tight against him. With his other hand, he pulled the freshly wiped knife from its case and held it up in front of me. I saw "D S" carved into the handle before he pressed the blade to my neck.

"I've got my van out front. Don't make me hurt you. I don't want to mess up your perfect body."

The tip of the knife scratched against my throat.

Sometimes I'm a smart aleck, flippant, and I minimize things, but I was scared out of my mind and don't mind admitting it. I'd always felt weird around Dennis Sharpe, and he was freaking me out. He'd killed George Carter in my defense, but I felt as threatened by him as I had by George.

Looking around the room frantically, my gaze settled on the squirrels Otis had made me bring home from the mortuary. Mother and baby mounted forever on the tree branch by Dennis Sharpe. Carefree Pets.

"Oh, Dennis, let's take the squirrels with us. It was your first present to me. I want them." I forced myself to lightly touch his arm, and it was all I could do not to flinch, but my touch made him drop the knife.

He grinned and said, "Okay. I'm glad to know you really liked 'em. I'd been thinking you weren't impressed with my work."

"Oh, Dennis," I said as I picked the dead animals up from the dining table. "This is a work of art. How could anyone not be impressed?" I wanted to grab the gun, but I was afraid that if I looked at it, Dennis would remember it. I had no doubt that if we went after it at the same time, he'd reach it before I did. If so, I might wind up being shot. I also didn't want him looking at the floor and remembering his knife.

No matter how impressed with the squirrels I may have tried to appear, Dennis pulled a piece of rope from another pocket and tied my wrists together in front of me. He put the squirrels into my hands and pinned my arms against my body. He lifted me from the floor and, half-carrying, half-dragging me, forced me to his van.

Chapter Forty

I'd never even wondered where Dennis Sharpe lived. He drove up Highway 21, cut off into a deeply wooded area, and made a few more turns before he stopped in front of a cabin with a couple of rickety-looking wooden tables in the front yard.

"Come on." He pulled me across the seat and out his side of the van. Not wanting to offend him, I brought the squirrels with me, clutched against my chest with my bound hands.

Inside, the cabin was filled with dead animals, preserved and mounted on wood and stone. A couch was covered with more examples of his taxidermy. He shoved the birds, cats, dogs, raccoons, possums, and squirrels over, pushed me down, and sat beside me. The small round table near his kitchen area was covered with small tools and animal skins.

"It's a good thing I've been following you," he said. "Carter would have spoiled you for me if he'd killed you. I don't want a mark on you." He smiled. "I'm gonna tell you a secret. Sometimes when people want a mounted dog, some special breed, I steal one and then euthanize it so I can preserve it."

The man's expression was so proud. Like I'd be

impressed. "I do it just like they execute people. I looked it up and ordered the same drugs off the Internet. It's painless. The animal just goes to sleep and doesn't wake up, and it doesn't mar the body at all. That's what I'm going to do for you. It will be painless."

Buh-leeve me, I'd rather die painlessly than in agony, but given my druthers, I'd prefer to stay alive. *Think, Callie,* I said to myself, *there has to be something you can do, some way out of this.*

"Then I'm going to preserve you forever and set you right here on the couch. I can watch you, and I won't be out driving around looking for you, peeking through your windows, or following you when I should be working to make my business successful like it used to be." He reached behind the couch and picked up a bag, which he handed to me. "Here, open this."

I shook the bag and out fell a wig. A cheap platinum blonde wig. "Put it on," Dennis said. "You'll look like you did the day I met you."

Obediently, I pulled the wig over my head and tried to stuff my own brown hair up under the blonde. "Don't worry about that," Dennis said, "I'm going to shave your head."

Don't ask me why, but the thought of his shaving my head was as terrifying as the realization that he planned to "euthanize" me.

"Dennis," I said, "you don't have to shave my head. I can color my hair back to blonde. Let's go to the beauty supply store or the pharmacy. I'll buy the color and put it back the way you like it." *I need to get him to take me to where other people are. Let me see someone to signal that I need help.*

As though reading my mind, Dennis said, "No, you're never going to leave my cabin. I'll put you to sleep and preserve you. Like that Eva Perón. Twenty years from now, you'll still be sitting here with me every day, and I can talk to you while I work." He sighed. "It gets lonely here."

He was thinking Eva Perón. I was thinking Norman Bates. I also wondered how painless his euthanasia would be. *Think,* I told myself, *what have I read? Is it better to fight or try to convince an assailant to stop by talking to him, making him relate to his victim as a person?*

If Dennis Sharpe was lonely and needed someone to talk to, I'd try to accommodate him. Surely I could speak better alive than dead. Of all things, I thought about one of my daddy's chauvinistic jokes.

"Why can't women ever speak their minds?" Daddy would ask. "Because it leaves them speechless," he'd answer himself, then laugh like he was the greatest comedian in the world.

Tears burned my eyes. Daddy had just opened up and really shown emotion toward me on my birthday. My disappearance would devastate him. And The Boys. And Jane. And the Middletons. And Rizzie. And maybe Levi Pinckney. And what would happen to Big Boy if I died?

Dennis pulled a handkerchief from his pocket and tenderly wiped away my tears. Cautiously, trying not to hurt my battered face. "Nothing to be scared of, Callie. And just think, your face will remain unlined and unwrinkled. I can use some makeup to cover what happened to you on the highway. I didn't even think it might disfigure you. I was so mad that I just wanted to scare you."

So George Carter really hadn't been driving that Tahoe!

"And your body," Dennis said with eyes filled with awe. "Your body will stay just as youthful and firm as it is today—twenty, thirty, even forty years from now."

"My body? If you're searching for the perfect body, you've made a mistake!" I squeaked.

"What do you mean?"

"My body isn't me."

"Well, I know that. Your body is only part of you. There's your personality and your sense of humor, and your intelligence. I can't preserve those for you, but they'll always exist in my mind while I have the physical you here with me always."

"Will I have to wear this black dress?" I asked, hoping I could convince him to take me shopping.

"No, I bought you a white dress. It's not like the one Marilyn Monroe wore in that famous photo, but I know from her picture that you'll look great with the blonde hair and white dress."

"Will you show it to me?"

"You want to see it?" His tone changed again. Now he sounded like a little boy, eager to show off.

"Of course. I want to see all my presents from you so I can thank you for them." I looked at the squirrels beside me with all the other animals that had been shoved over on the sofa. "Like my squirrels," I said and turned so I could pick them up with my bound hands. I actually petted the back of that rat-thing.

"You never thanked me for the flowers. Not for the vase or the wreath."

I was glad I'd never thanked Levi for the bouquet. I'd thought it was from him, but I hadn't been sure enough. I almost told Dennis, "I didn't know they were from you," but that might set him off. Instead, I mumbled, "I'm a little shy sometimes. I didn't know exactly how to tell you how much I loved them." I almost fluttered my eyelashes at him.

"I guess you knew I was mad at you when I took the wreath to your house. I'm a man and sometimes men get mad at women. My father used to scream at my mother. 'Sit down and shut up!' he'd yell at her. You won't have to worry about that because you'll always be sitting quietly watching me do my work. Men like that, you know. A woman should watch her man work and admire what he does."

"I could do that." My voice had taken on a pleading tone that was strange to me. "I could watch you work. I could admire you. I could even cook your meals and clean the house for you," I said, but I thought, *until I could get away or slam one of these rocks against your head.*

"You don't understand, Callie. I want you with me forever, but I don't trust you."

"You can believe me. I promise." I didn't even bother to cross my fingers. My words weren't a fib; they were an outright lie.

"I've been looking all my life for the perfect woman. Every time I find one it turns out that she isn't right or she leaves me. I've found you. I wish I could freeze-dry you. I can't afford the equipment, but I'll preserve you even better than if you was freeze-dried. It's going to be perfect. Wait right here."

He stood, then shook his head. "No, you'd better come with me. I can't trust you not to run out the door." He snatched me up by my arm, pulling me so hard that both hands flew up. He dragged me into a bedroom, small and crowded with even more dead animals, many of them reptiles. Snakes, lizards, and turtles of all sizes filled one side of the room. Foxes and wolves on the other side were poised for attack, mouths open with bared teeth. Suspended from the ceiling with wings spread, seagulls seemed caught in flight.

Dennis zeroed in on my staring at the seagulls. "You should have seen yourself that day when I was hunting seagulls," he said. "I don't usually kill them. I just try to break a wing so they fall and I won't have so much work to do to cover the shot. I was just playing with you when I shot the watermelon." He laughed.

He opened the door to a wardrobe and pulled out a white dress on a hanger. On the shelf at the top, I saw a jumble of brightly colored satin and laces. Jane's thongs. The thief who stole them from the back of the Mustang hadn't been a squirrel or raccoon. It had been a rat. A rat named Dennis Sharpe. He saw me looking and slammed the wardrobe closed. Then he picked up a shoebox from the floor and pushed me out into the main room again. "I need to get you still and quiet because I'm not really good with inserting the IV needle. I've got exactly the drugs used for executions, so it will be peaceful and painless, but I need you to be still, so I've got some animal tranquilizer."

He lifted a dart gun from the box. "I don't think this hurts much either. You need to lie down on the couch." He began shoving the mounted animals onto the floor. I strained against his arm, trying to pull away, with no success.

"See, Callie, you're fighting me all the way."

He pointed the dart gun straight at me.

He paused for barely a moment, but his grip on me loosened.

Only a second or so, but it was long enough for me to jerk away from him and run as hard and fast as I could out the front door. I crashed straight into my daddy. Sheriff Harmon ran beside him with his gun drawn. Dennis Sharpe came charging through the door still aiming the tranq at me. Again, the sound of gunfire. Not a tranquilizer dart. A forty millimeter. The sheriff bent over Dennis Sharpe's prostrate form and said, "I hit him, and he's out, but it wasn't a chest shot. How about you, Callie?"

My answer was silent, but dramatic.

I threw up again.

Chapter Forty-one

Jane and I lay on the sand at Hunting Island Beach, trying to get some tan in the late afternoon sun. With her naturally light skin, Jane avoids the beach in the middle of the day, and I had worked until midafternoon anyway.

I'd picked her up at her new apartment, which for the time being was *our* new apartment. Both of us were living in Jane's side of the duplex while our landlady had my living room painted and the carpet replaced. She'd even let me select what I wanted. I'd chosen a tan berber.

Jane suggested we come to the beach because she didn't like hanging around the apartments until the remodeling was completed. She had this weird idea that George Carter's ghost might be in my side of the duplex because he'd shed so much blood there.

I'd bought a bagged supper for us on the way home from work that afternoon, but we hadn't opened it yet.

Jane wore her skimpiest purple string bikini while I had on a modest black one-piece suit, yet I felt more naked than she looked.

I'd bought the bathing suit before my birthday because

it would conceal underwear if I wore an inflated bra and my booty-boosting panties beneath it, but I wasn't wearing any underwear. All I had on was the maillot, which made me feel bare.

"You seem moody," Jane said as she sat up and handed me the tanning lotion. I poured some of the solution into my palm and began rubbing it on her back. "I'd think you'd be happy that your friend Mrs. Counts won the Southern Belle Baking Contest and will be expanding her business."

"Well, those benne wafers of yours were mighty good. Wouldn't it have been great if you'd won?"

"You bet, but we don't need money to be happy, now do we?"

"I've been thinking a lot lately," I said without answering her question. After all, a lot of money *would* be nice.

"What about? I hope you aren't going out looking for another murderer."

"Buh-leeve me, my amateur sleuthing days are over. Not only did George Carter try to kill me, that psycho Dennis planned to stuff me and leave me sitting on his couch. *Ughhhh.* Imagine sitting around dead for twenty years or more. Especially wearing a wig and a white dress getting dingier with each passing year."

"Are you wearing your underwear under your bathing suit?" Jane changed the subject.

"Nope. Just me under my swimsuit."

"I never understood why you wanted to wear fake boobs and fanny panties anyway, but now I don't understand why you've stopped wearing them after you spent so much money on all that stuff."

"You know as well as I do. I fuss at you when you lie and steal, yet what I was doing was lying. There's lying by omission, but that was outright lying by deception. If I hadn't been wearing all that false stuff, Dennis Sharpe may never have noticed me. He was infatuated with my 'perfect' body, which wasn't mine at all." I'd finished her back, so Jane took the lotion and began smoothing it on her legs.

"What else?" she asked.

"If Levi Pinckney hadn't thought I had such a wonderful body, I might have let myself get involved."

"By 'get involved' do you mean get bonked?"

"No," I mumbled, "I mean make love."

"Well, may I remind you that your headlights weren't blown up the first time Levi saw you. That's something you told me yourself. Over at the Dawkins house. You'd forgotten to put on your bra. Remember?"

"I don't think he noticed. He wasn't paying much attention to me that morning."

"But he came looking for you that night. He wasn't lost."

I grinned. "Yes, I guess he did. Then I got mad because he stood me up. I even wondered if those flowers, the pretty ones and then the dead ones, were from Levi. Dennis Sharpe took both the bouquet and the dead funeral wreath to my house. He was playing Peeping Tom outside my windows and leaving notes for me, too. He's even confessed that he tried to drive me off the road in that stolen Tahoe, not to hurt me, but to frighten me because I'd made him mad by not paying enough attention to him. The sheriff said Dennis keeps saying that women make men mad sometimes and that when a woman made him mad, he liked to punish her by scaring her. Turns out that's why his sister Denise left home as soon as she could. He was always scaring her." I picked up the lotion and began smoothing it on my legs.

"And he was infatuated with your body. Wouldn't it have been a hoot if he'd killed you and then found out what a flatty you are when he undressed you?" Jane giggled.

I scowled at her, though she couldn't see it. "I don't think that would have been a hoot at all." Pulling two bottled waters from the cooler, I opened both and handed one to Jane. We'd gone on a health kick. Fewer sodas.

"You still haven't told me why your dad and the sheriff went to Dennis Sharpe's cabin."

"Frank and Jane got worried when I didn't arrive at Daddy's not long after they did. Daddy called the apartment. When no one answered, he got angry and thought I was being stubborn and had gone home instead of following Frank and Jane to his house."

"You had gone back," Jane said and took a long drink.

"I didn't go back to stay, though, just to get my cell phone. Daddy was so sure that I was just refusing to answer the phone because I didn't want to spend the night at his house that he went to get me."

"I guess when he saw the Mustang in your driveway, he really thought you were just being stubborn."

"Yes, but the broken bathroom window alerted him something was wrong. He kicked the door in and found Carter. He called the sheriff. When they read that suicide note, they knew it wasn't for real. Daddy and Harmon saw Dennis Sharpe's initials carved into the handle of the hunting knife, which he had dropped when he forced me out to his van." I trembled at the memories.

"Sheriff Harmon knew where Dennis Sharpe lived. He and Daddy arrived just in time to keep Dennis from tranquilizing me and then executing me by lethal injection. He really had the paraphernalia to tie me down and put in an IV to deliver the drugs."

Jane reached for the lotion. I handed it to her and she rubbed more lotion on her tummy. "Who trashed your apartment and wrote on the mirror?"

"Turned out that George did the trashing. He was looking for anything that would lead him to Mrs. Counts. He'd assumed we were friends because I was helping her at Dr. Melvin's visitation. Dennis went in afterwards and wrote on the mirror. He'd followed me when I was out with Levi, and it made him mad."

Jane stretched out on her stomach. "Did I tell you that Pearl White has moved back into the big house and wants me to rent the garage apartment again?"

My heart dropped to the pit of my stomach. I'd really enjoyed seeing more of Jane and had even learned to ignore Roxanne when she worked in the other bedroom—on the phone, of course.

"What did you tell her?" I asked.

"I told her no. I'm staying where I am. I don't want to live over there where that woman harassed me and where her blood's all over the steps."

"They tore those steps down and built new ones," I said. "How is Pearl doing?"

"Said she's fine. She's back in AA doing her steps again. She says if thirty-six don't do the trick, she'll do forty-eight or sixty."

"You know, she really loved that rotten con artist, and he would've killed her and taken everything she owned without batting an eyelash, but the worst thing he did to her was get her back drinking. You said she'd been dry fifteen years when she met him. I hope she can do that again."

"Callie, before Pearl rents the garage apartment to someone else, I want to ask you something." She set her empty water bottle on the towel beside her.

"Go ahead."

"You always say you'll never live with your dad and brothers again. How would you feel about one of your brothers living next door to you?"

I squealed and hugged her. "You and Frank are going to live together?"

"More than that. How would you like me for a sister-in-law?"

I promise, I knew I should feel elated and happy for her,

but immediately I went into anxiety mode. What if Frank cheated on his wife and she was my best friend? What if my best friend didn't do right by my brother?

"What's wrong? You've always said you felt like I was your sister."

"Oh, nothing's wrong. I'm just overwhelmed. It would be wonderful." *Liar, liar, pants on fire.*

"Well, we're not figuring on beating Bill and Molly to the altar. We're thinking December, so we don't even have to talk about it now." She paused. "Callie, you never told me about Dr. Melvin. Did Roselle or George Carter kill him?"

"Not at all. The heavy metal poisons tests showed nothing abnormal, but when Sheriff Harmon asked them to specifically test those vitamins and food supplements Dr. Melvin was taking, they found he was overdosing on about everything, including DHEA, which is sometimes known as the 'fountain of youth' supplement."

"So he actually died of an overdose?"

"No, the cause of death was determined to be heart arrhythmia."

"No kidding? I guess your heart is arrhythmic if it stops."

"That's not what they mean. Some people have arrhythmia for years without having a heart attack. Other people have massive heart attacks that show up during autopsy. They decided that Dr. Melvin's heart went into arrhythmia and didn't correct itself. No scar tissue. His heart died immediately." I sniffled.

"Toxicology showed no poisons," I continued, "but he was overdosing on all those supplements. DHEA or 'youth' can cause heart arrhythmia. Too much of that stuff can make even a young heart arrhythmic and result in sudden death. Thank heaven the toxicologist discovered it. When Sheriff Harmon told Roselle the cause of her husband's death, she was shocked. She'd been taking his supplements since he died. She'd thought her heart was racing because she was upset. She's still grieving. I think she really loved Dr. Melvin."

"Goes to show you never can tell," Jane said. "What about you? Does anyone want to meet Vanessa?"

"Yes, I've had a couple of hits, but you know Vanessa is a bigger fib than my boobs and booty were."

"As big a fake as Roxanne?"

"I wouldn't go that far."

"I'm getting hungry. What do you have to eat?"

"I've got meatball subs."

"You went to Nate's Sports and Subs on the way home?"

"Yep, and I asked Levi what he thought about second chances. He's taking me to the midnight movies in Beaufort tonight."

"Why the change?"

"Remember I said I'd been reading about Abraham Lincoln?"

"Uh-huh."

"I read a lot of his quotes. One of them was, 'You can fool some of the people all of the time, and you can fool all of the people some of the time, but you can't fool all of the people all of the time.' That's what I've been doing with my inflated bras and fanny panties."

"So, are you going to tell all this to Levi?"

"Don't know yet, but I can tell you another famous Abraham Lincoln saying. 'Most folks are about as happy as they make up their minds to be.' You know what, Jane? I'm going to make up my mind to be happy, and if I succeed with Levi, that will be fine. If not, I'll still be happy."

Jane grinned and turned toward the sparkling sand and whitecapped waves as though she could see them. She said, "You're so full of quotes. Here's a Jane quote for you to remember: 'People who don't get bonked occasionally might go bonkers.'"